Contents

Angeline

Illevante' Curse

Book One

By

Linda Kane

This story is dedicated to my brother

Kenneth (Kenny, always to me) for all those nights you would listen to my endless stories as I progressed from notepads to typewriters to word processors then computer! Love you always!

Angeline

1877

Tears dripped from the line of her jaw, and it was with a little touch of surprise that she realized how cold they were. Why did she think them to be warm? She wondered in a half-hearted attempt to focus her mind on anything more than the weapon that lay before her, memories continuing to haunt her, a love refusing to be disavowed. Reaching across the slight distance between the chair she sat in, and the desk where the weapon waited, ready, patient, a weary sigh escaped to the effort picking it up would take from her.

Slowly the solidness fit into the palm of her hand; nestled there with silent acceptance to its place in her ending life. A trembling hand caressed the barrel as with a start the chamber clicked into readiness. The iron ball and gunpowder carefully placed. '*What are you attempting?*' Whispered softly and at first, she wasn't even aware that the voice was inside her head. She wasn't aware she was no longer alone. '*Wouldn't you rather talk to me about this before you do anything rash?*'

Blinking to the tears as they continued, she managed, "I have nothing left to say; no one to say it to."

'*I am here, am I not?*' A slight breeze was felt to ruffle the collar of the silken wrapper as it hung loosely about her length; the heavy drapery of the window was seen to flutter with the gathering disturbance. '*You could talk to me.*'

"You're not here, only a sound in my head." Managed as the

cold metal was once again contemplated. The craftsmanship lost long ago to time was admired, "you simply keep me alive with a promise, a dream that will never come true."

A soft laugh was heard to swim about her head as the breeze once again stirred; the air seemed to ripple seeking her naked length in a familiar touch, '*you know that is not true. If you would only put that horrible thing away and look about you would find that I have always been here. I have always been attempting to come to you. And now we are so close.*'

"Close?" And this time she laughed at the idea of such sounds. "It would be so much easier if you would stop talking and allow me to do, as I must; as I should have so many years ago."

'*But what would I do without you---what would we do?*' Questioned with such sadness for only an instant, she contemplated placing the weapon aside and allowing the voice its wish. Moving steadily closer to the determination of the woman the voice managed, '*we could wait till tomorrow night and then if you insist on this nonsense still, I will allow you, as you must without a sound.*'

"Tomorrow night?" Was repeated with hopeful intent as she began to feel increasingly weary, so weary her eyes were felt to be too heavy to remain open and the hands so weak she could scarcely lift the readied weapon. "Yes, tomorrow." Was agreed as she came from the wooden chair with scrape against floorboards. "And you must remember your promise. Without a sound."

In a warming touch, the air wrapped her; shimmering in its need to surround, protect as it guided to the quilted bed. The warmth and comfort it brought her caused a smile even as her troubled mind could not quite grasp the idea that it still cared. Soft laughter was felt to caress the recesses of her soul as the thought came from her weary mind, '*I have always cared.*' Gently the essence began to ease her troubled brow as she drew the covers securely up and about her shoulders. Welcomed the help as she slipped into a sleep without thought to the darkness and then somehow managed to keep the horror of dreams from plaguing her weary mind as it had done for a thousand, a hundred thousand, nights. *'Without a sound.'* Repeated as a promise.

∞∞∞

Opening eyes to the sounds of the night; Angeline pressed the roughness of a scarred hand against the pound of her temple as realizing she had lost the courage to end what had begun so many years ago. "Why?" Questioned as her throat was felt to thicken to building emotion, eyes burn to the tears that would not come to fall when she needed them most. "Why have you prolonged this?"

Feeling the air, as it seemed to still and gather about her, Angeline waited for the inevitable sounds to fill her head, the essence haunting her to return, *'because I am so near.'*

"Near?" Was the ironic snort of laughter, "how long have you promised me you were so near?" Sitting up slowly from bed's engulf the veil of fiery hair was pressed back over shoulders and held there, clutched at for silent, contemplative moments. "How many times do we need to have this conversation; how many times do you need to instill your will upon me. I am weary of this isolation."

'You are not alone.' The stillness was felt to sweep up and about her length, *'let me be with you; comfort you.'*

Wearily the head shook for she knew such acceptance would only make tonight harder to face, would only force to break the promise made. "You said without a word." She reminded the whisper to the inevitable outcome of the evening.

'Let me be with you, then, if only now.' Persisted as Angeline resisted the air growing thicker about her; rejected the whisper of touch and moaned softly, weakly to the insistence.

Wrapping her arms about her head the words, "why can't I come to you, why do you torture me so?" Cried, as she seemed to curl herself into a protective ball from any attempt to comfort her. "I want to be with you, why can't you find your way to me, why are you torturing me?"

'You know it is you who will come to us, little one; you would be lost to me for all time if you persist in this frightening path.' Steadily the air eased till she turned to the bed, and her head returned to the pillow. *'Close your eyes,'* was the gentle command, and Angeline did as bid. *'Breathe for me, little one, breathe.'*

Strong arms came to enfold her, and Angeline could do no more than gratefully allow the strength to gather her. Protect, as it entered first though lungs then to spread out as if carried in her blood, along every vein to throb into every nerve till finally, the sweetness of touch came to her brain. Images of loving and being loved sparked much like a pictograph when flashed before an eager child's eye. Each picture, each sensation flicked behind the close of eyes, and she allowed the emotions to ease her. Allowed the voice to love her as it always sought to do. "You aren't fair." Came as the image of the voice was managed, as the details to face and body made her remember to a time long ago — a time when she thought love never to end when she thought life full of promise.

'I need you to remember us, little one. I need you to keep us in your being.' Whispered as something reminiscent of fingers were felt to stroke the length of her, caress the lines of her face as something once familiar with life pressed to the softness of her abandoned mouth and held there for silent moments. *'Remember, always.'*

Reaching up hands allowed the air to thicken about her, welcomed the warmth as it settled upon her and vowed, "how could I ever forget?" When arms returned to her sides, she allowed the images to come once again allowed the memories and sensations as they filled her.

One

1540

Naked feet were heard to slap over thresh of sweet herbs along the winding corridor to where the master's chambers laid, "Momma!" He cried coming to fling himself into the woman's opened arms as she woke to the demand, "Momma, I heard a baby." The words were breathless and in the wonder of such a thing. "I heard her Momma, I swear!"

Pressing back the errant raven curls as they came over his forehead, the gentle fingertips teased over the fullness of his cherub mouth before managing with a teasing smile, "Nico, love, you were dreaming. There is no baby." Snuggling him in the space between her and husband, she held him close as he could only shake his head to her easy dismissal of his words. "Sleep, my little love, sleep, and dream of your baby," Josephine whispered before sleep came to close her eyes, and the child was held close, secure in her warmth.

∞∞∞

Anton Belaveuta looked down to the screaming bundle in his arms and couldn't help the smile coming to his lips, the love felt to the daughter whose tiny fists rallied against the demands of childbirth and hunger. "She's a fine babe." He whispered to the worry of his weakened wife who watched the two for silent moments and with his words smiled and allowed emerald eyes to close to the exhaustion the last two days of labor brought her.

1553

The hood came to be adjusted into a deeper fold about his face as the man sipped from the tankard of ale placed before him. The piercing eyes scrutinized the gathering, mostly young men all carrying the colors of King and Belaveuta, that crowded the few benches of the village's tavern. Their brightly colored sashes banded across a single shoulder then gathered at the waist were held as a marking of loyalty and honor or so the stranger assumed from his men who also held similar badges to honor.

The heavy tankard was lifted, sipped from and slowly returned as he threw a few coins across the wooden planked barrier which kept the proprietor shielded from the nightly brawling which inevitably erupted once drinking was well underway. Now that his curiosity had been sedated, at least for a few days to the goings-on at Belaveuta, his own home and lands would be safe if only for a little while longer as the Baron of Belaveuta was busy rejoicing after his recent marriage to a woman it was rumored nearly fifteen years his junior.

"To the Baron!" Someone suddenly shouted as if reading the young man's thoughts, and all tankards rose in the toast. "May God bless him and his family!" Voices rose in echo, and gruffly, he murmured the words if only not to draw attention to himself.

"To the Lady Belaveuta!" Another shouted as all rose in tribute to the young blond woman who came from the confines of village shop to find the mass of her new husband's troops gathered in a tavern whose storefront opened onto the street. Tightening the hold about the wrist of the child who continually fought for freedom, the woman tugged her forward with a hiss of stern warning in her ear about running off.

The girl barely glanced in the stepmother's direction but raised glorious emerald eyes to the surround of familiar men, most of which she could name, and flashed them her brightest smile. "To the little Lady Angeline!" Another cried out to the child's delight as she dropped into a deep curtsy, her length of thick, fiery curls bouncing over shoulders as a fit of giggles took over her.

Staggering in return to the seat, the stranger became aware of the voices of his ancients as they repeated the prophecy which cursed his family, which was his to fulfill to a child who would one day be wife — pressing the hood back from the raven head as he came to push the others from his way. Blue eyes studied the girl who could be no more than twelve years old. How could this mere child be an answer to his deepest dreams, the reason for him to wish to go on? How could he possibly be sure she was indeed the one? '*She will be your life, Nico; she will be our salvation.*' Echoed once again as eyes of disbelief watched the impatient stepmother drag away the child.

Turning to the nearest of the men as they returned to their ale, the stranger demanded, "the child. She is Belaveuta's daughter?"

Placing the tankard to table the question slowly was met with eyes of suspicion, "aye, she is the daughter, Angeline, what would be your business with the wee one?"

Thumping the man's shoulders in reassurance to claim, the stranger announced, "she is going to be my wife." With a smile, the waiting horse was mounted, and the stranger rode quickly from Belaveuta.

Two

1559

Brooding blue eyes stared at the dark surroundings of a cave deep in the bowels of the Illevante` Keep waiting for the ancients to acknowledge him. Silently he remained, as they seemed to whisper among themselves before confronting his demands. "This is ridiculous!" He spat as coming to draw himself from the ornate throne of jewel and gold to pace the sandy floor. The path a familiar one over the years and the following of his previous steps retraced. "What do you mean it is not time; she is a grown woman!" Shoving an aggravated hand through the shoulder-length raven hair, he wished for something, anything to crush, to destroy under the power of his hands if only to take such helplessness from him. "How could you say this is not the time!" The torches that lined the cavernous room flared dangerously high as shadows leaped and voices battled, "it is a perfect time before another comes to claim her hand. Surely there must be one who will persist for her, how could they not?"

A soft ripple of sound seemed to vibrate off the very walls, the shadows wavered along with the glow of torch as it returned to a mere flicker, '*she is not ready for one such as you, Nico. We need to prepare for the one who is not; he is the key to the undoing.*' They responded as a single voice; as a chorus of voices. He turned as if attempting to catch one instead of the many as they explained. '*Now is the time for planning and preparing. When the markings on Mars are foretold, then you will be able to claim her, and then she will be yours as the prophets have heralded.'*

"The prophets!" With a fearsome string of blasphemy, he stormed from the room to the rocky shore beyond, the door slamming and locking it would seem by its violation of sanctity.

Standing in the blinding sun Nickolai Illevante' allowed the heat to calm him, willed his anger away, the constant of wind and wave to soothe the unrest of his soul. Slowing his wild pound of heart to match that of the beating surf, he willed the frustration and impatience to a more manageable emotion all with the calming image of emerald eyes and auburn hair. "Angeline." Whispered as for a moment he contemplated returning to the secret chamber where it was the easiest for him to speak to his ancients. He considered ignoring their visions and merely going to the woman and claiming her as his own. How long, he wondered, did they expect him to last as such, how long was he supposed to survive as such. He was tired of living alone, tired of not knowing the love of a single woman; he needed this woman who was capable of easing the constant burden of his soul, the loneliness of his curse.

The raven head shook with a sigh of disgust, in the six years from which he had first sighted the child he had done nothing but wait. Feigned patience he could no longer pretend existed; when his soul wanted nothing more than to gather her into his arms, bring her to Illevante` and see to her every need. Make her fall in love with him, make him the only one she would ever need, but such actions were strictly forbidden, or so the ancients had warned him. Any interference could be the undoing to all that was foretold, to all that was the future. So Illevante` waited, waited, and watched.

Three

Struggling the servant's trousers over her legs, Angeline swore silently to herself in the cramped quarters of the buttery as she tried to hurry in her redress. Once the waist was fastened, and the coarse muslin tunic tugged overhead, she peered from behind the cracked doors to ensure she had not compromised her hiding place. Stealthy she crossed the width of kitchen avoided the curious looks from servants who merely shrugged shoulders to another of her antics then gained the freedom of the yards beyond.

Running to the stables where her favorite horse was waiting, she dragged herself up over its back, breathing only as the house, and most importantly, the stepmother was left behind. For many miles, she allowed the animal to lead the way. Over familiar trails and winding paths, they raced till a favorite pasture was found and slowly the gait came to linger as preferable patches of sweetgrass came to be nibbled. "It's perfect, thank you." Murmured as she slid from the animals' back and allowed it to roam freely about the land with a grateful pat to its dark mane.

'*Angeline,*' and the nuance of her name caused all other thought to slip away. Here, now, she was safe and protected, nearly cocooned in the warmth of embracing arms as all worries swept from her with the soothing word of '*soon.*'

Four

1560

With a sigh of consent, Angeline allowed the hand to press over the plain of her belly, the curve of her hip, to the waist where it lingered for a teasing moment before rising to palm the fullness of her breast. Arching against the thumb's pad pressing over the rise of the nipple, her hand came to cup the masculine one, and she reveled in the power, and the trust of her desire. Her fingertips explored the hand under her own, felt each scar and callous, which only seemed to add to its perfection of strength.

"Lady Angeline!" Eyes opened with a gasp as a servant was heard to insist against dreams, "Lady Angeline, the Baron is requesting your presence in his library."

Nodding to acknowledge her wakefulness, though she was barely aware of anything beyond the imagines continuing to dance vividly before her mind's eye, Angeline waved the women from her with an aggravated flit of the wrist, "inform my father's messenger; I will be there shortly." Listening to the constant whispering beyond her chamber doors, she crossed the distance of the room and soundly slammed the wooden barrier shut. Leaning weakly to the coolness of the wood, she allowed a hand to rise in touch over the tenderness of lips, the ache of a sweet caress as it lingered at her throat. Forcing a breath from its held state, she couldn't help but look down to see if the wrapper remained about her length or if she was splayed naked as images demanded. “If the Baron knew what you were doing to me, he’d see you hang.” With a shake of her head, the haunting eyes and dominating impressions were pressed aside even as such left her wildly aware of femininity and desire.

Stopping before the silver disk trembling hands pressed to the heat found in cheek. “Why do you torture me so; if you are more than my imagination, why don't you come to me?” Was questioned as she quickly escaped the reflection suddenly afraid of the answers that would come, the ones that would not.

∞∞∞

Once appropriately dressed for the mandated meeting, Angeline dismissed the bevy of fussing servants about her and tugged self-consciously to the tightness of corset as it gripped her lungs. For a fleeting moment, she stared at her reflection and sighed to the image confronting her. “Please don’t let this be another uninterested suitor; not another for Antoinette to mock me with his rejection.” She prayed as with a determined sigh left the reflection and the massive room she claimed as her own. Lifting her hems, she managed the flights of stairs to the main floor and crossed the grand hallway leading to the library.

Sensing the urgency her father radiated to her appearance, she quickened her pace, '*a lady does not run!*' Could be heard mimicking in her head to stepmother’s voice, causing her to remain respectful and dignified, at least in appearance.

Stopped before the library doors, her father’s secretary looked down his crooked nose to her appearance and snapped, “you’ve kept him waiting. You've kept them all waiting. I’ve gone to your chamber door twice in summons!”

“Remind me to mention your diligence to my father.” Answered the steely eyes as they rose from his study of the scheduler within his palms.

With a startling *snap*, the leather-bound agenda closed.

Smiling smugly to Angeline's startled blink, the secretary couldn't help but admire the beauty of the woman before him the promise of her figure hidden beneath the style of gown. Her father had sheltered her for far too long, allowing her free rein over her destiny. Racing about the countryside without escort, milling about with villagers as if she were one of them and not Mistress over them. It was a behavior he would like to tame, as raising his stare, he found the curious emerald eyes fixed on him. And a momentary rush of heat spread under his embroidered waistcoat, nervously he tugged to the seemingly tightening of cravat adorning throat. "Don't you think you should announce my arrival, he has been waiting?"

Stiffly he turned and knocked soundly once, twice, to the doors at his back. "Milord," he announced, "the Lady Angeline."

Casting a final look to the servant as she was permitted entry into the room, Angeline wondered if had he not realized how obvious his intentions were? Though she was curious to the startled and near painful expression which came to mar his features.

Pausing as the gathering of strangers loomed at all sides of her, Angeline quickly took in those who surrounded. Guards, dressed in the colors of Belaveuta mixed with another, oddly familiar though striking in their dark contrast of her home. "Milord, please forgive the delay." She whispered in the vastness of the room, and the sound became lost to the parent who watched with full intent to her approach and struggle of her empathic gift. The curtsy before her father was maintained even though she couldn't ignore the nudging insistence of urgency, an unrelenting need causing her to seek the solitary figure remaining in the shadows. "Mother." Was added, as afterthought as her father's displeasure to her oversight reached her with tugging annoyance.

The breath exhaled in slow realization to the group of witnesses, as a barrage of emotions attacked her from all angles forcing her to mentally single each one out. Catch each of the sensations as they came to her then released once intent was known. To finally focus on the one shadowing the back of her mind, hiding there with the deliberate objective of consoling and easing her unrest. Angeline sought to recognize the hidden figure; how could he seem to know her so intimately that he could realize her gift. The ivory brow was seen to crease to the insistence of familiarity though she could scarcely make out a face in the obscurity of the dimly lighted room.

Anton Belaveuta set his eyes on his daughter and felt his heart weaken to the position he thought never to place her in. So young, it seemed as if only yesterday she was scampering about these halls in braids and bloomers and now before him stood a woman. A woman who was unsure of her place in the gathering which surrounded her. A meeting which pressed her naturals gifts to their limits, as they did his own. A woman unlike any within his protection, proud and strong, beautiful and innocent, worthy of the noble Belaveuta blood which coursed her veins. Wearily a sigh of concern escaped the Baron as a glance went to the Count of Illevante'. Would he be a patient husband to this innocence? Would he understand and accept the extraordinary gifts she possessed, or would he condemn her? "Angeline, daughter," came with slight hesitation; how could he even begin to explain the circumstance falling on shoulders never before burdened with the weight of responsibility, "the men who have gathered here today are of Illevante'." With an understanding smile, Anton observed Angeline's shoulders as they braced to the name. A name spoke only in terms of battle and betrayal, and he continued before the darkening expression could give forth heated words. "Count Illevante' has presented a proposition that I would like you to consider." From the corner of his eye, Anton contemplated the piercing blue eyes that instantly daggered his, felt the distrust of emotion directed toward him. Anton could sense that the Count wanted Angeline to believe she had no choice in this matter. With a rueful smile to the insistence, Anton knew his daughter would realize he would protect her from anything even if it meant his own demise.

Attempting to hold her father's intent stare, Angeline managed a furtive glance to the figure emerging from the darkness and held the stare for silent, awkward moments.

Once free of the shadows the Count sought to hide in, Angeline was allowed to contemplate the towering strength and handsome features, *'sweet mother of God,'* whispered inside of her head, *'so this is the Count of Illevante`*, the man her family had considered enemy for so long. Why was he not the monster she always imaged, how could a man she had been conditioned to loathe nearly from birth be more than breath-taking? Emerald eyes adverted the Count as a small smile was seen to curl the corner of his perfect mouth. A smile capable of generating a familiar longing to beat for this man within her heart within her blood. Feeling as if compelled, Angeline's eyes rose to meet the piercing stare, "I do not believe he would like me to consider anything, Milord. I believe he has come with the intention of me accepting what he has to offer and nothing less."

Pressing a hand over the smile, which unwittingly came to lips, Anton cast a sharp glance to the woman beside him who gasped in fearful admission to the knowledge of the child. "It may be true, my daughter," came with solemn repose. "However, he does have my wishes to consider first, does he not?" Anton could see the fear seeping into her eyes, the breath to deepen as if a frightened animal cornered by the most ferocious of beasts.

As the Count was witnessed to approach and Angeline to regress, Anton cast all from his wake with the command; "I will speak to my daughter, alone." Seeing the objection come into the man's stance, he repeated, "alone."

Waiting the moments for the room to empty, Anton motioned Angeline closer to him. "Come, sit here beside me. There is much we need to discuss." He instructed before gathering needed words to him, "you know we have been at odds with Illevante' long before your birth. His father and I have clashed on the battlefield more than once; Stephen plans an invasion even as we speak." And without realizing a finger's pad repeatedly traced over scar marring his cheek, an injury Angeline had learned long ago came from such men mentioned. “It’s been a bloody time, and the son has come asking for a solution to war; to death." Anton pointed to the document on the table between them, explaining the Royal seal that he could not ignore. "The Queen Mother has approved a proposition of marriage, though she would never order such a marriage, she has advised to its advantages. She believes the joining of our families will end hostilities; together, we will become a formidable force. “

Casting only the briefest of glances to the document she allowed a steadying breath to be inhaled before continuing. “He would take me to Illevante’, would he not, father?” Escaped from the child who had never ventured further surrounding lands, to the woman who was still unknown by the touch of a man beyond her dreams. With his rueful nod, the head lowered as lip was tugged between the clasp of teeth, “what if he doesn’t understand me, what if he believes me different?”

For long moments the father contemplated her fears, “if rumors about Count Illevante’ are correct, you may need to accept differences from him as well." Casting the quickest of glances to the child at his side, he reminded, “you know your mother and I were brought together under similar circumstances?" Anton allowed himself the pleasure of caressing the silk of her cheek if only to remind him of love still mourned. “It must be your decision to leave with this man; I have always protected you and will continue to do so with whatever you decide on this day. Eventually, these battles will end with or without your delicate hand evoking its demise.”

Angeline acknowledged his sacrifice for Belaveuta, “you have sacrificed much for our protection, Father, and I know how this is hurting you. You believe you will be sacrificing me this time for Belaveuta.” She came to stand from his gentle expression, the pain he fought so bravely to hide from her. “I know how important this is to you, to all of us.” Her hand came in warning to any words that he may attempt to lessen the burden of such denial should she choose not to marry the Count, “Don’t. Don’t attempt to mask what you know I already feel." Pressing away tears, she managed in a voice sounding far stronger than felt, "I will have him ask me to marry him, and we will marry here in one month. That is my request to such a joining."

Rising slowly to the task, Anton gathered her into his arms, held her for silent moments before pressing a kiss to the plain of her forehead. "You have made me proud to be your father, Angeline." With a reassuring nod to the decision made, he moved to the doors to summon the man found to be pacing the hall beyond. "Illevante, please, you will come." Explaining the conditions of his daughter's consent, with a nod of approval the man entered as the father stepped out to join the others. Looking down at his wife, who came instantly to take his arm, Anton reassured, "she will make the right decision, never fear." And her ringed fingers were patted with reassurance.

The leaded-pane of diamond-shaped glass windows held Angeline's attention as the doors were heard to come to a close. Silently she contemplated the words he refused to acknowledge her in as they seemed to swell to the very seams of the room. The emotion and hesitation in his approach of her caused a reluctant smile to full lips, "you can't possibly find me that intimidating." Turning Angeline found the need he radiated caused blood to fuse hotly into her cheeks, "nor has any man found me desirable."

"I am hardly any man, little one." The voice, soft and gentle, caused Angeline to feel as if her body reached for him, yearned to end the division, and she felt her mouth dry to the burn of such need. How could this be possible, she rebuked her own body, this man was her enemy, and the single reason so many of her own were dead? How could such betrayal be possible? Simply because a handsome man appeared interested in her, she couldn't be willing to give up all instilled since birth.

A single step brought him before her, barely touching in the slight separation towered over, Illevante' willed the glorious eyes to raise in the appraisal of him. Longed for the moment when fear would be replaced by love and desire as he knew it would be within their grasp if she would give them the chance to achieve it. A knuckle, roughened and battle-scarred, came to trace the silk of cheek, press over the part of lips forcing her to face him entirely as he enforced, "and never doubt your effect on me, nor my desire."

Angeline fought the urge to draw the touch into the warmth of her mouth as his touch continued to worry over her bottom lip. Learn the taste of him on her tongue. Instead, she concentrated on her need to breathe as her body clenched to an overpowering need. '*How is this possible?*' Resounded within her heart, as she considered the man before her. Towering and massive, she had to crane her neck up to fully contemplate his face as she realized the top of her head barely touched his chin. Had she ever seen such a mouth before, had she ever seen such a man? "Goodness!" Escaped in a breathless sigh before managing, "you would end this constant battle of our families? You will keep your word, honor, toward Belaveuta? Our marriage will not be an easy alliance; there have been many years of mistrust."

"I would do many things for you; little one, my word and honor are amongst the easiest." Chuckling with a knowing arrogance, he promised, "and perhaps you find it a little more than difficult to curse what you wish to keep unto yourself." Nickolai witnessed the uncertainty and distrust which tugged her mouth to frown, "I only ask that you trust in me...in us." His hand pressed through the thick of hair and cupped the nape of her neck, pleasing him to feel how perfectly the head nestled within his palm. "Angeline be my wife. Allow me to know you, love you, like none before."

The air gathered in caress against her face, stroked her neck, and laved the heave of her breast, causing Angeline's eyes to close to the feelings building deep within. "How?" Wondered to the sweetness of emotion flooding her in an undeniable need from and for this man. "How is this possible? How can my body mourn the loss of your touch, ache for your lips as if I miss them on my own?"

Nickolai tugged her to his towering length as confessing, "I could ask the same of you, little one, could I not?" His lips teased against the hesitation of her own till resistance was felt to waver.

Instantly Angeline cleaved against the body burning into hers, recognized the length fitting flawlessly against her own, and her soul she knew it was finally whole. Pressing her hand up over Nickolai's chest, through raven hair, she drew him to the warmth generated by the brush of his mouth over hers. "Sweet Jesus, how can this feel so right."

Reveling Angeline's touch, Illevante' felt his body hardened in demand to the woman who already held heart, who exclusively held desire. Once only speculating to the powers of his ancients, Nickolai now believed in the force that drew him to her, knew she would be his only salvation. "Because we are as one." Whispered as his mouth returned to entice the perfect mouth in search of his return. "You know this is true, little one, you can feel it with your heart, your body, as each call to me. As mine, in turn, calls to you."

Angeline contemplated his words; the words, and actions of a stranger. A shaken breath escaped if only to understand the conflicts raging inside of her; how can this be? How can it ever be? How could he be the one so different from the others, how could he be the one to bring to life her desire by a single caress, a touch? She tried in vain to remember one from her past capable of delivering such expectation, such need, and she knew they all paled in comparison. None had even come close to the desire this man was capable of inspiring. Had any sought to bring such emotion before? She vaguely wondered to the callers who presented themselves; to the days they managed to be in her company before abhorrence or overwhelming greed sought to circumvent their revulsion. This revulsion forced Angeline to peer into her looking glass, wondering to the reflection which caused men to avoid touching her, shun wanting to be alone with her. How could this stranger radiate such beauty in her, such desire by a touch?

"You are thinking about this far too hard." Nickolai teased pinching the chin between thumb and finger to raise the features to meet his. "It is right between us, little one, forget that we were once enemies, forget everything you have ever known of me before this moment. Know I will do everything in my power to protect the precious life, the beautiful woman, you have placed in my hands."

"Beautiful woman?" Angeline questioned as the hurtfulness of his boast caused her to recoil as if physically injured, "no one has been so cruel to name me as beautiful; know that you will be questioned by those who wonder to your choice in me as wife."

Frowning to the voiced insecurity, the pain etching glorious eyes, Illevante' could do no more than stare into the brilliance of eyes as they searched his. Caress the perfection of features as his fingertips came to touch ivory flesh with trembling reverence. "Little one," Nickolai forced Angeline to keep her eyes focused on him, "no one would ever dare to question why I have chosen you." His sincerity caused a stray tear to escape to what she knew could never be true. "I will cherish you always, Angeline, and only hope you can find it in your heart to accept me as your husband. To understand all that is coming with the name Illevante'. Please know that I never meant to insult, only to praise the woman who will be wife."

For silent moments Angeline contemplated the man, and when she could sense no malice, only an overwhelming need to love and protect her, she consented. "I will be married here in one month with my father to give me away, Milord." Whispered, relieved to feel the demands of his body become under control, the needful emotions diminish to a more manageable state.

Nickolai visibly relaxed to the words she shared, the way she sought the solace of his easing thoughts even without the realization she did so, "if that is your wish. However, we will be in Illevante' by nightfall of such night."

Mustering the little courage, she could, Angeline met his stare; knew of the circumstance of the nightfall to follow once she was in the Illevante' Keep. "if that is your wish."

"At the moment, Milady, my only wish is to hear you call me by my given name." Reluctantly Angeline came from the sureness of his protection, "my name is Nickolai, Angeline, and I hope you will address me as such in the future." With a nod in agreement, she moved to advise all who waited for the outcome of their mediations.

Opening the door, Angeline became immediately engulfed by the rage of her brother, Stephen, who appeared from the practice fields as the rumor was quick to spread to the arrival of Illevante' on Belaveuta; to the rumor of betrothal. To the treaty which would join the two families into an unbeatable force. Angrily he side-stepped Anton, who sought to curtail his direction, reaching for the door's handle only as Angeline opened the barrier and availed herself to his assault.

Had the circumstances been different, Angeline would have been able to prepare for the onslaught of attention he bestowed her. Would have braced herself against the degree of his fuming jealousy, "what in the name of God do you think you are doing?" Stephen demanded as he grasped her upper arms in the crush of his powerful hands, drew her hard to the demand of his body. "How could you allow them to do this to you? To be used when victory is so near, we can claim these lands for our own without the sacrifice of self."

Closing her eyes as twisted emotions swept from confusion to desire and then greed, Angeline could only manage, "Stephen, please don't do this." As the very fiber of her being cried out to be far from this man, to be safe and protected in the arms of a stranger whose thoughts only seemed to ease and comfort her. "Your victory will only mean death to many, is that how you would claim these lands?" Turning from the demands of the brother's anger to the mounting distrust of betrothed who came to draw her from the punishing hold, Angeline nearly held her breath to the reaction of the Count.

With a pained gasp, the hands bruising her tender flesh released, and Stephen looked to the palms, expecting burns to mar them. "Stephen, I allow them to do nothing against my will." Angeline stepped back from Stephen as he had to face the end of their future together, "I will marry Count Illevante'. I have given my word."

"But what of us?" Stephen whimpered in an attempt to fight the encroaching chaos as it sought to surround determination. Visibly the blond head shook as if attempting to clear the mind's fog and an accusatory glare passed to the man who had been his enemy for more than half a decade. How dare the spawn of the devil think to possess such a woman, as the idea of allowing her to be wife to another more than Stephen's breaking heart could tolerate? "He is forcing you to do this; I have heard rumor of this man. The conjuring whispered of behind his back in Court, whispers none would dare to say to his face. He will make you into nothing less than a whore for the devil! Use and discard you as he has with all the other women in his life, the whores who lust after him even as he comes entreating us all with peace." Stephen felt the years he had worshiped her crush upon him; nights when the others would turn her away, he would be there. The times he had comforted the defeated, often broken spirit when she was found alone on the outskirts of parties. The nights he longed to bridge the fine line of siblings to gather her into his arms to heal the solitude she believed was hers alone to bear. To see her reach for a man, he cursed as his worst enemy, was more than he dared to comprehend. "Please do not do this to me, to us."

Looking to her father, who was seen to pale to building anger as his wary eyes darted from Illevante' to surrounding guard, then to the display of stepson. Angeline cast a weak smile to the man who would be husband, and she prayed he would understand her actions, prayed Illevante' would show patience.

Armed with little knowledge of the gifts she possessed, Nickolai forced his overprotectiveness to Angeline's well-being kept under the strictest control. Refused to have her witness the destruction he was capable of as he would not have her fear him.

"Stephen," reaching in the distance between them, Angeline soothed the lines marring his features, pleaded to his anger and mistrust. "Please don't instigate a battle you will not win, a victory that we will not celebrate. Allow me to do this, allow me to secure the treaty that will bring an end to death, and secure a path to the future. Already Count Illevante' given his pledge to father, what battle is there for you to win, what victory to gain." Slowly the touch came from his features, her voice no more than a whisper to the growing confusion. "Please, trust me."

Turning into Nickolai's protection, Angeline proclaimed, "there will be no violence in my father's home. Not from the man who will be husband." With Nickolai's nod of consent, Angeline allowed him to lead her away.

Visibly sagging with relief, Anton confronted his trembling wife with the hiss, "get that boy of yours under control before I have to do it myself. He nearly ruined any peace this land will see in over fifty years." With a raised brow to her hesitation, Anton left her to join his daughter and her soon to be husband.

As the couple shared a private moment, Anton felt the tension gathered as a knot at the base of his skull ease to listen to the tone which Illevante' addressed his daughter. The reassurances the Count continued to share with every question, and every demand confronting him. The aging head lowered to the gentle amusement of Count's tone to Angeline's questions and inquiries of Illevante' Keep and its daily operations. Anton knew he should have placed the proper restrictions upon her upbringing as all other young women in this day and age. However, the idea of squelching her spirit seemed ludicrous, even as his new wife came time and time again to report Angeline's outlandish behavior.

Her daring to press tutors, who came for Stephen to verse him in the rudimentary skills needed in his life as noble, to further her need for additional education. She quickly had the scholars smuggling books, instructing to different languages, and further broadening the mathematical skills that seemed to come naturally. Of course, Anton mused; she seemed to go from one extreme to the next. When her nose was not within a book, she could be found to be riding unescorted about the endless lands which surrounded Belaveuta. Donned in a servant's stolen pair of trousers, she would diligently see to the villagers and their immediate needs, gaining their respect and devotion.

"Young women do not do such things!" The stepmother implored as Angeline's lessons to needlepoint and sewing were soon abandoned with a groan of boredom. Endless practice scales on piano only hampered the natural ability as she only to hear a piece a single time to be able to play note for note. As Antoinette sought to instill the duties of wife and mother, Angeline pulled further from her, deciding in a moment she had little use of such things in her life. "Anton, you have to curb this wildness. You must tell her she is no longer a child to do as she pleases. No wonder the callers never return; no wonder they flee as if she carries disease. Soon she will be past her prime for a good marriage, then what are we to do with her? No decent man wants an old bride, least she is barren." He never could. Summoning Angeline to him as promised to his wife as he had every intention of reprimanding her, Anton would take her by the hand and allow the stories to flow. Her eyes shining in excitement, keen to share her experiences of the day. He recognized the beauty and joy she radiated, as Anton had also witnessed the sadness as caller after caller refused suit, refused the pleasure of her company. He had seen what Antoinette chose to ignore; the pain and insecurity as it grew with Angeline's years. A beauty the woman did not embrace as a gift but as a curse. Instead of blossoming as he had seen many before in the natural beauty possessed, she seemed to shrink in a lack of self-confidence. “Angeline,” he managed to make his presence known, curious to see how the two cleaved as if intimacy was already shared. As if one could already anticipate the action and reaction of the second, “you must remain with your woman till the wedding day, child.”

A soft coloring was seen to tint her cheeks as she realized the intent of the parent, and Angeline joined her father. Embarrassed to the emotions which made being beside the Count so right, "of course, Father, forgive me."

Smiling to her realized impropriety, Nickolai entreated, “Baron, with your permission, I will leave the Captain of my Guard here for Angeline in my absence.” Drawing her fingers into his palm, he apologized, “as much as it pains me to leave you, little one, I must return to Illevante’. With your consent, I would like to return before our wedding day so that we may become better acquainted.”

Angeline studied the blue eyes as they contemplated her, as his lips pressed to the presentation of her knuckles, “I look forward to your visit, Milord.”

∞∞∞

In the days which followed, Angeline quickly became accustomed to the towering wall of the Guard that followed her from the moment she left her chambers till the moment she returned.

The Captain proved to be imposing enough to keep Antoinette a fair distance from her and Stephen, even further, making her days blissfully peaceful without the interference of either. Angeline found that with the Captain being at the beckon of her every whim, he had little to say to the way she spent her days.

Silently he would follow her as she would visit surrounding villagers, who all knew her by name, or to ride aimlessly about the countryside in men's trousers.

He merely secured each situation as it was presented, or whenever he believed a threat to her could be possible. Though most times, she glared at him to his ridiculous concerns to her safety. During the few times, she had found herself in Stephen's brooding proximity; the Captain had only to make his presence known to make the brother quickly disappear. Antoinette, on the other hand, seemed to be more than happy making ready the few trunks Angeline would leave with once the Count would come to take her to Illevante'.

In her father's library, Angeline skimmed the pages of stories that had always held her interest only to find herself distracted and unable to focus. "Do you believe you could ever come to love him?" Questioned, as Stephen remained in the frame of doorway careful to keep his distance from Angeline and but more importantly, the imposing figure always guarding her. "He is only after Belaveuta and is using you to get to the land." The arms held in cross over his chest only seemed to emphasize the mocked patience held for her response.

The Captain, already alert to the fear coming to cloud the woman's face, drew to attention, waiting with a tensed demeanor to the woman's reaction. "You know that is not true; you have read the agreement between the two families; the Count has no interest in Belaveuta." Drawing herself up from the engulfing chair behind the desk, Angeline came to remind Stephen, "unless father begets a son, Belaveuta is yours as it has always been. The Count is only interested in securing peace to this land." Angeline reassured, "there is no reason to doubt the word he has given our father."

Stephen allowed only the smallest of breaths to escape

him as she was now so near, so near he could sense the essence of her. More to him than a mere scent, it was the beat of her heart. The warmth of blood rushing her veins, a heat that caused his own heart to accelerate in need of her. "No reason?" Sneered the demand twisting any gentleness he wished to express toward her. His anger only seemed to feed with the idea of another soon possessing what was rightfully his. "Only days ago, he was your enemy as he is mine. Only days ago, you would have seen him dead; now you await him as a lover." A wary look was given to the guard as the man's hand came to rest at the hilt of the sword. "So easily, you will spread those ivory thighs; if I had known, I would have pressed my intent years ago."

Angeline took a hesitant step from Stephen, realizing how jealousy and anger twisted him beyond reason. "Stephen, if you would put aside your anger, speak to Nickolai, you will find there is no reason for him to covet what is already yours."

"Nickolai?" The name spat with disgust to how easily it slipped from her tongue. Already he could imagine the sound of her beckoning Illevante' as she would reach for him in the night, welcome him in want and need. "From a mere caress and kiss, you are ready to forget all that has been instilled upon you, forget all I have done to protect and keep you. Already you are ready to lay on your back and welcome him."

Visibly repelled by his words, Angeline spat with disgust, "we have nothing to say to each other, you will not listen to reason, and I no longer have the patience to deal with you." Angeline suggested only wishing to have him from her, "perhaps you should ask father to travel, obviously the business before you now make you weary."

In the distance between them, Stephen sneered, "business is hardly keeping me up nights, wanting you tears at my soul far deeper than any business. All I ever think of---dream of, is being deep within your flesh, hearing you call my name as I slam into the depth of your need."

Squaring her shoulders to the insulting and hateful words, Angeline managed, "it's not proper for you to speak to me as such." Nervously hands pressed into the flair of the skirt as she sought to draw her eyes away from his growing anger, from the towering strength she realized he possessed. "I will speak to father about allowing you to attend Court; you have been putting off a suitable marriage for far too long."

Stephen raked his cold, dark eyes over Angeline's length before confessing, "there will never be another but you. I will always want you, and I will not rest until I have you."

As the Captain began his advance from the shadows to see the absolute fear as it invaded the woman's features, Angeline stayed his approach with a single hand, then confronted the wickedness of her brother. "I am sorry you feel this way, Stephen, for I have pledged myself to Count Illevante` and all that I have will be his. His is the loyalty I will cleave to, and the love I will welcome."

Stephen's hand caressed the silk of her heated cheek, stroked the line of the jaw, "Illevante' will not live long enough to embrace you with his love!" And if he thought he had a chance against Illevante's damnable Guard, Stephen would have grabbed her into his arms, taken what was rightfully his. Damn the consequences, damn his soul!

Angeline felt her stomach cramp to the sickness which rose from his touch, and it was hastily pressed away, "you are not the man I thought you to be. Leave me before our father learns of such threats." Returning to the desk, she settled into the chair, waiting with bated breath till he turned with a soft chuckle to the fear seen to rise in glorious eyes and left the room.

Coming from his place in the shadows, Captain DeLeon stated, "Lady Angeline, the Count would expect me to address such a situation. The young man needs to realize his place in the scheme of things. More importantly, he must realize yours."

Trembling hands clenched against the weakness and fear experienced before she reassured the Captain, "I will not have the Count at the center of a controversy where my family is involved. The treaty between our two families it is still too new to be tested. My brother is hurt and confused, assuming something that was never meant to be; I will see it goes no further." Determined eyes set upon the towering figure above her, and for silent moments, the two clashed in their devotions and loyalties. "If I have a reason to believe such threats have validity, I will inform the Count personally."

Recognizing the stubborn line retaking her shoulders, the Captain explained his duty to her, as well as his Count. "Count Illevante' will not be pleased to learn I have not addressed the situation. How am I to protect you if you won't allow me to do what is necessary?"

"I will address such with the Count when the time is necessary." Realizing her answer would have to appease him momentarily, the man returned to the obscurity of shadows.

Angeline lowered her head as fingers worked over the tension seeping into her brow; closed her eyes as she sought to press the anxiousness Stephen provoked away. '*Nickolai.*' Sighed as the image, she kept secure in her heart of him, was allowed to mind's eye, '*what do I do if he attempts such threats?*' Vividly she pictured the piercing blue eyes, the line of the prominent jaw, but more importantly, the perfection of his mouth. The lips which seemed to beckon even from memory, "sweet Jesus," managed to escape before realizing she spoke the words, "where are you?"

∞∞∞

The thin cotton sleeve, rolled back to catch of elbow, came to press the sweat gathered on the brow away as she drew the brush through the thick of mane in repeated strokes. Softly she crooned to the animal who would occasionally toss her great brown head in appreciation to the efforts of the woman at her side, "you are too spoiled." Angeline teased as fishing in her skirt pocket a treat was offered to the mare as a final swipe pressed over her length. "As soon as I've finished helping

Thomas, we'll go for a ride to your favorite place where the grass is sweet." She promised, turning from her labors as a commotion was heard to rise from the courtyard beyond the stables. "What in the world? Thomas," she called to the horse-master as he stumbled into the stable, "what is the uproar about?"

"Lady Angeline," nearly breathlessly, he gasped, "it is Count Illevante', he is here!"

"Here?" She gasped, horrified, as hands pressed into the simple blouse and skirt worn for her day of helping in the stables; the smell of horseflesh as it clung to her. "Not now!" Groaned as fisting the length of the skirt, she ran toward the house. Hoping to return to her rooms before the Count had a chance to spy upon her appearance. *'Did the man not have the common sense to send a messenger so I may have prepared for such an arrival?'* Grumbled inside her head as her naked feet flew over the lawns that separated stables from Keep.

Count Illevante` entered the courtyard with the clatter of hoofs to stone just as Angeline rounded the corner, for long moments, she stared to his startled appearance before the exclamation, "damn it." Slipped over her lips and the heat of blush slipped up her neck to bloom over cheeks, "double damn it." The fiery head shook to her timing as he stared at her from the back of his monstrous black mount. The image of him instantly burned into her memory as she felt her breath catch to the towering perfection of his mounted height. *'Did this man always have to be so breathtaking?'* Angeline scorned only moments before the tips of his leather boots came into the line of her lowered eyes.

Capturing her chin between the pinch of finger and thumb, he raised the features to confront him, "Lady Angeline, I presume?" Teased to the woman cowering before him. The hair a wild mass of auburn curls caught the sunlight and reflected it in a thousand points of light as it danced about her shoulders. "I hadn't realized you liked to run about barefoot."

The skirt was instantly returned to the proper length, as toes sought the protection of hem, "pray, forgive me, Count,

I was not aware you planned to visit Belaveuta." A retreating step was attempted from his towering closeness, only to find Nickolai followed, "I've been helping Thomas in the stables for most of the day. I usually see to the care of Astrolabe, one of my favorites; she always enjoys a good brushing and a treat at the end of the day." Meeting the amusement of his expression, Angeline realized he would be another person in her life who would not understand or accept her differences. The little hope of him being different, open-minded, and understanding disappeared. "If you will excuse me, I will tell my father of your arrival; he will be most pleased with your visit."

"It is my understanding the Captain did not make you aware of my arrival. It will not happen again, I assure you." Tossing the reins of his mount to his Captain, Nickolai managed, "allow me to escort you." Casting a deadly glance to the Captain from beneath her lowered lashes, Angeline managed a nod as they began walking in the direction to the front doors.

Angeline hesitated to the prospect of walking across the gravel that crunched thunderously beneath his boot. "Milady?" Nickolai questioned as she remained at the edge of the drive, and his eyes returned to her toes. "Ah!" His amusement only seemed to deepen to her obvious distress. Returning to her, he scooped her up into his massive arms as if she were no more than a child.

Clinging to the breadth of his shoulders with a squeal of surprise, Angeline felt the hard expanse of his chest under her pressing length. The strength of arms through the blouse. "I---I came out of the kitchen doors---but your men now filled that courtyard." Angeline attempted to explain, only to be confronted by the indecent closeness of his face, the line of his mouth seeming to twitch to the laughter he fought to tamp. "You can let me down; I'm perfectly capable of walking on my own." Escaped weakly, as the heat rising along her spine could not be damned as blush, the strange churning in the bottom of her belly no longer dismissed as nervousness.

As if she didn't say a word, he continued only to pause

with the question, "the horse is named oddly, is she not? Whose choice was it to such?"

Frowning to such observation to a name she had pondered in selecting for days and days, Angeline snapped, "it is not odd, merely different. I named her after an instrument---" only to be cut off by his knowledge.

"---it measures the distance to the stars." Nickolai finished instantly recognizing the anger that sparked eyes.

"I prefer to think of it as a way to measure the distance to heaven." Came with a touch of righteous indignation to the opinions he formed to what he knew not.

Cocking a dark brow, Nicholai questioned, "and she has achieved this for you?" Not entirely understanding the relationship between the two.

"She has brought me to a place as close to heaven that I've ever known, a place of peace and acceptance." Came softly as the memories of the afternoons caught safe in the imagines of mountains and oceans came once again to enfold her, the wildflowers and sweet grasses as they surrounded her. To a place that always came as a comfort to her. "And her name is not odd!" Nickolai was sure if she had her footing, she would have stamped her foot in indignation to his observation.

Reaching to address the front entrance, Nickolai was greeted by, "Lady Angeline!" Lorrie gasped horrified to Angeline's outlandish appearance, "in the name of all that is holy; what were you thinking---you can't---" The words seemed to die as the questionable expression from Illevante` was more than enough to halt further criticism. "Count Illevante', forgive me, but this is not acceptable at all; you must put her down this instant." With his nod of agreement, Angeline was allowed to slide down his length. When her feet finally did return to the ground, she had to hold to him for silent moments until the weakness invading her knees passed. "The Baron is surely going to retire me!" Lorrie mumbled as grasping the woman's wrist sought to tug Angeline back into the house where she would be appropriately attired to greet her betrothed. "Please, excuse us,

Count Illevante`, Lady Angeline will return when she is more adequately attired."

∞∞∞

In the sanctuary of the bedchamber, and far from the scrutiny of the Count, Lorrie hissed, "Lady Angeline, do you want the Count to think of you as nothing more than a serving wench? A Lady, who is going to be married to a Count, does not work in the stables. Nor does she allow the man to carry her about as if she were nothing more than a child." Obediently Angeline agreed with the woman as she was at first happy to have an excuse to leave his side yet miserable to go.

∞∞∞

Nickolai allowed his eyes to linger in follow of his betrothed before turning to the Captain who came to join him in the entranceway, "all has gone smoothly?" With Deleon's hesitation, Nickolai questioned, "not as smoothly as you desired?" Looking briefly in the direction of the woman's escape, Deleon sighed as it seemed his loyalty split between the two. "If you do not tell me what I need to know, I will learn it from Lady Angeline. Now, which decision would better suit your position at Illevante'?"

Nickolai had sensed the longing and need for his protection as he was practicing with his fencing-master. A need nearly painfilled washed over him. So powerful, he almost lost an ear to the momentary loss of concentration, and he knew he had no other choice but to come to her.

"I do not wish to betray Lady Angeline's trust." Armand managed as escorting his Count to the library where the Baron Belaveuta awaited. "She was quite adamant in her decision of not bringing you into a family confrontation."

Stopping before the library doors, Nickolai assured the Captain to their place in Angeline's life. "If there is a threat against Lady Angeline, her concerns to my involvement must be put aside if only to ensure her safety." With a nod, the man quickly recounted the moments of the stepbrother's confrontation. "Very well," came with a troubled crease to brow, "go, see that the Lady Angeline is not left unprotected."

∞∞∞

The smell of stables was scrubbed away in a barely warmed bath as a swarm of servants, who came to do Lorrie's bidding, washed and rubbed, then pulled and tugged. Angeline, barely dried and wrapped in a robe, was seated before vanity as Lorrie attempted to put the auburn curls into a semblance of order. "Enough, Lorrie!" Angeline finally snapped as the fiery length was gathered into a thick plait down her back and tied off with a ribbon. "You'll have me bald before styled." Grumbled, as another woman stepped forward with freshly laundered undergarments and still a third with a gown.

Confronting her image in the mirror, Angeline frowned to the reflection greeting her, "do you think this gown the wisest choice, I seem so pale." Fingertips came to travel the line of cheek as a critical inspection was conducted, "maybe we should try another, and my hair---maybe a different style. Something more elegant, perhaps a wig. Wasn't Antoinette saying they are at the peak of fashion now." Her delicate hands clutched into fists as the disgust of such a reflection more than she could bear, "nothing is right; I look hideous."

"Nonsense, Lady Angeline," Lorrie admonished the young woman, as she drew the hands attempting to release the ties which lined her spine away, "the color is perfect with your ivory flesh and perfectly complements your eyes."

Angeline frowned to the woman's reassurances and with fading determination turned from the reflection. Knowing if she remained for a moment more, she would hide behind chamber doors and never leave again. “I don’t think I’ve ever been so nervous in my life,” Angeline confessed to the surprise of the doting woman. “What if he’s disappointed? What if he’s like all the others and loathes what he finds when looking at me?”

With a wave of her hand, Lorrie dismissed the servants making themselves busy about the room, and came before the uncertainty of the woman, touched the heat of her cheek, “Milady, the Count Illevante’ is enchanted by you. All you have to do is look in his eyes to see such. And as far as the others?” She spat to the uncertainty of the woman; “they were fools, where could they find someone to top the beauty and graciousness you offer? There is much talk about the Count in the Crowned Prince Phillip's Court, and the woman he awaits as a wife is most anticipated.”

A blink brought forth building tears; “I look in his eyes, and all I see is amusement and waning patience to all of my shortcomings. And if such anticipation is true, he will only find disappointment in the woman he has chosen as a wife. I am nothing like the others which frequent the Court.”

“Perhaps this is true, my dear, but with all of his conquests, it is you he is marrying, is it not?” A square of linen came to dab away the trail of tears as she coaxed a smile before urging the woman on her way.

Opening the chamber door, Angeline stood before the Captain, who was never one to even hint to emotion or conversation as he confronted her. “Captain, have you been in the Illevante` service for very long?” She questioned.

“For nearly as long as you have lived, Milady.” He responded, unsure of the thoughtfulness which came to the crease of her worried brow, the tug of lower lip by teeth as specific questions were wanted to be asked.

Nodding to such information, Angeline managed the smallest of smiles, “are rumors true to his conquests at Court?” Feeling the prickle of tears at the back of her lids as she could see his reproach to answer the question, she wondered, “will he be disappointed in me, Captain?"

"Disappointed, Milady?" He echoed to the woman before him now. The perfect features, marred by a crushing emotion he could not understand, a heart and demeanor which radiated the goodness in her soul, Armand pledged, "nay, Milady, I swear as Nickolai Illevant's Captain and companion, he will not be disappointed."

"Not even if I'm barefoot?" She teased, easing somewhat to the sincerity of his words.

"Not even barefoot." He encouraged.

The dazzling smile was flashed to his palpable relief, "thank you, Captain, and I forgive you for not telling me of his arrival." With a sigh of building resolve, she quickly descended the stairs, stopping as she came before the closed library doors. "You're positive?" She questioned once again as he hurried to keep her pace.

"Positive, Milady." Before announcing her to the room, the Captain apologized, "I never meant to deceive you to the Count's arrival, I thought you were aware of his plans." With her appreciative smile, he opened the doors. "Lady Angeline." He presented before stepping back to the shadows, only to make himself known should the Count require his services.

Dropping into her most perfect curtsy, she held the bow for long moments as the words, "ah, Angeline, perfect timing, come---I have a few things I need to attend to before dinnertime. Antoinette can't abide me working through a meal." Anton chuckled, coming to draw his daughter deeper into the room. "Count, please excuse me."

Watching as her father bustled from the room with a mumbling of apologies and reassurances, Angeline turned back to find Illevante' had bridged the distance between them and now stood no more than a breath from her. "I hope I haven't kept you waiting."

"Only a lifetime." Presenting his hand, Nicholai was pleased to feel the fingers curl protectively about his touch, "I trust my Captain has kept you safe?" Managed as drawing her into the separation of their bodies, he found her searching eyes met his with a hesitant, nearly hopeful smile in greeting to him.

"Quite safe, thank you." Releasing the gentle lead of his hand, Angeline came to nervously flutter over the volumes of books she had left unattended earlier in the day.

Frowning to the distance placed between them, Nickolai persisted as the width of the desk separated them, "so there are no concerns that you wish to share with me?"

Casting a look as naive as possible over her shoulder, as she was sure he would recognize the worry as it came to her, the fiery head shook. "Nothing that I can't handle myself." Angeline pondered sharing Stephen's threats, then immediately decided against it; instead, she sought a different, safer, subject. "Father is very generous with his books; however, he becomes quite perturbed when I forget to put them away." As she made herself busy with the straightening, he lifted each volume to inspect her interests, and the dark brow rose in question to the subjects of her preferred reading. "I wanted to get out to the stables and when Thomas called to let me know Astrolabe was in from the fields, I rushed to be with her."

Watching her nervous avoidance for silent moments, Nickolai wished to question her; hoped for her to confess the words the brother used if only to justify his anger. The threat against self was of little consequence to Nickolai, having had to face adversaries before. However, the idea of Angeline living under the same roof as this man caused him to wonder if waiting for the desired time to wed a wise decision. "So, your interests swing from horses, heaven, to conquerors." He managed to see some of the most notable names of conquers holding her interests. "Are you planning an invasion?"

"Only a tiny one." Came in retaliation as the book was drawn from his hands and replaced in the allotted spot on the shelves which lined an entire wall of her father's library. "Stephen's last tutor had just introduced the strategy of war before Antoinette came to the deduction further teachings were no longer necessary. When Stephen no longer had an interest in furthering his education, consequently, she curtailed mine as well." Angeline watched as he moved slowly about the room though he seemed to keep his eyes forever focused on her. "My interests were not considered in the decision."

Watching her for silent moments as the very breath of him was robbed by merely allowing himself to remember that soon she would be his wife. Nickolai forced a distance between them, as he wanted to concentrate on her words and not the need as it grew between them. Wanted their relationship to build on more than mere passion; he wanted her trust and commitment. "Ah, yes, Stephen. And how is your brother? I did not see him when I arrived." He fought to keep his suspicions under strict control as he recognized the color which drained from her to the mention of the man, the hesitation in facing him to such questioning.

Shrugging off such knowledge, Angeline managed, "Father keeps him very busy. He is expected to learn all of Belaveuta, as it will one day be his." Wishing only to change the subject, even if it meant returning it to her, so fast and confusing were his emotions coming to bombard her.

"Stephen is the only son?" He asked, aimlessly wandering about the room.

"Stephen is Antoinette's only son," Angeline quickly corrected. "My father married Antoinette with the stipulation Belaveuta would be Stephen's once my marriage was secured, and father begot no other children. My mother was unable to give my father a son. She, as well as the babe, died shortly after the birthing."

Frowning to such knowledge, he paused for only a moment, "why did the Baron not leave you Belaveuta? You are his legal heir." And the endless roaming resumed.

Smiling to the simplicity of such a notion, Angeline enlightened, "I am not a legal, male heir. The Queen nor the Crowned Prince would ever sanction such succession." Angeline lowered her eyes as she watched his powerful body move. The muscular legs strained and flexed beneath the catch of hugging material. The shoulders solid, tightly honed layers of strength caused her to recall artist renditions of black panthers. Unfailing to the power carefully captured beneath a thin veneer of control.

"You are more capable than most, more educated obviously." His hand waved over the spread of text. "Surely your father had plans for you, or he wouldn't have allowed your education."

Following the wave of his hand to the text which still scattered the desktop, she confessed, "Father wasn't aware of my education until Stephen told him." A small smile came to the memories; "Stephen was never very interested in their teachings. I believe it upset him when the tutors were paying more attention to my studies than his."

"Perhaps it was the phenomenon of a young woman wishing to learn," Nickolai commented, knowing of few women who desired to read, let alone study with scholars. Most were concerned with learning the fine art of finding the wealthiest husband.

Arching a brow in surprise to such a statement, Angeline questioned tersely, "do you find my interests so different from the other women in your life? Is a woman who knows how to read and write such a phenomenon?"

"Hardly a phenomenon, Milady, however, most women, who *were* in my life, wouldn't know what a library was, let alone to be found barefoot in a stable with the knowledge of an astrolabe." Nickolai could see the stern line of Angeline's lips ease into a small smile of sad understanding. '*How*,' he wondered, '*could I have ever thought to leave this woman unattended for so long. How was it possible for none to push aside his administrations and seek to claim her for their own*?' He watched as she turned without comment to the remainder of books and seemed to fuss over their placement for silent moments. "I hope I have not insulted or demeaned you in any way, little one, I assure you it was not my intention."

Focusing on the books, and not the insistence of the man

at her back, Angeline confessed after thoughtful consideration to his words. "I am nothing like the women you've attracted previously. I don't understand why you have chosen me as a wife. Why are you so kind and considerate? Why you feign such interest in everything I do? If we were a fairy tale, you would be the handsome prince, and I would be the toad. And not even one of your kisses could turn me into a beautiful princess." Turning into the circle of his arms, Angeline braced herself against his towering strength, fought the solace of his warmth as it encompassed her. "Why do you believe I am the one who will make you happy? I have never been able to make any man happy, make any man want me. I know that you could have any woman, at any time, that you've had your choice." Valiantly tears were fought as she attempted to control the tremble of her chin. "Why me?"

"Angeline," Nickolai managed as he confronted the misery of her features. "If only you would believe me when I say that for every woman I have ever looked at in my life, I have been looking for you. For every breath I have ever drawn into my body, I have done so with the hopes of finding you. You have made me happier in mere moments than I have ever been in my entire life." The pads of his thumbs caressed away her doubts as he teased, "how many times do I have to remind you, I am unlike any man who has come into your life before? Know that I love you, Angeline, I will love you always. And you, little one, are hardly the toad in this relationship."

The fiery head was shaking with rejection, even before her words could be formed, "you profess to love so easily when you don't even know me. Of my differences." With a sigh of defeat to her insecurity, to the emotions she knew to be true from him with what she could sense, Angeline asked, "what if my differences are too great, even for this love you so easily proclaim?"

Chuckling to the question, his lips pressed to the top of the nestled head before stating, "my god, Angeline, you are like a breath of fresh air. Do you not realize how the women in Court are like one mind, one mold? Money and marriage. To be able to have a conversation; to share an idea; is a marvel, I assure you. This is hardly a difference, little one." Smiling to the features which eased to his words, the length relaxing against him, Nickolai offered, "and once properly settled at Illevante` you must make the library your own. We have an extensive collection of titles covering many subjects. Many, I'm sure that will hold your interests for years to come. And with Antony, my assistant, you will find a wealth of information to all that you seek to study."

∞∞∞

Waiting in the shadow of the door's frame, Lorrie felt her heart ease to the words the Count used to console Angeline. Watched with a tender tugging of emotion as he caressed her beneath loving hands. '*How,*' Lorrie wondered, '*could this child not see the emotion he held toward her? How could she not guess the gentleness and caring used during each interaction with her?*' Once satisfied to the direction the relationship had taken, the woman took a deep breath before barging into the room, "Lady Angeline! Not again!" Lorrie cried in disgust, "I leave you alone for a mere ten minutes and look what happens!"

Pressing a final kiss against the nestled head, Nickolai allowed the escape wished for and for silent moments paced the room waiting to see where the servant would settle before doing so himself.

Once Lorrie had decided on a chair before the desk and settled with satisfaction to her vantage point in the room, Nickolai pointed to the chess set and with Angeline's nod, drew out the heavy wooden chair for her to join him, "I assume you play?"

Settling on the chair he attended, she was acutely aware of his closeness as he came to lean over her shoulder, waiting for a response. The cheek nearly pressed to her own, his radiating warmth as it seemed to beckon her beyond reason and decency, "you assume correctly, Count."

∞∞∞

The game that Nickolai presumed would be over quickly, lasted far longer than anticipated as the woman before him seemed to predict his every move and have a counter in defense. More than once, he found his attention waning as he studied her concentration of the pieces, his eyes lingering over the perfection of mouth as the lower lip was repeatedly tugged between teeth then nibbled. Finally, moving to take his king, *'checkmate'* was announced with a sigh of relief. "I would like to say I let you win." He teased to the realization his soon to be wife had bested him.

"I promise not to tell a soul." The forever watchful Captain was given a furtive glance, as it seemed he barely looked in their direction for the many hours of their game; however, her woman, it would seem never took her eyes from them. "She, however, may be a different story." Angeline teased as they rose from the game once replacing the pieces to proper order. Looking away as the hall clock was heard to chime, she realized no one had come to summon them to dinner, "I fear we may have missed dinner; would you like me to have Lorrie direct the kitchens? They could prepare a late sup if you so desire."

"I asked your father to sup without us," Nickolai informed as pressing his hand into hers he led her from the room with a leading tug. "I thought a private dinner for two more appropriate." Nodding with pre-occupied thoughts, as she couldn't help but concentrate on the hand engulfing hers, the size and strength of it causing her to wonder to the control that he maintained to remain so gentle in touch. "Does it bother you?" He questioned, and seeing the questionable eyes as they rose to confront him, he persisted, "me; holding your hand, does it bother you?" Quickly skirting her eyes from his probing ones, the fiery head shook with embarrassment as her cheeks were felt to color once again. "Good, because I had no intention of relinquishing the hold."

Entering the dining room, Angeline gasped to see the usual massive dining table replaced by a table designed for two. "How could you have managed all this? I can't believe Antoinette approved of this." And it surprised her that she had not seen her stepmother for the entire time of the Count's arrival.

Chuckling to her apparent approval, Nickolai teased, "you don't think I travel with all those men just for protection, do you? And the Baron pleaded my case to your stepmother." The candles set about the room cast a warm glow as she ventured closer to the table to inspect the bouquet of roses that adorned a vase to overflowing, "they're from our gardens." He managed as her fingertips came to caress the velvet petals.

"They're beautiful." Managed softly as with a motion of his hand, servants began to appear with steaming delicacies. Nickolai pressed conversation as he sought to learn more of her. Questions from childhood to as recent as the previous week were asked, and not wishing to interrupt the stories she shared; he insisted on selecting only foods she showed an interest in from among the many presented. Till finally, a sweetened custard came to be presented, and she had to beg off another bite. "Not even if you threatened." She laughed to the disappointment as it came to his features.

"Are you sure?"

"Positive." And she laughed to the dubious expression greeting her.

As the dishes were cleared away, Nickolai motioned to the wine server, who promptly opened the champagne and poured it between the two glasses remaining on the table. Watching Angeline sip to the bubbling wine, he couldn't help but feel his need for her to clench at his body. Watched as her tongue teased over the mouth's perfection to the bubbles which dared to caress where he had not, and he wondered to his sanity of such a need.

Angeline studied the stem of crystal with a thoughtful preoccupation of his inevitable feelings. She knew it only a matter of time until the hope and happiness of their evening would thin to troubling emotions, emotions which brought a frown to her mouth as she had thought the evening to be perfect. "You're frowning." He observed, wondering what he had done to displease her.

The fiery head shook, and the curls which had managed to escape the braid in teasing wisps about her face, "I'm afraid you are not pleased with this evening's outcome. I'm sorry, I tried to make it as tolerable for you as possible." Angeline managed, as the unfinished wine was placed aside with disappointment to the obviousness of his frustration and desire to be from her presence. "I'm quite surprised you were able to mask such from me for so long; you are far more diligent than most to be sure."

"Contrary to what you may think you know; I am very pleased to any time I can spend with you." Seeing the doubt which came to mar her features, Nickolai settled back into the chair as he carefully considered sharing his observations, "I have come to realize you are very sensitive to other's emotions; that you can sense the disappointment or conflict within them." Nickolai clarified to what she sensed from him, "little one, the only disappointment I feel at this moment, is that I will soon have to leave you. You need to believe me; you need to trust me when I say these things to be true."

"I am trying, however, sometimes it is difficult to trust; to believe so blindly in all that you share with me."

"All I can do is ask you to search your heart, as well as mine, and know that I would never deceive you." With her hesitant nod, Nickolai shared, "you remind me of my mother. She came to my father under the same circumstance. The stories she would tell me of her mistrust. He was adamant in his love of her, so adamant on the day they were to sign their marriage contract, he had fashioned a gift for her. A gift, he stated, which would win her heart forever." Smiling to the memory, he explained, "there are jewels in the Illevante' coiffures my ancestors have collected for many years, jewels from the four corners of the world; from the kings of many countries." Nickolai managed as reaching into his tunic to retrieve a small box, "on my sixteenth birthday, my mother presented me this gift for the woman I would marry. Though she assured me it had nothing to do with winning her heart, she hoped the sentiment behind it would help me achieve such." Coming about the table, he presented Angeline with the box, "I would like you to have this."

Angeline cherished the history behind the gift as she accepted the offering, "your mother sounds like a wise woman. I wish I had to chance to meet her."

"I wish you could have, as well." Rising from the chair, he assured her, "she would have loved to welcome you as daughter to Illevante'."

Lifting the lid, Angeline revealed a teardrop-shaped emerald as she drew a pendant, nearly the size of her fist, from its resting-place, she requested, "would you mind fastening it for me?"

"It has been waiting for you." He managed softly, warmly over the ivory column of her throat as Nico secured the ribbon. "Its beauty rivaled only by your glorious eyes." Caressing fingertips lingering over the line of jaw pleased when she was felt to press into the touch of his palm as it cupped the warmth of cheek. The interrupting cough of her woman caused a mutter of oath to escape as Nickolai reluctantly relinquished the touch to pace the cavernous room for silent moments. Moving to where the Captain remained, a few quick words were shared before Nickolai turned once again to the forever watchfulness of Angeline. Coming to her side, he apologized, "it has been many a year since I have required a chaperone, please forgive my forwardness. Do you think she would approve if we were to get a breath of fresh air?"

Casting a glance to Lorrie who rose with them, Angeline directed them to the terrace doors, silently she led him from the dining room to the night beyond. "Lady Angeline," came the warning as the woman followed onto the terrace, "this is not proper, Milady. What would your stepmother have to say if I allowed you to wander about in the dark?"

Inhaling deeply of the scents of rose and lavender as they carried in the gentle breeze, Nickolai suggested, as drawing Angeline close to his side, “Lorrie, I was hoping you would show my Captain about the gardens. I assure you your Lady will be safe here with me.” The woman turned to confront the towering strength of the man at her back, gave him a weak smile as his features became lost in the shadow of night. “He would greatly appreciate the diversion to duty. You must take your time.”

Waiting the moment, it took for the woman to make up her mind, Lorrie turned toward the gardens and stepped into the paths beyond, “she’ll realize her duty and quickly return. She has always been very faithful to my stepmother.” Angeline cautioned to his towering closeness the warmth of his pressing strength, as she became acutely aware of him. The man he was and the havoc he could create on her senses. Angeline realized as the sounds of the night settled about them, Lorrie was entirely correct. It was not proper for her to be alone with him, not even for a moment, not with the images capable of haunting her to his nearness.

“Perhaps.” Sounded and Angeline took an involuntary step back from his towering closeness the warmth as it was felt to lick the length of her spine in terrifying intent. “But then again, perhaps not.” Teased as he reached in the slight distance between them to caress the heat of her cheek, the column of the throat where fingertips tripped over the ribbon bound there. “Do not fear me, Angeline, search your heart and know that I would never hurt or force you, under any circumstance.”

Allowing the breath to escape as the fire deep in her body was felt to flourish; she acknowledged her place in his life, “I am to be wife, of what say would I have?” And she turned to the laughter heard to come from the direction of the gardens only to be suddenly muffled with a quick gasp.

Emerald returned to find the amusement of such implication in his study of her, of the heat, deepening along the cheek, "you would have every right to say how and where this evening will end."

Exhaling to the implication of his words, Angeline managed, "it may be best if I retire now, it is getting late."

"If you wish," came as he sensed the anxiousness engulfing her to what was still the unknown, "allow me to escort you." Stepping about the protection of his length, Angeline maintained her lead along the many halls and passageways before stopping before chamber doors. "Thank you for allowing me to spend this evening with you, Angeline."

Before the doors, with her back pressed to the barrier as if in support, Angeline lifted her features to confront the conviction of the man before her. Daringly she allowed her eyes to search over the perfection of his features, the beckon of a demanding mouth, and felt a shuddered breath escape to the moments raging between them. Nervously her hand came to close over the gem, which weighted her throat, her fingertips to caress the coolness as it seemed her body blazed to his nearness. "Thank you for my gift; it is beautiful."

Inhaling suddenly as his hand came to confirm the warmth of her cheek, his thumb to caress the perfection of her lips, Nickolai professed, "you know, little one, it may have been best if we had kept that chaperone between us." Slowly he came to press his lips over hers. Softly he searched the mouth as she seemed to tremble beneath the insistence, pulling back from the crowding of his length; she nearly gasped out loud as his arm circled her waist, dragging her hard to his strength. Reacquainted her to his need as it raged as never before, "Angeline," whispered as his mouth traveled throat, and the pulse nuzzled, "what sweet torture you have always been."

Angeline felt the immediate surrender of her traitorous length as it seemed the bones within her body turned to nothing more than jelly and the blood in her veins burned to the teasing he was capable of, "Milord," escaped in a haggard breath as her arms rose to encase his breadth to her, caress the strength of shoulders.

Pressing into the softness of her cradling length Nickolai nearly growled to the overriding hardness of his body as the softness of her belly was felt to caress his need. Her hips a welcome to all she promised, to all she held. Smothering an oath in the surround of fiery hair, valiantly Nickolai fought the release pounding in his ears, resisted the impulse to lead her to the bed, he knew to lay beyond, and claim his right even before their wedding day. "Little one." Managed before all thought, all reason was gone from him as the softness of her body was felt to arch into his with the growing need of her own, the insistence of her womanhood offered with the cradling of thighs as they embraced his urging, "sweet Jesus, you have no idea how much I need you." His hands seemed to be everywhere and then nowhere. Teasing and caressing, exploring, and beckoning as she whimpered to the burn of her desire growing with an unfamiliar ferocity. Pulling himself away from her welcome, Nickolai exhaled a steadying breath as he commanded, "go to your chambers, little one, go before I can no longer control my need of you."

Opening the door with a trembling hand to knob she nearly staggered into the room beyond only to turn to him before his escape could be possible, "will I see you in the morning, Milord?" She questioned unsure if she wished to put the distance that he so urgently demanded between them. How could he demand that she leave him now, now when her body was trembling with anticipation of his next touch. Yearning to grasp what now seemed the unattainable though only moments ago was within her reach.

"I will give you a proper goodbye, little one, have no doubt." He promised before turning in the direction of his chambers.

∞∞∞

Nickolai's caressed Angeline's features hoping to ease the worry recognized in her expression, "I'm sorry I can't stay longer, little one." Meeting the eyes of his Captain and the men of his garrison which surrounded, he reassured the concern found in her eyes, “I have assigned more of my garrison to remain with the Captain until I return. You must allow them to protect you; keep Armand near you always.” Angeline's eyes remained steadfast in the study of his boots as the words Stephen had used to threaten her came to haunt. “Please tell me you will give me this small consideration.”

Slowly the eyes rose to confront his concerns, his insistence for her safety when he was the one in danger. “But what of you? You will need the protection far more than I.”

“Why is that, little one, who could try to hurt me?” Nickolai pressed her, hoping Angeline would express the concerns so obviously witnessed in her wondrous eyes. He needed her to trust him if only this one time.

Exhaling, with a defining conclusion to the task before her, Angeline shared, “I'm afraid my brother is still bitter, Milord. I don't know what he is capable of doing.” Came as she refused to acknowledge the sudden burst of relief felt to swamp her, “I'm not sure what the Captain shared with you if he has shared anything at all, but Stephen believes himself in love with me. Believes if you had not appeared, he would have convinced my father to accept him as my husband. He is making such horrible, vile threats against you.”

Nickolai pressed his lips into the warmth of her cheek before acknowledging, “thank you, I know how important it is that the peace we have only begun to experience hold. I will overlook your brother's bitterness with the stipulation that you accept the protection of my additional men.” Seeing the objection rise once again to his safety, he promised, “and I take only enough to see me safely home.”

Her smile caused a small dimple to dot her left cheek to the stipulation and concession made, “very well, I agree.” Shyly she pressed her lips to the closeness of his cheek as whispering, “thank you, Nickolai.”

∞∞∞

The monstrous black mount had long left the drive to Belaveuta, and still, Angeline remained unmoving on the front steps. Again, her fingertips came to touch the tenderness of her abused mouth as a smile came to ease the worry that clouded her eyes, "ten days." He had promised as his mouth sought hers, "ten days and never again will I endure such separation between us."

Five

After endless days of frenzied preparations, Angeline found herself standing reverently beside the man who would be her husband and felt quietly at ease to the decision. She watched the priest, who had heard her father's confession for many years, ready the necessary documents to their joining. Felt her breath hold as Illevante's flowing signature scratched across the marriage contract. Surprising Angeline, as he turned to her with the request, "I will have you sign our agreement, Lady Angeline, I will have your consent." With her father's silent approval, her named joined his.

A mumbling of words sounded over their bent heads from the priest; words she was not quite ready to comprehend, and they were joined as one. With a steadying breath, Angeline turned to confront the witnesses as they expressed each sentiment in a flood of emotions. Illevante's guard dismissed to the loyalty held to their Count. Her brother, attending only because of their father's insistence, glared with a deepening hatred and loathing. To sadness, and Angeline's eyes found her father helping him to realize she readily accepted her fate.

Finally, relief and this emotion puzzled Angeline as her stepmother's guilty eyes swept quickly from the curious ones. Poor Antoinette, Angeline mused, to the young woman who came into a marriage not quite knowing or understanding the child who realized the scorn and contempt harbored. Emotions that only festered within her as husband seemed to be far more content to spend his time with the daughter than the new wife.

The scorn which forced the child to flee the house in hopes of finding one capable of understanding her differences and talents.

The hand claiming hers tugged, drawing her from troubling thoughts, and she turned to her husband. '*Husband*!' and the idea of him loving her seemed a nearly impossible thing. Could he be the one she searched for all those years ago, all those moments ago? She wondered with a touch of sadness. '*Nickolai*.' and the name filled her heart, breaking any barriers she tried to build between them, '*if only I could hold you to my heart forever.*' Lowering scrutinizing eyes, as his amused expression turned toward her and winked with a somehow knowing to the emotions which pinkened her cheeks. "It is time, little one; we have a few hours of travel before us."

Angeline turned to the cheer of, "Illevante'!" from the surrounding Illevante' men as Armand bent to a kneel before her to swear his life to her safety. Angeline couldn't help the smile that seemed to ease the last of her worries to such a decision. "Thank you," she murmured to the Captain, "thank you all."

"It is all that you deserve, Angeline," Nickolai whispered before turning to address the silence of her family. "Milord," he began as her father came to embrace him in the way of warriors. Hand to arm, sureness, and strength tested in a matter of moments to each, "you do me a great honor today, one I will never forget. One I will repay to you a thousand times on the battlefield when our forces join when our allegiance is most tested." Ruefully Nickolai watched as the Baron's stepson was heard to curse violently under his breath before leaving the gathering.

"Pay him no mind, he is young and a fool." Anton spat with a disgusted shake of his head to Stephen's display. "My little flame," was spoken with heartbreak as he came to gather his daughter into his arms. Holding Angeline close, Anton fought the emotion building at the back of his throat, "I will miss you, daughter, and I will always love you." Drawing her back to arm's length, he advised, "it has always been my experience to hold no secrets, my love, to trust is to love." Taking her father's words quickly to heart, for she alone understood the meaning behind the message. Angeline held him for a single moment longer before turning to share a brief, cold, exchange with her stepmother. "Antoinette, thank you for everything you have tried to instill upon me."

Raising a pale brow in surprise to her stepdaughter's words, Antoinette confessed, "you have never made our relationship easy, Angeline. Perhaps if your father did not spoil you as he has, you would have appreciated my guidance and accepted it more willingly."

Nodding to the honesty of the woman, Angeline conceded, "perhaps, I was never a willing student." A step brought her back into Nickolai's hovering protection.

Escorted into the confines of a massive carriage that left Belaveuta by a team of six restless stallions Angeline watched as the only place she had ever called home became nothing more than a dark line in the distance. Settling against the cushion, she confronted the silence of her watchful husband, the thickening of expectancy as it came to swamp her. Not wishing to think of the hours before her, instead Angeline thought of all she left behind. To the home which held all the memories she cherished of her mother, “I should have paid attention to the many things my stepmother placed into the trunks. What if she has coveted items my mother wished me to have upon my wedding day?” She managed, “how could I have allowed myself to abandon all that is dear to me. All that I have held to my heart for many years?”

The linked metal covering his chest was released as Nickolai confronted the distress of her parting, “all of importance to you is safely in Illevante’. I requested as much from Antoinette, and I have no reason to doubt her promise to see all arrangements.”

"No reason to doubt Antoinette?" Confronting the smug sureness of his actions, Angeline snapped, "how could she possibly know what is of importance to me? Of the precious items left to remind me of my mother. She has been waiting with bated breath for the day I was to leave Belaveuta. For the day, she would have my father to herself; as you heard, I was nothing more than a spoiled, willful, brat."

Capturing her hand, Nickolai held it close to his heart, as he reassured, "I do not doubt that she has completed all requested of her."

Tugging her hand from his, Angeline deliberately avoided Nickolai's niggling concerns to her doubting him, "you don't know anything of Antoinette, and you know even less of me."

Reaching in the distance between them, no more than the press of thigh to thigh, Nickolai reclaimed her hand, pressed it to the warmth of his mouth, before persisting, "I know you, little one, I feel your heart as you feel mine." Looking over the knuckles he lavished to the questioning stare, he pleaded, "do not fear me, little one, or have suspect toward my feelings. Only know that they are genuine and sure to grow in the years that stretch before us. I can do no more than pledge myself to you, like my guard before me, and swear you will always be safe. You will want for naught and cherished for the woman that you are, for being my wife."

Contemplating the warmth of his touch, Angeline sighed with little resolve against the arrogance of the man before her, for what else could it be if not pride, she mused, if he thought to know her very heart. "You speak to me of years, Milord, when we have yet to complete a single day."

"Or night." Nickolai mused, causing him to nearly laugh out loud to the look of repugnance directed at him. With a sound, '*humph*' Angeline refused to acknowledge his staring silence or the damning heat invading her cheeks. "Do you not agree we should cherish each day as if it could be our last?" He finally spoke, breaking the long silence that stood between them.

"I believe I may wish this to be my last." Wearily the head rested back against the cushion as she attempted to find sleep, only to feel as if she was being bumped and jolted from every rut in the road. Moaning, her hand came to massage against the stiffness creeping into neck and shoulders, and still, she disavowed the natural call his length seemed to beckon. Avoided the comfort his strength cradling hers would bring.

"Little one," whispered, as he could take no more of her constant agitation in her seek to find sleep, "come here." An arm circled her shoulders, drawing her to his strength and willingly Angeline came. Welcomed the sureness of his length as it shifted to accommodate her weariness better, as it seemed the natural thing, secured in the fold of his arms.

Closing her eyes, she welcomed the warmth of his cloak as it came to enfold her. With a murmur of his name, Angeline welcomed the beckon of sleep, and the piercing eyes that invaded dreams with a haunting need to understand and accept. Shifting in the surround of arms, Angeline buried herself into the strength as images caused her body to undulate in rising demand and whisper in plead of her desire. The elusive image that would bring to an end desire always teased at, to the need only a dreamed touch would end.

Slowly Nickolai exhaled and allowed the images to escape him if only to end the torture he brought to self. How much longer could he dream of what making love to his woman would be like when she was now warm and beckoning in his arms? If only he could win her heart as quickly as her pledge.

It seemed as if an eternity had passed since he had first found her, sensed her through the ancient power that coursed his veins. For countless years he believed himself cursed never to be loved, never to be allowed to love.

Images to years ago came as a smug reminder to the day Angeline came into his life. To a time when he was young and willing to take any risk in pleasing his father; Nickolai would often disguise himself as a villager and move freely about Belaveuta. He found it the easiest way to learn strategies and rumor to planned incursions. Vividly remembered the moment when a child came along by the tugging hand of a newly acquired mother, but mostly he remembered how he found himself lost to the emotion conquering heart. The whispers of his ancients, who foretold of a woman destined to remain at his side for an eternity.

The child soon became an obsession, and in the years that followed, Nickolai's visits to Belaveuta became more frequent. Each with the hope of catching a mere glimpse of the child who quickly grew into a woman. A woman, the likes of he had never seen before. One look from her emerald eyes more than enough to melt even the most apathetic of hearts, and he was no exception. With a face and body befitting a goddess, Nickolai found himself helplessly lost to the unknowing of the woman as he secretly watched her for the many years to womanhood.

Visits, no longer sanctioned by father or secreted to the victory of the war, became more frequent. When a confrontation between the families was unavoidable, Illevante` ensured no harm came to any of her loved ones. So worried was he to irreparable damage such an act would have on the relationship they would share.

For hours he would study battlefields and possible scenarios all in the hopes of never having to confront her father or brother. Situations he soon found himself an expert at as he grew the power to foretell of battles and their outcomes. Such a power quickly drew the attention of Queen and then her son, the now Crowned Prince. Making him an indispensable friend and ally to the Crown.

With passing time, Nickolai found it more and more difficult not to introduce himself to Belaveuta's daughter; before another, the Baron deemed worthy of her sought to do. On more than one occasion, either through rumor at Court or visitor to Illevante', Nickolai would learn of an enthusiastic suitor. Such talk caused Nickolai to do everything in his power of persuasion to turn the man's interests away. But Nickolai found she was a woman too few were willing to forget no matter what images or suggestions he invoked to defer them.

With a frown, he remembered the ardent suitor who realized warts and blackened teeth Angeline had acquired in the many days of his persistence. Or the Nobel who became conscious of the horrible hump she carried to back and how it bent her perversely crooked. All rescinded their intentions gracefully. It was never Nickolai's wish to hurt or dampen the young woman's spirit only to keep others from winning her heart till the time played into his favor.

However, with regret, he looked down at the beauty before him and sighed. Nickolai had never been privy to the extraordinary gift she possessed, enabling Angeline to realize what others were feeling or how it affected her. The moment Nickolai stepped from the shadows, he realized how Angeline could read each of those surrounding her. Knowingly absorbed the emotions they projected, then just as deliberately dismissed them. It was at that moment Nickolai felt the shame of his actions, the knowing of his selfishness. The horror and repulsion projected to her innocent mind enough to make Nickolai want to confess all; if only to help regain her injured confidence if it wouldn't mean she would hate him for always. Her insecurities voiced, 'othe*rs wonder to your choice in me as a wife'* caused him to nearly scoff out loud to the absurdity of opinion toward self. He should have realized the ancients would not have sent him an ordinary woman, a woman who would not understand his secrets and considerations. If only he had been courageous years ago if only, he came forward as always intended instead of waiting till his ancients thought her ready to accept him. If only---sighed wearily.

Even now, it was only because of circumstance that forced his ancients to agree to his demands; Nickolai learned of the impetuousness of her brother and the relentlessness of a planned invasion on Illevante' that determined the future. He would come forward before more bloodshed would be possible and pledge a future of lasting peace all for the hand of daughter. Illevante` was weary of battle and knew if peace did not reign soon, he would forego all planning and take Belaveuta, as his father always planned, by force, by death.

After months of secret negotiations, first with the Queen Mother, then with Belaveuta, an agreement was settled upon, a contract dependent on the acceptance of Angeline. Illevante` knew he wanted her to come to him willingly, to believe she had a say in the course her life was taking. However, Nickolai was unwilling to open himself to rejection and willed the father to press her, demanded that her refusal not be an option. When he ventured from the shadows to confront the woman, who goaded his presence as no one had dared before— as she faced him without fear or hesitation to the position and rumor held, he knew that he had to have her willingly, body and soul. She was a woman who seemed to sense him in a far different realm than what he was comfortable with from others allowed near. A woman who was bold and daring one moment then scared and cringing the next.

Feeling the slight weight in his arms shift into a more comfortable position, bury herself deeper, closer to the length as her arm came to circle waist, clutched in the splay of hand caused Nickolai to groan to her pressing softness, the sweetness of her scent as it engulfed in rose and vanilla. And he wondered how much longer he could endure such sweet agony. Gently drawing away the wig, of powder and feathers she donned, he sought the fiery richness hidden beneath, allowed the length to tumble free about his hands and arms. The splay of vibrant color seemed to surround in a thousand burnish blazing fingers coaxing from him a desire nearly painful in its intensity. Brushing aside errant curls clinging to cheek and lash gave Nickolai leave to caress the perfection of her features, trace the line of flawless lip. Pulling from the flesh before he pushed beyond the limits of her innocent understanding, Nickolai heard, '*she will be your life, Nico; she will be salvation. She will keep you unto her heart for many lifetimes.*' Eased the direction of his troubled thoughts, and with a moan of frustration, Nickolai removed his touch, and Angeline's sleep deepened in the knowledge of her safety, and the travel continued.

∞∞∞

Nickolai knew the moment she woke, could sense the limbs as they nearly vibrated to the closeness of his length, to the images that came in a reminder of her dreams. Pressing up from the chest supporting her, her hand lingered on the thick of a rock-hard thigh as she pressed the palm of the second against the weariness of eyes, "they call you Nico." Angeline managed, turning on the seat to confront his suspicious eyes for her to have such knowledge. No one had called him such since his mother, and she had passed years before.

"Pardon?" Nickolai questioned the statement that seemed to make his heart slam within his chest. Could she be such a strong empathic to read his deepest secrets, seek his most sheltered memories? Could he trust her with the secrecy and mystery surrounding his life, did he want to trust her? Nickolai wondered, and instinctively he closed his mind from further probing, nearly shut himself off emotionally.

Confused to the information, Angeline shook her head to what was shared and what was the truth, "in my dreams---voices, shadows---they called you Nico. They promised me all that I sought if only to keep you to my heart. The words were mere whispers and shadows, '*when blood is shed of one who isn't so shall you remain to claim your love.*'" She repeated, looking to him for answers, answers she was sure only he would know. Desperate eyes searched his hooded ones; bereft with the realization she could not sense what he was feeling, could not gather the needed information from his emotions, that all passion from him was gone. "What are you doing!" Cried to the dark void engulfing her, her eyes wide and wild to the black pit threatening to overcome her sanity. "What have you done?"

"Angeline?" He questioned to see the tears as they clouded her eyes, the terror that caused her slight length to tremble as if injured. "Angeline!"

The mouth worked to speak, but no words could come from her as emotions thickened her throat, and she felt sure to faint to such a longing, "you closed yourself from me." Angeline whispered, scampering to the far corner of the cushion, "never has one been able to make me feel so---alone." A violently shaking hand pressed to the pound of her heart if only to ensure it wasn't breaking, "it was as if everything I have ever known to hold my sanity together left me." The sobs came in a shuddering strength causing Nickolai to gather her near. Poured forth all his understanding and worry to the reaction felt, and slowly he felt the length within his arms ease to the comforts expelled.

Gathering her onto his lap, Nickolai held her for silent moments, cradled her to his length till the trembles were felt to ease and the tears to cease. Nico realized the moment he closed himself mentally off from her, emotionally blocked her from learning any more of him; she became frantic. Had he been foretelling his emotions to her all these years that when he suddenly closed his heart from her, it was painful, obviously dreadful to her mental state? "Angeline, I know you can sense other's emotions. You are a strong empathic reader. The first night we meet at your father's I felt that about you, but how could this be possible? How can you understand the words of ancients, my ancients? How can closing my emotions affect you so?"

The fiery head shook against the length of the chest she clutched. Angeline's arms circled his torso, held to the strength of hardness and muscle, as she needed to absorb all of him if only to keep the vast barrenness at bay. "I don't know I have never been affected as such, and no one has ever been able to block me from their heart, from their mind. I have always had the gift to sense others' emotions," came as she swallowed thickly over the decision which brought forth-such words. The advice of her father, convincing her to trust shadowed her thoughts, and with a deciding breath, Angeline began. "When I was a child, I remember being afraid to be about others. Somehow, I always knew what they were feeling, what they were attempting to hide from me. My gift was never a true surprise to either of my parents. It was something they dealt with from the very beginning. My mother would always seem to rescue me from such distress, she always knew when I needed her most, and perhaps she too could sense such things. She always managed to have the most calming of images to envisage, and father, when he wasn't attempting to protect me, allowed me to bask in his love. Together they taught me to control the onslaught of a crowded room, to soften the explosions of emotions, as they would come. To single each out and cast them away, even to block such feelings if I so desired. Even as I learned to control this gift, Father was always fearful the prosecutors would come. He had heard in so many other countries of the burnings and stoning, certain his enemies would speculate about me. You were his biggest fear, as nothing would have hurt him more than you to learn of my differences and using it against him." A snort of laughter escaped Angeline to the ironic circle her life had taken, "I don't believe he ever anticipated this when he was protecting me." Smiling to her words, Nico waited as Angeline continued with her reminiscences. "After mother passed away, he nearly forced me into being a hermit, hidden from others, forced to hide my talents. With her wonderful images gone, it seemed my gift was something to be ashamed of, not normal. It was a difficult time, he mourned her so, and I don't believe my resemblance to her was a benefit. As time passed, it became a necessity for Father to take a new wife, Belaveuta needed an heir, and my father needed a son. He married Antoinette. I knew how much he longed for a son, and when the young widow came with Stephen, how could he turn her away?" Shaking her head to the memories as they returned, Angeline confessed, "I wanted a mother so desperately. So many times, I would come to her, if only to have the embrace of a woman, the answers to questions Father could never answer. However, she never understood how I could look at her and know the loathing and jealousy in her heart. Look at my new brother and see the desire behind his sympathetic eyes. Father never trusted their small-mindedness and made me promise to never share any of my secrets with her or Stephen. I was thankful enough for being able to escape the house on my own during such times. I would often leave for hours visiting the surrounding villages, meeting the people would help to be accepted, if not loved."

Tugging, with indecision, to the bottom lip, she wondered if she should continue in her explanations? Share the development of her gift as it took her in a different direction, "about that time, I began to experience images; places presented as if looking through the eyes of another. Wonderful places filled with serene mountains and turbulent oceans, of a dark ominous, Keep, high on the cliffs with the crash of ocean below. I would run from the house all in hopes of such images coming to me, of such peace and understanding as it would wash over me."

"In the fields surrounded by grass and wildflowers. Astrolabe in the distance, it's her favorite place, the only place where the sweet grass grows." Nickolai finished as grasping her upper arms into the crush of his hands; he drew Angeline from the protection of his body and held her at arm's length. "Such joy, undeniable beckoning." Murmured, as Angeline's confused eyes searched his incredulous ones for understanding. "She brought you to this heaven, and I gave it to you."

He felt the trembles as they fed upon each other as the moments passed, and still, he stared at her, "how could you know?" Angeline questioned, feeling the icy finger of fear trace her spine to the look of misunderstanding and confusion that came to mar his wondrous eyes.

"You don't understand," the mouth moved as if to speak, only to close with the lack of words at his disposal, to the impossibilities of such a joining. "I need to show you something." The carriage's leather shade lifted, and he urged her forward by the hold maintained. "This is Illevante`."

Moving to the window, Angeline peered to the structure looming above them, as below the crash and roar of the ocean could be heard to battle the shores. Her eyes could only widen as they swept from the view back to the man before her, “how is this possible?” She whispered as her eyes returned to the approach of her new home, a home she had often wondered and dreamed of now stood dark and warlike before astonished eyes. As it seemed to Angeline a thousand shadowed windows looked down at her approach from high on a rocky cliff where it perched. Recognized her nearing and readied for her arrival. “You were always there.” Stated matter of fact to the realization of all images; of all dreams. Dreams! Emerald eyes widened then swept guiltily away, “Sweet Jesus, was it always you?”

Watching as she physically drew from him. Nickolai could only shake his head and shrug shoulders to all revealed, “I don’t know.” Nickolai's curiosity piqued to all conveyed over the many years of his waiting, wanting, which caused the color to spread up over her neck to flame across her cheek. “I swear to you, I never knew of such a connection. I thought of you, of course, wanted to share things with you, but I never thought it would be with my mind.” Raising a brow to memories and fantasies as her womanhood became irrefutable, and he denied himself the company of another, “you have sensed---everything?” He managed incredulously to realize everything he had ever dared to dream had been channeled to her. With a pained wince to such fantasy, he managed sheepishly, as raking hands through the length of raven hair, “nothing was censored I take it?”

“How could you not know what you have been doing to me?” She gasped, feeling the color pinch at her cheek to the embarrassment of such intimacy, “you’ve come to me night after night. It made me feel things---want things---” The fiery head shook as Angeline sensed his deep confusion to such matters as he questioned the ancients which coursed his blood. “These ancients,” she began dropping the leather shade back to place to muffle the roar of the ocean as it seemed to beat at them, “your ancients, could they have done this. Could they have forced such a link?”

Pressing an aggravated hand over the sweat at it gathered to the upper lip, Nickolai admitted to what he knew to be true, "they drew me to you when you were merely twelve years old. Beckoned me to find the woman who would be my salvation, and there you were a slip of a thing being dragged along by the hand of stepmother." He ventured honestly into the separation between them, "I never truly believed together we would be this powerful. Together we would be intertwined as none other."

Dropping back against the cushion Angeline could do little more than stare at the hands in her lap, replay every image as it burnt onto her brain, every caress this man was capable of granting and wanting from her even as miles and years separated them. "Beyond this connection, they have forged between us, is there anything else I need to know of you? Anything else you keep secret from me?" She questioned as lifting her eyes; she found his piercing blue ones trained on her, waiting for action, hoping for a reaction. "How is it possible for you to channel such images to me, to come to me time after time?"

Chuckling softly to her questioning, he contemplated sharing such knowledge with her, and his fingertips came to scrub across the crease of his brow. "There are things you will learn about me, little one, many that you may find disturbing. Some handed down from one generation, in my family, to the next, others I have come by naturally. Talents," the word was plucked from her head as his mouth softened to her knowledge. Nickolai felt his soul reach to hers; he never dared to believe it possible to share every secret and difference tainting his family's name. Secrets keeping him apart from the rest of the world, as his world was shrouded in mystery and distrust. "Talents that have grown while others have diminished. Talents others can't quite seem to grasp. It has always been my strength to enforce my will upon weaker, unsuspecting minds. Have them see things not there, feel things, even do my bidding, whenever it became necessary."

"Antoinette? She questioned with the realization of his words and reassurances earlier. "Lorrie, in the gardens. I wondered how she could be so agreeable." And she nearly laughed to the circumstance of his interference.

Nodding with a smile, "Antoinette was easy to influence, to say the least. And your woman; she had been eyeing Armand for hours; it was just the push she needed to overcome her---hesitation." Raising a brow of amused understanding of the women, Angeline silently urged him to continue. "When an Illevante' is born, we are marked with our powers." Taking her hand, he directed it to the raised symbol found behind his ear. Angeline's fingertips traced the marking, realizing it felt more like branding than a birthmark. "Each has the same birthmark. It is a mark visible to those we trust and only after touched by another Illevante' at birth who also bears the mark."

"So, if we were to have children, you would need to touch them for the marking to show?" She questioned attempting to understand all that he was telling her. "And all born of Illevante' have the marking?"

"Yes, every one of my ancestors have borne the marking." Gathering thoughts to the mysteries of his world, Nico confessed with indecisiveness, "I don't know where to start. I have never had reason to share my family history with another." With her gentle smile to his hesitation, Nico started, "My talents came to be known to me at a very early age, powerful and nearly overwhelming. I remember being seven or eight years old, wanting to be with my father's guards. Of course, my Governess denied such a request; yet the next thing I knew she agreed to everything I had to suggest to her. I was quite a horror story to the Governess' my parents employed, they could never quite grasp how I was able to get what I wanted, even when they knew it quite against my father's wishes. Though I seem to remember when Martine came into our employ, she quickly put an end to such flights of fancy she has always understood me like none before." Looking down at his hands as if in awe of the power they contained, he explained, "as I matured the dominion over elements developed. Fire," flexing his hand, Angeline watched as a blue flame grew along the tips of Nico's fingers; traveled in the distance of their separation to dance over her hand, "and air has been easier to control," a ripple of air extinguished the flame, and it amazed her no burn existed. "Water has always been a little trickier, and the earth is easy enough to move as desired." The voice evoked such a need to understanding and acceptance; she could do little else than raise her eyes to confront him, encourage him to continue as it was so obvious his wish. "Illevante` is a name and place rich in history; not all of it will be to the liking of one such as you. One who is sensitive to the feelings and thoughts of others, only know nothing I possess will ever come to harm you, will never come to influence you in an adverse effect."

Gently Nickolai brought forth images he sought to impress upon her mind to a time long ago. A time of darkness and death when most of his family was haunted and tortured for the talents they possessed. The differences they shared in the healing arts or foretelling the future, even those that had once beckoned them to cast away the shadows now condemned and accused. It was during such dark times his ancients appeared within their bloodline; the most powerful of his family tormented and cursed to forever roam the earth in a world of shadow and myth. Forever able to communicate when the link was forged correctly yet destined to be alone. "There has never been a time when death hasn't surrounded Illevante'; either by the prosecution of our differences or wars waged. To reasons I no longer carc to have to worry about, I wish to spend the rest of my life in service to you and my Prince. To love you, to have Illevante` associated with more than the death and destruction of so many years ago. I wish to end my family's curse; Angeline and I need you to do it."

Pressing tears, which clung thickly to lashes, away to hear such sadness in his voice, feel and experience the heaviness as it crushed his heart to the history. Angeline confronted the man who yearned for her understanding, for her acceptance but mostly her unconditional love. Allowing the touch as it came to caress, Angeline knew that it was indeed he who had come to her all these years. "Nico," came in sweet ebbing resistance to desire, “you are no more than stranger to me, yet I know you like none before. I feel as if my heart has somehow wound itself about you and will never want to let go.” Touching the worry of the stern cheek, the line of his exacting mouth, Angeline reassured: "I know the fears you have lived with; the differences you have endured all in the name of belonging and together we will surmount such obstacles.” Coming to her knees beside him, Angeline pressed into the muscle of the upper arm, lent into the strength of shoulder as reassuring, “together we will bring light into the darkness of this place, of such a heart and we will learn to love each other.”

Gathering her close to his chest, he held her for silent moments until he controlled emotions, and the heart beating within his chest once again sought normal rhythm, “most definitely learn to love.” He reassured to demands placed on him to the murmuring reassurances of ancients seeming to clamor in unison to the path chosen.

As the clatter of the horses' hoof and wheel crossed the wooden drawbridge to the Illevant’s stronghold Nickolai reassured Angeline as she peered out the window to spy the many who were gathering at the gates to witness their arrival, “there will be little formality this evening, little one. It is far too late for servants and townspeople to make themselves all known to you, I will see to introductions over the coming days; once you are comfortable with your surroundings." Smiling as Angeline turned from the scenery back to him, Nico explained the moments to come, "I will show you to your rooms, and then with Martine’s help, you will ready to retire.

Nodding the carriage doors opened under the capable hands of his guard and Angeline was barely allowed breath to escape before she secreted from the many seen to be peering from every window, and pouring from every doorframe as all hoped for a glimpse of the woman who had stolen their Master's heart. "Martine will see to your every need; she is well aware of the demands my life will place upon you. If you have any questions or concerns about such arrangements or accommodations, we can address them in our chambers."

Brought through the towering twin arches of doors into the massive stone structure, Angeline quickly looked about her as the interior came with far more appeal than the exterior.

The entranceway was of high arched ceilings adorned by massive chandeliers, all of which were lit casting the shadows of the night far into the recesses of its vast marbled width. Richly embroidered settees were alternating from right to left in the lead to a massive pendulum clock that guarded the center of a thickly wooded staircase. Wandering from Nickolai as he became involved in the direction of her few belongings from the carriage, Angeline stopped before the massive swinging mechanism to stare at the odd pictorials adorning it. "Christian Huygens personally constructed it for Illevante'. We began corresponding a few years ago, as he was doing similar studies in astronomy." Nickolai explained as he came to join her before the piece.

"Similar?" She questioned, casting only the quickest of glances to the man beside her.

"Mars has always held my family's interests, Huygens was, at the time, studying the markings." Pointing to the clock's adornment, Nico explained, "though many have questioned the adornment of Mars, it has a great bearing on my family, past and future."

Turning from him only as the feeling of urgency was sensed, a figure was found to be waiting in the shadows of the massive hall, hoping to gain his attention, "yes, Antony?" Questioned as following her distraction, Nickolai motioned the man, who handled most of his correspondence, forward, "come here. Angeline, this is Antony; he coordinates my life, Antony, my wife, Lady Angeline."

"Or at least I attempt to, Count." Antony added with

all seriousness of his position as bowing elegantly before the woman, “welcome to Illevante`, Milady, it is indeed a pleasure to finally meet you. And even greater joy no longer having to juggle about a demanding schedule so the Count could abandon duties to oversee preparation for this day.”

Frowning to such words, the intensity of his emotions, Angeline managed softly, “I never realized I was causing such inconvenience, pray to forgive me.” As the odd statement was felt to wound her, had she been causing such a disturbance without knowing?

Seeing the disappointment as it came to his Count’s features, the man was quick to apologize, “no, forgive me, Milady, I never meant to infer you were an inconvenience, simply the Count and his many demands to detail in preparation.” His nervous eyes quickly danced between the couple, “ah, so the Count has not advised you to the preparations he has been making to this joyous day.” The fiery head shook as her emerald eyes came to peek up to the silence of her husband as she experienced his displeasure of the man’s loose tongue. “Let me just say he has turned Illevante` around, from Keep to home. All in the expectation of your arrival.”

An interested brow rose, as she heard Nickolai grumble to such revelations, “Antony, I will join you shortly.” With the curt dismissal, Antony scampered behind the door leading to his very cluttered desk. “I didn’t think you would appreciate my primitive style of decorating,” he tried to explain without going into great detail as he ushered her through the many halls and passages making up the interior of Illevante`, “to say the least I was quite obsessed with war and books. All of which seemed to spill into the very halls. For now, the books are in a library, and the war held in the Garrison House I have begun constructing, where my Guards have more appreciation to the weaponry.” Stopping before a set of double doors where an older woman awaited their arrival, he instructed. “I will leave you in the capable hands of Martine, little one; she will acquaint you with your dressing and bathing rooms.” With a touch of lips to her hand, he left her to the servant who looked upon her next movements with knowing patience.

Apprehensively Angeline looked upon the barrier before her, and with her hesitation, Martine opened the doors, swinging them wide for her entrance. With a welcoming hand pointing the way, Angeline stepped into the indulgence of what would be her dressing room. An elaborate room of multi-fireplaces and groupings of deeply cushioned chairs in the softest of mauves to the deepest of burgundies all seeming to center about the silk and lace layered vanity table and its massive polished mirror. "Milady," the elderly woman prompted in her hesitation to all she took in, "Count Illevante` requested these items be available for your satisfaction to their safe arrival." Settling on the cushioned bench before the vanity, Angeline gingerly touched all her most precious belongings and blinked to the tears which misted her eyes. How could she have ever thought to doubt him?

"Did he do this?" She questioned as the precious wooden jewelry box, which came to her at her mother's death, was touched with a trembling hand.

"If you mean the Count, Milady, then I would have to say I'm sure he had a hand in arranging such." A knowing smile lifted the many creases and wrinkles which adorned the woman's face. "You will find the Count has many ways of making all of us at Illevante` as comfortable as we can be. Though I am sure you will learn of such things yourself, in due time."

Observing the woman for silent moments as she made herself busy about the room, Angeline inquired to the history she shared with Illevante' and Nickolai, "you have been with him for a very long time." The apparent ease in which the woman conducted herself before and about the man Angeline was still in her infancy of learning.

Again, the smile returned with the memories, "yes, since he was no more than eight years old. He was a spoiled terror." And a reluctant chuckle passed to the hellion she had taken responsibility of, "everyone always let him have his way that was until I stepped into his chambers. He was quite baffled to the fact that I recognized his special-ness, his uniqueness if you will. He learned quick enough that his wild days were over when he tried to persuade me into allowing him to join his father's Garrison on their next patrol. The look on his face when I said no, how he concentrated on convincing me otherwise; his beautiful little face all crunched up and furious."

Smiling to the memory shared, Angeline inquired, "how were you able to recognize such---differences?" Curious if her differences could be so readily acknowledged.

"Just as I was able to recognize yours, Milady. I have always known his ancients would direct him to someone, unlike any other. His true other half, as his mother, the Countess, would often say." Martine watched as the curious eyes dropped to the hands folded in her lap, "you have no reason to fear me, Count Nickolai is as my own, and you will be held just as dear, to be sure."

Angeline contemplated the woman's sincerity, and it eased her heart to know she had come to a place where she would not have to be guarded because of her differences, fearful of those which surrounded her. Never had she been entrenched as with the sincerity this woman was capable of radiating, "how long ago did his parent's pass?"

"Many years have passed since they left us. The Count was into the second half of his twenties when he became responsible for all that you see. He has shouldered it well, brought Illevante` to such heights I know his father is quite proud of him, his mother has always been."

"His mother? Was she happy here, there is naught of her history in any of the books I acquired to the Illevante` lineage? If not for being the birth mother to Nickolai."

"Milady, the Countess Josephine Illevante` though brought here under a similar circumstance to your own from a far different land, came less than willingly to her new husband. Nickolai is much like his father. They are very determined, not easily swayed. It was his father's quest to have the young

Countess fall in love with him, which she eventually did. The Illevante` men are indeed a rare breed; it is as if the sun and moon revolve about the woman they take as a wife. When Nickolai proclaims, he will do anything to make you happy, rest assured he will."

Feeling blood rush to cheeks in remembrance of such declarations from Nico, though, she had to admit she smiled away such words as a way of winning her favor. Angeline felt an odd sense of relief to be able to hope that at least it would be possible for one such as he to love someone so unlikely as herself. "He has no brothers or sisters?" Questioned wishing only to change the subject from her newly acquired husband and his boasts to loving her.

"No, the Countess was allowed a single child, though she did try for more. It was not meant to be, not within these walls. Now if you will excuse me, I have much to ready for you this evening." The woman smiled before allowing Angeline a moment of privacy to reacquaint herself with the many items adorning the vanity top, from perfume bottles to patches, Illevante` had not overlooked a single detail.

"Where is he now?" Angeline questioned as the woman was found to be preparing her attire for the evening, a length of filmy material that seemed to reveal more than it would cover.

"Matters of Illevante' needed immediate attention; he will join you in the master's chamber shortly." Coming to touch her shoulder, Martine pointed to an adjoining room, "you will wait for him there." Then with a gentle hand, drew the child from the security of things she knew too that of her future. "Now, it is my position to ready you for the evening. If you would, please follow me, Milady."

Lifting a massive tapestry of hunters and horses, Martine lead her to the passageway beyond, silently the artwork fell back to conceal the way as Angeline found herself in a cavernous room of blue and gold. Water was found to be rushing from the very wall in a fall to the pool beyond as steam could be seen to rise in slow circling threads. "The Count thought you might like to bathe before retiring," casting the quickest of peeks to the astonishment of the woman, Martine quickly explained to the wonderment of the room, "the water comes from deep within the mountain and is always heated. There is always a constant flow, so you need not summon a servant whenever there is a desire to bathe." Drawing the cape from about her new Mistress's shoulders, Martine inquired, "will you require more than my assistance with your undress?" As thick Turkish linens came to be laid out on one of the many settees adorning the room, and when the fiery head could only shake in response Martine quickly had the elaborate wedding gown stripped from about her length leaving Angeline to clutch a crisp linen about her nakedness, "when you require my further assistance, please call for me." The call cord in the far corner of the room pointed it, "I will see to the organization of your items. I believe the Count made arrangements for the delivery of your trunks."

Looking about as if trying to ingest all exposed to her in so little time, Angeline allowed the breath to escape, and it felt as if it was the first had taken since being whisked into the wonders of Illevante`, "Nickolai." Whispered, to hear the sound of his name on her lips, to remember the sweet rush of emotion, he was capable of bringing time and time again. "What manner of man are you to have managed such wonders?"

Turning to step into the depth of the heated pool, Angeline found her reflection in the massive polished mirror which dominated an entire section of the wall. It was then a little of her resolve to make her life with Nickolai Illevante' work seemed to seep from her. How long would it be till he too would sense the revulsion the others had always been aware of, when he would come to loathe the simple act of touching her, being with her. "Please." She pleaded to the reflection as it stared silently to her, mocked her dreams, "please let him want me, let me have the family I so earnestly desire." Then turning away from the answers, she knew to come to such a plea, she stepped into the waterfall of warm water, allowing her to feel as if for a moment she was as beautiful and desirable as his images projected her to be.

∞∞∞

Alone in the center of the master's chamber, Angeline stood, willing herself to breathe over the anxiety stopping her heart. When the servant, Martine, was questioned to the chosen attire, all she received as an answer was "it is the Count's request." The Count's request! '*What were you ever thinking? You don't know the first thing about being with such a man.*' Angeline admonished herself as the newly assigned servant completed her toiletries and left her standing in wait for her husband.

A chill was felt to race her length, and hands came to press over the exposed flesh of her arms to warm them. Or perhaps it was only to hold her from the trembles felt to rack her body with growing and multiplying tremors. Why didn't she listen to the lessons Antoinette attempted to instill on her all those years ago? Perhaps the woman wasn't as useless as Angeline always thought.

Gathering the hair cascading naked shoulders in hopes of covering the revealing nightwear, Angeline spun about as a tapestry at the opposite side of the room was pressed aside. Standing there, Nickolai hesitated for only a moment to stare upon the woman awaiting him and had to remind himself to breathe. How could a single woman hold such beauty and not realize its effect over him? How a look from her enough for him to pledge his soul to her safety, his life to her happiness. After a moment of hesitation, Nickolai entered the room and recognized the wide eyes of fear as they confronted him, reminding him of the innocence she held.

The silken ivory robe Nico wore was a striking contrast

to the darkness of his raven hair as it flowed freely about his shoulders, and Angeline couldn't help but notice how the garment, unbelted, opened with each of his approaching steps revealing the cinch of trousers at waist. A narrowness of waist that seemed to amplify the mass of bronzed rippling muscle making up chest, a breadth only hinted to beneath the covering of cloth, and a soft, terrified sound managed to escape over the tremble of her mouth. "Forgive the delay, little one; one would think no one capable of a decision in my brief absence." Nickolai forced himself from rambling as it seemed the very heart in his chest was pounding hard enough to escape and the need to possess her an overwhelming thing as he forced himself to remember her innocence, how easily he would be able to frighten her if so pushed. "Thank goodness for Antony; he manages to handle most of the inconsequential business that always finds its way across my desk."

Taking a hesitant step back from his towering closeness, Angeline managed, as she sought to look anywhere but to the magnificence which was her husband's body, "there must be many who seek your guidance and assistance as Count of Illevante`. You must be kept very busy. I'm sure being away for most of the day has left a significant number of problems needing your immediate attention."

Forcing a smile from coming to his otherwise stern lips, if only to hear the hopefulness of his attendance elsewhere in Illevante' but before her now, Nico reassured, "you'd be surprised how easily I can rearrange my schedules no matter how much Antony may complain." A single step bridged the distance she insisted upon, and when he was no more than a breath before her, he touched the warmth of her blood-fused cheek, the tremble of lips as her fear was seen to rise ten-fold into the brilliance of sparkling, watchful eyes. "Angeline," caused her heart to clench and body to yearn for his as never before had her name been spoken with such stark desire, such need, "don't be afraid of me, little one." Cautiously his hand tripped slowly from the touch of her mouth, down to splay the length of her throat, the flesh of shoulder where the material there was pressed aside down over arm till his fingers meshed with her own.

When the mouth opened as if to speak only the rush of a nervous breath managed escape as tears found their way to her lashes, “Milord, I would not be here if I were afraid of you, only the unknown now seems quite terrifying.” She confessed as swallowing thickly over the emotion claiming her throat. “Please forgive me.”

“There is nothing to forgive; I would have you no other way.” His mouth curled into a small, patient smile as Nico traced the pulse of the wrist with a pressing pad of thumb trying not to feel quite so affected as her glorious eyes rose to meet his with tears shimmering their depth. “Angeline,” came with a sigh to her escalating fears, “come.” Settling into a massive chair that cradled his length, Nickolai drew her down onto his lap. Instantly cuddling into the fold of his body, she sought the naked flesh of his chest to rest upon as her head came to tuck under his chin. Angeline realized how right it felt to be in such a place, how easily he could calm her most overriding fears by a simple touch, “little one, I want you to trust me, know that I would never hurt you.” Came as he captured her chin between thumb and forefinger to draw her features up to confront his. “Look at me,” he beckoned, nearly smiled as her cheeks were found to burn in blush, a state he realized with amazement that seemed to bc constant as of late, as she stared nearly breathlessly to the handsome face before her. Silently she studied the beautiful blue eyes and felt as if all fear, all hesitation was melting from the very core of her being. “Do I strike you as a heartless monster to force you into something you do not wish?”

Fighting to lower her head, she managed, as the head shook slowly, “it might be a little easier if you did not strike me as being so beautiful, Milord.” Whispered, gasping to the admission, had she allowed such words to escape her? What, in the name of all that was holy, was wrong with her? She admonished self to confession.

“Beautiful?” He suddenly laughed, and the sound at first

surprised her, “did you call me beautiful?”

“Nickolai,” the hands laying within her lap were twisted painfully together as she could no longer lift her eyes to meet his amusement, “there have always been handsome men, pretty boys, coming to Belaveuta but none that gave me more than the briefest of considerations, but you take my breath, Milord," in fact, she reflected silently, he was unlike any man she had ever seen before. To merely look at him caused her knees to weaken and a strange yearning to grow in the pit of her belly, to feel his hands on her more than enough to make her forget all believed on how a woman should act and beg him to touch her again and again. Even now, as he sought to end her worries, she could do little more than wonder when he would bring such fire to her flesh, yearning to her soul. When would the perfection of his mouth come once again against her own?

Pressing his lips into the crown of her head, he held the action for silent moments before forcing the features up to confront him, “as you take mine, wife.” Slowly he lowered his face to hers, first to press a teasing kiss to the plain of the forehead, then the tip of her nose, “let me kiss you, Angeline.” With a timid nod, his mouth found hers, pressed in gentle awareness of the trembles that persisted — reveled in the innocence in which her mouth accustomed itself to his attentions.

For long moments he held to the kiss, pressing, searching for the moment when she became soft and warm in his arms. For the moment when her delicate hands came to venture to the naked flesh of his chest, up over the corded muscle of shoulder then to cup neck, drawing him closer with gentle pressure to the exquisite torture his mouth invoked. The fire as his tongue ventured in stroke over hers once he was able to coax her mouth open then deepened to taste the very sweetness of her. “Angeline.” Groaned in controlled emotion as his mouth slowly, teasingly, ventured to the ivory column of her throat as his hand came to clench possessively to the softness of curves as they pressed ever so suggestively to him.

Pulling from the spiraling dangerousness his kisses

brought her, Angeline fell back against the arms cuddling her close to his length and stared at his amused expression as he couldn't help the smile growing to the woman he held in his arms. The mouth red and wonderfully abused by his causing him to bend in the capture of it once again. "Sweet Jesus, wife, do you realize what a sweet torture you have always been to me? How long I have waited, planned, for this very moment when you are in my arms. When you are as my wife?"

Rising from the chair, with her still held in his arms, Nico allowed her feet to settle upon the thickly woven mats which donned the stone floor as she stood before him. Pulling herself to stance, as she suddenly realized he now intended to take her to his bed, Angeline once again felt her body tense to the terror of what he would expect from her, or when he would turn from her with the evident disgust of so many others.

Touching the wan of her cheek to such realization, he reminded gently, "you have nothing to fear from me, little one, lest you forget what we have shared over the many years with our minds we are hardly strangers journeying into the unknown."

Miserably the auburn head shook as she professed, "I am not that woman you dream of, the woman you caressed with such tenderness. Loved with such gentleness, the woman who responded to your every touch. No man has ever touched me, and none have sought to bring passion to me---I don't want to disappoint you. Not tonight."

"You have never been, nor will you ever be a disappointment, Angeline, not tonight, not ever." Motioning to the massive bed, Nico he drew her gently toward the drapery concealed confides that beckoned even as she sought to move in the opposite direction. "If you do not wish me to touch you, Angeline, I will not," he promised as he felt her tug with dreaded hesitation in the opposite direction, "however, you will find it far warmer in here instead of the middle of a room where even the fires are now failing." Pressing the quilted drapery aside, he lifted the corner to blankets and furs, waiting for her to gather enough courage to comply with his bidding as she watched with a touch of regret the fires in the hearth flicker to final light then diminish to a smoldering glow. "Come, Angeline, we need to rest."

Pressed under the heavy bedding, Angeline followed his progress about the bed as he quickly shed the robe and climbed in at the opposite side. With a motion of his hand, the candles surrounding the inner chamber flickered to life, and the soft glow filling confides caused an unsuspecting gasp to escape her. "Would you prefer darkness?" He asked, plunging them into black, and with her whisper of *"no"* the candles returned to a flame.

"My goodness." Escaped as she settled into the surrounding warmth, clutched hands over the hem of blanket till knuckles were nearly white to the tension of her fears. Settling to his side, so his head was propped against hand, Nico studied her avoidance with a gentle smile. Watched how carefully she sought to avoid all contact with the beckon of his naked chest even as he crowded her a little too daringly, as he was sure she would flee if he instigated a single touch. "I would have never imaged." And the chuckle of amusement only caused the heat to deepen in her cheeks, the tremble to return to length.

Catching a thick curl about his fingers, he studied the tendril as it encased knuckle for silent moments before agreeing, "no, I'm sure you wouldn't have." Releasing the curl, he settled back to piled pillows with a deciding sigh to be patient and watched her through lowered lashes.

"Do you only have to think about it, to make it so?" She questioned. Lifting his hand, he reached for a thick column of wax. Bringing it before him, he looked to the column to have the wick extinguish then as suddenly sputter then leap to fiery life. "And the hearth, it is the same?" Leaning across her length, a motion of hand brought the smoldering ashes to life, the fire to rise with a blast of welcoming heat. "And the wind?" The air came to smother the fire dancing in the hearth's protection. A brow rose in realization as she accused, "you forced the flames in the hearth to die just now, didn't you?" With a shrug and sheepish smile, he returned the candle to the holder. Greeting his amusement with her most accusatory of glares, Angeline focused her attention to the fire beyond and not the weight and warmth of the man above her, "though you don't play fair, I have to admit your gifts are far more impressive than simply feeling others' emotions. It's truly amazing."

Remaining in his lean across her length, he conspired as his face was only inches above her own, "I usually don't put on quite so much of a show without charging admission, Milady."

The tongue swiped nervously over lips before she was able to draw breath to answer his obvious tease, "regrettably, my husband doesn't allow me an allowance."

"Ah," sounded soft and the head lowered till it was nothing more than a touch from her flesh, till he heard her inhale with expectation, "then perhaps we'll have to barter for the price." The breath was felt more potent than any caress as it came over the heat of her cheek, the sense of his building desire more intoxicating than any touch could ever achieve, "I have been known to be ruthless in my bartering skills, I always get what I want."

Nickolai stared to the fullness of lips, as a nervous tongue swiped repeatedly leaving them wet and inviting, and with a soft moan he forced himself to remember how easily he could frighten her, how easily he could break the trust growing between them, "I fear I have nothing of value, Milord."

"Haven't you?" The question seemed to hang for eternity as eyes were held fast to the piercing blue. As her body already surrendered to the will of the man who teased her without a single touch.

Forcing a breath to come and body to regain a moment of ease, Nickolai could feel every inch of him scream to join with her. He needed to hold her within in his arms, love and cherish her always, Nickolai reluctantly returned to the pile of pillows. "I fear you possess far more value than even you realize."

Long moments passed to the stillness between them, to

the emotions seeming to thicken the very air they breathed. “Nickolai?” Questioned, as Angeline remained at his side, waiting for him to press advancement as a husband. Act upon his intention, which was so evident in every breath he took, in every emotion radiated from him. “Are you going to sleep?” Was asked, and the clutch of blanket relaxed momentarily to the idea.

“No, little one, I am not.” He managed folding his arms behind his head so that the muscle of shoulders strained and swelled to menacing proportions in his struggling patience.

Angeline forced herself not to stare from the perfection of the man beside her. The arms bronzed and corded seemed to be muscle upon muscle, the chest a finely chiseled sculpture hard as stone yet she knew the flesh to be warm and welcoming from the precious few moments she was allowed to nestle against it. With a thick swallow, she forced herself to breathe over the breathlessness any of his movements stirred within her as whispering, “did you mean what you said about not touching me?”

Shifting his head on the pillow, he held her stare for merely a moment before responding, “I said if it was your wish, little one.” Amused by her overwhelming nervousness as if wishing to finally end the suspense so she may finally sleep with the knowledge of his objective. “Is that what you wish?” *'Sweet Gods,'* Nico nearly swore out loud, *'how was he expected to lay in the same bed beside her, without touching her, possessing her. What would her reaction be if he moved to a separate bed?'* He briefly wondered if she was aware of the torture she was inflicting upon him.

“So, you don’t wish to fulfill your duty as a husband?” Came in a rush of nervous breath as it felt as if her entire body burned to the humiliation she was being forced to share with her husband on their wedding night. And her heart crumbled within her chest to realize he would be no different than the others who had sought her company, who fought to overcome the natural aversion she was able to conjure within the hearts of men.

"No, little one." Stated as he continued to stare to the vexation and then the confusion of emotions as they played over her features.

"No?" Came with more pain than intended. With a glance to his study, she lowered her eyes to the pattern as it spread over the blanket, her bottom lip quickly tugged between teeth before the tell-all tremble would make him realize her disappointment. Nervously the fiery length of hair was gathered over a single shoulder as she sought to hide the tears that she knew to be welling within her eyes, to the heartbreak crushing her chest. Why would she had even dared to assume him to be different, why would she believe his attraction to be genuine and not the practiced response of one who was capable of deception. "May I ask you another question?"

"Of course, as many as you wish."

Nodding thoughtfully to his consideration, Angeline blurted, "why?"

"Why what?" He tormented nearly enjoying himself to see her burning cheeks and growing agitation to such rejection.

Looking up to him, Nickolai nearly gasped as he found the face was to be a mask of heartbreak and confusion, as a single blink brought tears to her lashes, and Angeline managed to fight for her words, "if you find me as such, why did you marry me? Why did you want me as a wife if you can't even consummate our marriage? What could you possibly want from me?"

Rising from the pile of pillows Nickolai looked down to the woman beside him, touched the beauty of her features with a cupping palm as he pressed away the tears of misunderstanding and betrayal with the press of his thumb, "because, little one, we will be making love to each other." Beneath the pressing covers, Angeline could feel the material about her loosen to be replaced by his knowing touch, felt the coolness of sheet as it pressed upon her suddenly naked length. "Do I frighten you, little one?" He questioned as the clutch of blankets she held were gently drawn away, revealing the ivory length she wished so desperately to conceal, and blue eyes stared with silent appraisal to the woman before him. Felt the air leave his lungs in a rush of emotion, seeing her now in his bed, having her here after the many years of dreaming, planning, and scheming to achieve this moment. “Sweet Jesus, do you realize how beautiful you are?”

The fiery head shook slowly, “please don’t, Nico.” She managed as she followed the splay of his hand over her flesh with watchful eyes only to close them as the sudden spears of pleasure were felt to shoot from somewhere deep within her up to the strain of breast.

“Please don’t what, little one? Don’t touch you as such?” He questioned as the hand splayed across her glorious flesh, reveled to the touch as it moved slowly in exploration as if wishing to capture and memorize every inch.

“Please don’t call me beautiful.” Whispered as her eyes rose shyly to meet his surprised expression.

Tugging the pillows from behind her head away and throwing them aside, he pressed his lips to the plain of her forehead, then tip of the nose before confessing, “but you are beautiful, my love, you have always been beautiful to me.” Covering her silken length beneath the blanket of his strength, his mouth, then tongue lapped to heaving flesh, tasted the sweetness as it proved too quickly intoxicate.

The tongue trailed hotly, slowly over the rise of ribs, the plain of the belly to tease the navel, lower to press reverent kisses to the fiery tight curls where the thighs were clenched in protection to innocence only to retrace the path up to the heave of her breast. Slowly, deliberately, the pale flesh was teased, the pink stone breathed over once twice till lips captured the puckered flesh. Demanding reaction as Nico's hands explored what his mouth had conquered only moments before.

“Nickolai?” Questioned to the driving need as it filled her to the heat and strength of his flesh coming in a cover of her own, and he knew the question did not need an answer. For the answer would only come from the touch of his hands, the caress of his mouth.

Forever mindful of the delicate length beneath him, Nico braced himself above her before his mouth came to explore the perfection of her throat, up to tease the lobe as he whispered, "touch me, little one, know me as I will know you." And he watched as her hesitant fingertips came in exploration of his length.

First to travel the strength of his corded arms, across the breadth of shoulders, down over the mantel of his chest where she faltered in journey unsure, unprepared for the manhood which rose between them as she realized clothing no longer remained between them. "Trust me, little one." Whispered as his mouth returned to lavish the length, his hands to caress and splay to the flesh that cried out for him. Knowing fingers teased and probed, delved, and demanded as the body was felt to react to every touch.

Angeline warmed in a heated rush and offered herself ultimately to the man, a man who seemed to become the center of her world. Her very need to live and breathe for a moment more, "please, Nickolai." Became chant as finally he sought the tenderness of her desire, caressed the essence of culminating need till the scream of her release came with pleading to further pleasures and still Nickolai teased her; again, he stroked and lavished. His hands seemed to be everywhere yet nowhere, his tongue a constant battle to be sought against her flesh as it eluded all but to the most teasing of touches. "Please, Nickolai." Cried as she came to lead him to her need, cupped the thickness of his length within the palm of her hand and nearly lost self to the sensations washing through her.

"No, little one, let me please you." Whispered as his mouth teased ear, nibbled to the sensitive lobe with tantalizing touches. "Let me touch you forever."

Leading his length to her, Angeline felt the silken flesh as it met hers. She coaxed the thickness presented to the tightness that rose to engulf him. For long moments she allowed the new fullness of him to penetrate her, let the thickness press endlessly into the depth of her as with a slight hesitation the barrier of her innocence came to be pierced, and he laid deep within her. Still, as the gasp of pain caused her to tense and for a moment struggled to be from beneath his pressing weight as it trapped her to the deepening act, the thickness as it seemed to fill her like nothing before, "no, Nico, I can't do this, I don't know what to do. What you want!"

"Ssh, little one," and his hands came to cup the fear found in her searching features, stilled her movements till the tenderness eased her discomfort, "you're already doing everything perfectly." Again, he captured the mouth as it opened in protest, silenced her fears with teasing touches till she was felt to relax beneath him. Emerald eyes opened to meet his, and the arms circled his shoulders and drew him down to her softness. "And all I want is to feel you like this forever."

Burying her face in the crook of the neck, she hid the tears as they escaped into the fall of raven hair, the scent of him hard and sure above her, within her, before confessing, "but it hurts, Nico."

Cupping the back of her head within the palm of his hand Nico drew her face from the protection she sought; studied the uncertainty which marred perfect features to reassure, "only for a moment, my love, I swear." Gently he found the exacting line of her mouth with his own, his tongue teasing over the lips dipping in to do battle with her own and his hips nudged deeper into velvet depth of her warmth. Lingering in the caress and stroke of tightness which engulfed him, Nickolai was sure he had died to experience such sensation in his life. "Angeline," whispered in the strictest control as he fought the instinct to deepened and intensify his strokes; to seek deeper depths as her heat beckoned. "Sweetheart, does it still hurt?" When the shoulders shrugged with uncertainty, and the eyes confronted his shyly, he managed, "love, let me make everything perfect, just hold onto me and let me do what I must." Reaching between them, he caressed the nub of her desire. Teased it with gentle touches as he felt her react to the attentions granted, the unexpected gasp which breathed over her lips to the culminating sensations he introduced to her. "Let me love you, little one."

"Nico!" Escaped in a smother as he once again captured her mouth, trailed the arch of the throat, then suckled the need of breast as they pressed in demand of further attention. As he sought deeper depths of her want, urging her, needing her to fulfill such desires as his own were peaked. His palms pressed over her length, grasping and holding to her hips, holding her to his increasing depth. Splayed to the flesh, he sought more and more to caress as he ravaged the tenderness of her offering.

"Sweet Jesus, Angeline, I love you like none before." And all control was lost only the feel of flesh against flesh, of muscle fighting muscle for the ultimate release and when Nickolai was sure of her fulfillment he cried out to the release which encased him; to the woman who clung to him taking him to the depths of his soul then brought him to heaven in a single clasping touch.

Laying safe in the haven of her arms, the gentleness of hands as they caressed the thick mane of raven hair from features Angeline pressed her lips to the plain of forehead as he laid cradled in the joining of their bodies, lavished the strength and breadth of him beneath adorning hands and Nickolai couldn't help the content sigh which escaped him to the woman he claimed as wife. A wife who held him still deep within her, her tightness seeming to beckon with every movement of muscle, drawing him, coaxing him to harden. "Angeline," he warned to the actions of her body to the tightness of her depth, "I don't wish to hurt you, little one, it may be too soon, and I have not been the gentlest of lovers." Whispered as his lips caressed the swell of breast, teased the tender underside before the strain of puckered flesh came between the pull of lips, and he felt the creamy heat of her inflame him even as the stain of her innocence marred thigh. "I have waited so long to have you here, to be able to touch you, I fear I will never have my fill of you."

Arching her back to the sweetness of his assault, to the body deep within her own she sought to explore the muscles of his straining back with hands that grew bolder with each of his caresses, caressed the ripples as fingertips traced and beckoned along each rise of rib, till finally she caressed the strain of his buttocks, drawing him harder, deeper to her constant, unquenchable need of him as her silken legs rose to enclose about the power of his thighs, to lock about his back and hold him tight, secure to her. "Nickolai, I need to know this isn't some wonderful dream that you are finally, really here." Came in soft pleading to release any resolve he held in coming to her too soon, to any control he thought he held to the moment before them. "Please." And instantly, Nickolai lost himself to the woman, to the flesh that beckoned him.

"Never a dream again, little one, never again." Managed as he emptied himself deep within the beckon of her womanhood. "Never again." Reiterated as Nico moved to his back, drawing her over his length nearly bereft from leaving the joining of their flesh, and he cherished her in the strength of engulfing arms. Tenderly his hands caressed the silk of her flesh, gathered the fiery hair as it beckoned him with a thousand teasing touches, "are you sure you're, all right?" He implored to the feel of her now so small, so delicate in his arms.

Brushing his sensitive skin, Angeline smiled softly to his concerns as she lifted her head to confront him, "I am perfect, Nico, I swear." Gently her hands came with timid caresses to the thickness of his upper arm, the corded muscle of shoulder defined in a spectacular show of strength, pressed palms across the shelf of the breast as her lips pressed into the pound of his heart.

"I know your perfect, little one; however, are you sure I didn't hurt you?"

"Do I act as if you've hurt me?" Teased as the head returned to his chest and her eyes closed to the weariness of their endeavors.

Tightening his hold about her delicate length, he smiled to the contented expression as it came to her weary features, "you must be exhausted, go to sleep, little one, sleep."

Reaching to pull the blankets back over their lengths, Angeline managed softly, “don’t try that persuasion stuff on me, husband.” Smiling to feel the soft chuckle as it rumbled within his chest. Twisting about in his arms, so the swell of her bottom was cupped along his length, she whispered sleepily, “thank you for my things, Nico, thank you for everything.”

Closing his arm about her length as seeking the flesh of neck to rest his head against, he managed, “it was the least I could do once forcing you from your home, your family, to come here with me. I will never see a day you will regret such a decision, little one; you will be happy here.” With a soft nod to his words, Angeline allowed the compelling call to sleep to have its way, and she laid content in the strength of protective arms. Before sleep could claim her completely, she prayed silently to any of the god’s which may be listening that Nickolai would keep every promise made to her.

When he was sure, she slept, Nickolai pressed his lips to the nestled head and extinguished the candles with a single thought to darkness.

∞∞∞

Eyes opened with a start to hear the soft scratching at chamber doors, “Antony.” Growled to realize already a new day had begun, already the man awaited his presence to a pressing schedule, at least, Nico reflected he had enough sense not to barge into the chambers as he had done every other day of his employment. His hand instinctively caressed the softness as it cuddled protectively under the press of his claiming arm, palmed the perfection of her breast as the pad of his thumb teased over the nipple, causing it to harden in search of further attention. For a terrifying moment, he thought the night before nothing more than the dream it had been for the many years of his waiting. How many times had he awoke to look expectantly about to find he was alone? Only this time the dream was laying quite contently beside him. Drawing his arm from its possessive drape across her body, he turned to stare at her sleeping face, the spray of fiery hair as it crossed hers as well as his pillows. “Angeline.” Whispered if only to hear her name; to know she was finally beside him as she always should have been.

Drawing the hair back over the shoulder as she murmured a response in her sleep then snuggled even closer to his length, Nickolai couldn't help the smile as she sought his hand with her own and brought it into the protection of her grasp. Though he had had his share of women, more than his share, conscious reminded with a grimace to his indiscretions; Nico never remembered sleeping as soundly as he did with this one beside him, he never knew how right it felt to have someone so soft and delicate lay cupped to his length. It was always his practice in the past to be far from a woman's bed before the light of dawn could bring about the allusion of an unwanted involvement. Who would have imaged he could get used to a woman as quickly as he did this one, who would ever think to need a woman as much as he needed this one? “Ah, little one, if you only knew how much I love you, how much I need you.” Whispered as his lips press to the exposed shoulder, causing her to swat at the teasing touch before turning toward his length with a murmur of distraction from dreams. Softly Nickolai allowed his fingertips to trace the outline of her body, over the shoulder to the slope of ribs down to the hollow of waist, over the sweet swell of her bottom where he cupped the perfect flesh in his massive palm pleased to feel her press back to her body's validation of the attention granted. Turning to her back, her leg thrown over the two of his Nickolai felt his entire body respond to the woman who seemed to stretch as contently as a cat before him. Instinctively his hand moved to caress the flesh offered, only to hesitate as the bloody smear of her innocence was found to stain the ivory of inner thigh. Instantly he was reminded of the virginity she gave to him, and the need to be with her now seemed to elude him. Instead, he cherished the woman whose body stretched and arched toward him before turning once again into the protection of his side, where she snuggled with a smile to the warmth sought. "Sweet Jesus!" Came in a hiss from lips, "will I ever be able to leave this bed again?"

Reluctantly turning from the sweet unknowing beckon of her warmth as she continued to sleep, Nickolai opened the heavy drapery from about the bed and squinted to the invading sun. A weary sigh escaped to the work awaiting him. The men and duties which called to him every morning in the last five years since he lost his parents, how he wished for a morning they would let him be — for a morning that would allow him to lay here and stare at the woman who was his wife. Watching as she slept, he surmised, would soon be his favorite pass-time. One, he was sure he would never truly grow tired of experiencing.

Six

Stretching lazily from the utter contentedness of strained limbs, Angeline opened her eyes to the enclosed darkness that surrounded her. Sometime shortly after sunrise, Nickolai pressed his lips to her forehead to whisper of business and a promise to return soon. Pressing back the covers, she stared at her body as if it belonged to another and wondered to the feeling it was capable of, to the emotions it brought her to. "Nickolai." Whispered to the instant ache her body felt to wake without him beside her. To the need to touch him as it became consuming. Drawing her legs up against her chest, she hugged the knees within the wrap of arms only to witness the dried stain which came to her inner thigh; a testament to the night they had shared. "Where are you?" Was wondered out loud and the air was felt to stir warmly about her length, seeming to caress her where eyes inspected only moments before. "You're not playing fair." Teased to the instant warmth spreading up and over her sensitive length, to the sweet ache taking limbs.

Coming reluctantly from the warmth of covers, Angeline looked about the massive room which surrounded her in deep dark woods and thick tapestries. For silent moments she stared to the portraits as they hung with staring, knowing eyes. Unknown eyes that seemed to follow her movements as subtle shadows could be seen to move slowly about the room. Her eyes darted from one portrait to another, but it seemed she was always a moment too late to see the change which had taken. The movement completed before her realizing caused breath to exhale in a sudden gasp, a wisp of fear to chill along the length of her spine. *'Only you will save him,'* came on the wisp of air causing Angeline to spin about if only in follow of such words, *'only you can save him.'* Reinforced before the shadows retreated and the room stilled to silence. *"The curse is so his; now you must be the one."*

"Who?" Was managed as Angeline confronted the depictions hanging in startling familiarity to Nickolai, "who must I save?" Pleaded as she remained to stare to the silence now engulfing her, the torture of the unknown plaguing her. Pressing the length of hair back over shoulders Angeline managed softly, "how can I help if you won't help me?" Teeth came to tug worrisomely to bottom lip as she waited with bated breath for a response, any response.

As the moments ticked into minutes, Angeline felt a frown tug to the concentration of her features, "I must be losing my mind." The robe, of the night before, was tugged up about her length with the self-admonishment, "if anyone ever knew you were speaking to an empty room, they'd lock you in the highest tower and throw away the key." Leaving the master's chambers behind she sought the luxury of her bath.

A tray of fruits and pastries awaited her appearance as steam was found to be rising from the waiting depth. Slipping into the waters, a sigh of contentment came as the rushing, and swirling waters eased her tired limbs, and she selected a fresh berry with a smile to such indulgence. *'Let him come to you, allow him to know of your need of him. Already your need for him grows, your desire to be with him warms your blood. Beckon him.'* A nuanced thought beseeched Angeline, causing her to hesitate to reach for further delicacies. *'He's thinking of you even now, waiting for you. Beckon him.'*

"How can this be?" *'Trust in what you know is true.'* Sounded in wonder as she looked about the room knowing someone had to be hiding there; speaking to her in a whisper for how else could she explain the voices she heard. How else? *'Think of him, beckon him, two as one.'* "Come out, show yourself!" Shouted to the surroundings as only silence seemed to ring. For long hard minutes, she studied the surroundings, and when the realization she was alone finally settled in, it caused her heart to quicken its beat within her chest. *'Listen to your heart, two as one.'* "What do you want of me?" Questioned as images of their lovemaking came to haunt, the feel of hands to tease, "who is doing this?"

"Why are you doing this?" Closing her eyes, Angeline refused to allow the fear to overrun her, "there has to be a logical explanation." Mind whispered to heart, forcing its wild racing to under control. "Who are you?" Demanded into the echo of the room as she spun in growing fear to catch the smallest of glimpses of who could be playing such a horrible joke on her. Wild eyes searched in vain to the creator of the voice, and still, she found none, *'Nico, where are you?'* Whispered within her heart; allowed the need to emanate in concentration as she thought of Nickolai, sought to sense him as he was preoccupied with thoughts of warriors and strategies. *'Beckon him.'* Insisted once again and she allowed the emotion to reach him; call to him. *'Two as one.'*

∞∞∞

Captain Deleon watched the Count as he pondered the plans for battlement and sleeping quarters before him. Nikolai planned to have his guard assigned to quarters and not roaming about the Keep where his wife would be spending her days. "Have the men begin with a wall, here along the buttress," and the parchment was traced off with fingertip, "take as many men from the village you will need---" The wisp of fear clenched to his heart, the uncertainty to tug him to distraction as his brow creased to the realization of such feelings, "---to gather the readied stone. I'll have Joseph begin on the doors and windows." Turning toward Illevante` Nickolai contemplated the emotions which crept into the back of his pre-occupation. The soft stirring of her seeking as it instantly caught his interest. *'How is this possible, little one?'* He questioned forcing himself not to smile to the longing which came to conquer the fear that was only moments felt, the heat of need as it radiated with the touch of uncertainty, a shadow of a doubt. Mentally he envisioned the ivory length laying pressed against his own. With the mind's eye, he watched his hand caress the swell of the hip up along the dip of waist further till the swell of an ivory breast filled his palm, and he teased the perfection of the nipple as it hardened to demanding attention. *'What are you doing, little one, do you even know?'*

Pressing back from the tub's rim Angeline looked down to her length expecting to see hands beneath the water's edge caressing her, "you're letting your imagination get the best of you, actually listening to the voices in your head!" Even as she banished such thoughts as being ridiculous, she found herself breath-held waiting for Nickolai to come bursting into the room with the realization she had called to him, had needed him to be here now for her. "Simply ridiculous, Angeline, to think that he would come as if reading your mind. This place is making you crazy."

Rising from the bath's depth, the last of lather was rinsed away from her hair under the rush of the waterfall when she heard, "I thought you required me, little one?" Though his voice held a touch of amusement, his breathlessness was evident to see her under the fall of water. The hair a thick, wet flame down the slope of her back, teasing to the fullness of her bottom as the remains of soap could be seen to follow the ivory perfection of her length.

Turning to confront Nickolai's amused voice, the hair and water were pressed from the surprise of her eyes, as she managed, "then It's true."

"And what would that be?" He questioned as shrugging off tunic and overlay before bending to pull the leather boots and trousers away.

Appreciative eyes remained fixed on the naked perfection as it became exposed before her, found herself nearly breathless to the strength and breadth of the man she called husband. “Sweet Jesus.” Whispered as the legs long and muscular slipped into the depth, the thighs thick and hard forged through the water bridging the distance between them. “You would come if I beckoned you.”

“What I felt was hardly a beckon, little one.” Nickolai teased, the fiery hair pressed back over her shoulder as his hand lingered to the flesh there, pressed up to cup the column of throat forcing her to bridge the distance between them. “And if what you say is true, our life together will be more than a little interesting, would it not?” Nickolai could do little else then smile down to the woman whose cheeks seemed to burn as if in a fever even as her body already cradled him.

Angeline was all too aware of the formidable chest she was pressed against, the hard plain of his belly where her breasts seemed to pound in growing need. The soft tickle of hair spreading across his chest down to where she couldn’t even bring her eyes to follow without allowing the heat to spread to her cheek. Lifting her face to the gentle pressure of thumb under chin Angeline nearly sighed as the mouth was found to be only inches from her own, the lips already beckoning her with surrender as they touched first gently then with growing intent. “Nico, how is this possible?” Whispered as her hands splayed over the expanse of his shoulder, down the strength of arms, bolder to caress the area of his chest, the narrow of waist, “how can you know what I’m feeling, what I’m thinking?” Trailing fingertips she teased the muscle of thigh, dragged fingernails over the definition of muscle smiling secretly to feel the breath he inhaled quickly to her searching.

Wrapping his arms about her length, his hands pressed down the length of spine to mold over the perfection of her backside, drawing her hard and without question to the need which rose between them, “all I know is I can feel you in my heart, I know your emotions as if you were speaking them to me. Something you do quite eloquently to be sure.”

Giggling to the intent Angeline welcomed the press of his mouth over hers, the feel of hands as they reacquainted themselves to the ivory length cleaving to him, needing him, "Nico," whispered with waning patience to the teasing of hands, the suckle of mouth, "please."

"It's not too soon, my love, are you still tender?" He managed reminded to the stain of blood as it colored her inner thigh, the force in which he had used in the taking of her virginity. As the mouth sealed over his, Nickolai felt his body respond to the answer of her own. The straining length lifted into his arms, and the legs about his waist; grasping his shoulders in surprise to the depth he achieved in a single motion. Nico groaned to feel the thighs clasp about him; the ankles locked at his back. He relished in the tightening of her muscles as he moved deeper into her warmth, harder into her heat, "you feel so good, little one, like velvet and silk." Murmured as his mouth sought hers and the tongues danced in rhythm of their bodies. Tightening her arms about his shoulders, Angeline drew up his length, teasing him to withdrawal only to lower to the thrusting in deepening strokes. Over and over she brought him to the brink of release; till the hands palming her bottom clasped possessively about her waist holding her down to the assault as he quickened to the creamy depth beckoning him as the muscles caressing him tightened and the quivering of her release caused him to lose all control. His body slammed into her, battered her new-found desire with an unquenchable ferocity leaving them both weak and exhausted at the finale.

Lowering them into the bathwater, refusing to relinquish the hold about her length, Nickolai pressed teasing kisses along her throat up over jaw and then across cheeks before managing, "you have to learn to control these beckons of yours."

Snuggling close to his length she lapped the beads of water trickling over the collarbone, trailed tongue over the breadth of his shoulder as her giggle teased his flesh, "I heard voices telling me to beckon you to me, shadows that seemed to enforce such a decree."

“They are attempting to strengthen the bond between us.” Nico surmised studying her expression as it came with slight vexation to such a statement. “They want to make sure you can’t live without me.” He teased.

“They? Your ancients.” Tugging to the lower lip for silent contemplative moments, Angeline confessed in confusion to that was happening about her, “but I heard them; it was no dream. They were speaking to me, not out loud but I heard them. I hear their whispers all around me, and I see them moving over the walls.”

Caressing the curls which began to dry in wisps about her face, Nico confirmed, “they were never a dream, little one, they live in this Keep as surely as we do.” Watching as her eyes searched his for long moments, he reassured, “they would never hurt you; I would never allow them to do so. You have nothing to fear.” With an unsure nod and tugging frown, she settled against the brace of his shoulder as her eyes continually searched the walls about her wondering if they were there with them now.

∞∞∞

With a start, Angeline woke to the soft knocking as it came to the chamber doors casting a quick look to Nickolai; as he slept soundly beside her, she managed to crawl out from under his capturing arm as it crossed her length. Pressing the riot of curls and snarls from about her shoulders after pulling on a robe, she crossed the great distance of the room to confront Antony as he stood beyond the barrier in wait of his Count. “Lady Angeline,” he managed to avert eyes from the woman before him; her hair a wild mass of fiery curls about perfect features making him regret summoning the Count so early in the morning. '*What man,*' he wondered, '*could ever leave this woman for any reason?*' “Pray to forgive me, I didn’t mean to disturb you; I usually summons the Count at this time, I have appointments awaiting his direction as Count of Illevante `."

Nodding thoughtfully to the man's duty then looking to her husband who remained contently snoring, Angeline informed, hoping she wouldn't regret her decision when Nico awoke, "the appointments will have to wait, the Count didn't sleep very well last night. I will send him to you as soon as he has adequately rested. And I would appreciate it in the future if the Count's appointments are arranged for later in the day." To Antony's surprise the door closed to the man's objections. *'Didn't sleep very well?'* Angeline questioned the white lie stated, *'well,'* she consoled conscience as the pitcher of water came to fill the basin, and she washed the evidence of the night before away, *'it's not a total lie.'* Taking a quick peek to mirror she rinsed her mouth with minted water she requested Martine bring to her every morning then dabbed her wrists with a dot of perfume. *'Once they had collapsed with exhaustion they slept very well'* With a giggle, Angeline crawled back into the bed they had occupied for most of the previous afternoon and evening. Long, wonderful hours wherein each other's arms they spoke of their futures, of their pasts, touching and exploring. Making love time and time again until finally, they slept.

Drawing the blankets up about their lengths, she gasped to feel the arm as it draped about her waist, dragging her back to his side, "was that Antony?" Growled against the length of throat Nico nuzzled with warming intent. When the head nodded, and she snuggled closer to his warmth, he managed, "damn him and his agenda."

Raking her hand through the length of raven hair she drew his mouth to hers and when the kiss ended told him, "I had Antony rearrange your appointments for this morning; I informed him you didn't sleep very well, and would require additional rest."

Drawing her up over his length, he teased, "did we sleep at all?" The robe was lighted away as his hands marveled in the vibrancy of flesh, the heat of her depth as he was lost to her once again.

∞∞∞

Twisting about in his arms, Angeline listened to the mantle clock announce the afternoon hour and smiled to the time which had slipped away, “Antony is going to be furious with me.” She managed to trace the muscle of forearm crossing her length, “he’s done nothing but juggle your schedule about since we’ve wed and now, he’s more than a little perturbed to have to take orders from me.” Craning her head about she looked to his silence, “you have a great deal of work to see to, don’t you?”

“Nothing so pressing to take me from this bed at least for another hour or two.” Teased as his hand pressed up over the dip of the waist, across the narrow ribcage to cup the perfection of her breast into the palm of his hand. Nearly absentmindedly the thumb came to tease over the hardening nipple causing it to rise and pucker in demand of the attention granted. “I love touching you; the feel of your skin.”

Cupping her hand over his further, halting his endless exploration emerald eyes met blue as Angeline suggested, “perhaps it’s time for you to see to other responsibilities while I need to take a bath and attempt to comb the knots out of my hair.”

Twisting her about and drawing her down into the mattress, he covered her length as asking, “what if I don’t wish to see to anything other than you, my love?” Tugging the piled pillows away from her nestled head, “what are you going to do then?”

Sighing wondrously, Angeline surrendered, “exclaim my weariness and demand a moment of repose. I swear you’ll wear me out by nightfall.”

Laughing out loud to her exclamation he lifted his weight from her length but not before suckling the puckered flesh into his mouth, relentlessly his pursued reaction only stopping as the body was felt to undulate beneath him and the thighs spread to encase his pressing, “very well, go to your bath while I still have the taste of your flesh on my lips."

Opening her eyes, Angeline glared at him for silent moments, "I knew you didn't play fair." And with a *'humph'* to his chuckle she watched as he lighted from the bed and disappeared into his dressing rooms.

∞∞∞

Once pulling herself from the tangle of their bed, Angeline soaked in the steaming waters of the tub. Welcomed the relaxing aroma of vanilla and rose as it eased exhausted senses and seemed to erase the weariness from her limbs. Listening as the mantle clock was heard to chime out the second hour reluctantly Angeline came from the water, wrapped herself in the length of a sinfully soft covering, and went to explore the dressing rooms beyond.

Opening the first of the many cupboards which lined the cavernous room, the brow was felt to crease in confusion to the items found. Cupboard after cupboard opened, drawer upon drawer searched, and still, Angeline found none of her clothing. *'There must be some mistake.'* She thought wildly as all manner of images came to crowd her head, "how can this be?" Her heart cried to the evidence placed before her, every cupboard, every drawer was filled with another woman's clothing. Found nothing she called her own no matter how hard she searched no matter how many drawers were opened, and their contents rummaged through.

"Yes, Milady, you sent for me?" The servant questioned as she found the young woman wrapped within a Turkish linen inspecting contents behind every door and within every drawer.

Turning with great distress upon her beautiful features, Martine was sure she witnessed tears in the young woman's eyes as Angeline managed, "my clothing. I can't find anything that is mine. There are all other women's clothing here." The delicate chin trembled fiercely against the onslaught of her breaking heart. To the evidence that Nickolai wouldn't have at least cleared out such reminders of his lovers before settling her here. "How could he have allowed this? Why would he have permitted this?" Eyes searched those of the silent servant *'because she is the one he wants,'* came with a whisper to her heart as the tremble she fought valiantly to keep from chin was seen to have domain over pain, *'She's the one he thinks of when touching you. That's how he's able to touch you, want you.'* And already her heart was crushing to such assumptions.

∞∞∞

Working in his library, Nickolai looked up from the smattering of paperwork holding his attention. *'She doubts the place she holds in Illevante,' questions the loyalty given so freely.'* "Count?" Antony inquired to see the man faltered in verse to the response he was scribing. *'You must gain her unconditional trust.'* Demanded much like a drum within his brain, pounding, enforcing their will. *'All this means nothing if she does not find a place for you in her heart. Nothing! You cannot fail us now, now when the time is so near!'*

"Leave me." Nico demanded as the papers before him blurred and his hand shook violently to the sudden surge of emotion, the gathering of power as it emanated from the very walls in demand of his attention. *'You need to secure her before we can move on; before all can be achieved. All this will be for naught if she is not secure within you.'*

"But, Milord, we are not finished---the change in schedule this morning has put all of my plans into disarray---there are appointments awaiting an audience." Antony cast his eyes from the distraction of Count only as the shadows cast suddenly upon library walls seemed to move of their own volition, the air to stir in growing temperature. "Milord?"

"Finish this senseless dribble on your own!" Bellowed as flinging aside pages he felt his forehead crease to the awareness as it swamped him with engulfing misery. '*All will come in time; she will love me!*' Instantly he recognized the pain and heartbreak she emanated, could nearly feel the pressure of her tears as they threatened. How could she have gone from such utter contentment to agony in a matter of moments, one moment he felt her longing and need of him only to be quickly replaced by despair and doubt. "Angeline." Escaped to the crushing pain and he traveled the length of halls, took flights of stairs in only a matter of strides till he slowed before her dressing room doors.

∞∞∞

Gathering up handfuls of silk and satin, of bows and ribbons, Angeline presented the lengths to the astounded servant who could only shake her head to the conclusions of the young woman, "but, Milady, you don't understand!" Martine attempted, as the air that surrounded her seemed to thicken and still, the shadows to move and whisper of their discontent, "the Count---"

Instantly the doors to her dressing room flung open, and Nickolai stood in the frame. His towering breadth filling the opening as he managed in the strictest control, "Martine, leave us." His eyes never left those of his wife, as she was pale and shaken before him. The hair a dark, dampened flame about her naked shoulders, causing a stark contrast to the pristine white of the linen enfolding her, "you should have allowed Martine to explain. She is well aware of all the goings-on at Illevante`." Managed once the doors to the room closed behind him and he assured their privacy. "She would never lie to you or for me, little one." Nico confirmed before the accusations that were quickly coming to lips, once disappointment crushed to heartbreak, were spoke. "It is nothing like you suspect."

A single blink allowed a tear its escape and lowering the fisted items back to the drawers where she found them Angeline closed the drawers and presented her back to explanations that she knew were to come. Swallowing nervously over the exasperation and impatience proceeding him into the room, Angeline briefly wondered how she could face him when he blatantly slapped the truth in her face. How could a single word that he spoke be trusted, when everything he had ever dared to convince her with was nothing but a vile misconception? Was she so desperate to believe that someone as beautiful as he could want her, need her in his life? "What I suspect is that she is aware of the other women who frequent here. So aware that she has yet to remove their clothing from a dressing room you claim to be mine." Looking up, she briefly caught her reflection in the polished mirror and quickly looked away, hating the face that confronted her, hating the very body which betrayed her. *'You were a fool, Angeline, a fool to hope, to believe he would truly want you, would truly desire you.' 'Listen to your heart.'* Tears gathered thickly and burned to the humiliation of her dreams, "why couldn't you let me believe in you only a little longer? Why couldn't you be different from all the others?"

"Would you believe me if I told you none other ever came to this Keep, no one but you have ever shared that bed with me?" Seeing the look of utter disbelief as it came to her features Nickolai felt a frown tug to the corners of his mouth, a defeated sigh to escape him. "Very well, allow me to prove it to you." Quickly he moved to one of many overflowing wardrobes and drew from it a wrap. The material nearly shimmered to its purity and the black ermine fur trimming it a perfect contrast to its simple design. Releasing the tuck of linen, he allowed it to fall as a puddle about her naked feet, as he insisted to her disbelief; "do you honestly believe this could be made for anyone but you?" Urging the material up about her arms, across the shoulders then turning her to fasten the single clasp, which closed the length under her breast. "You are the only one, Angeline; you will always be the only one."

"You don't need to explain or hope to console me, I understand perfectly." The lingering of his hands at her waist was pressed away, the splay of fingers across ribcage removed. "It was what I expected; how could you be different than any other man. I have always known of the loathing as they attempted to spend more than a moment in my company. I only thought after---" and the tears rushed in choking words that fought for release, "---I thought last night---"

"Last night was perfect, little one, this morning was spectacular, and this afternoon was beautiful. Your passion was more glorious than any man could ever hope for in a wife." Nico nearly shouted to the anger as it grew to his own disappointment and realization that he brought her to this place in her life, in their life.

"It meant nothing to you!" Cried to the all-engulfing humiliation, to the voices which seemed to bombard her, confuse her continuously. Instantly her defenses were drawn about heart, about mind, in protection, "why did you do this? Why did you make me want you? Why couldn't you have stayed away, stayed with this other woman, what can you possibly need from me?"

"Angeline, how can you deny the beauty that you are, the effect you have over me?" With a disgusted sigh Nico moved to the wardrobe doors and opened them one after another; drew forth gown after gown before her till they piled about his feet in an array of exquisite materials and color. "Summon Martine, have her try any one of them, and you will see they fit you perfectly. Only you, there are no other women, all this I made ready in preparation of you joining me; of you becoming my wife. The redecorating, the gowns---all of it was a wedding present for you. I wanted you to feel at home, here, with me. I wanted you to be happy." A low moan, nearly growl, escaped him to see her in such pain and he spat a loathsome string of blasphemies as it was apparent there would be no other way to explain the long and tedious care he took in preparing for her arrival without confessing all. "Look at me, and you will know I am telling the truth, touch me and see into my heart, you above all others will know what I am saying is true!"

Miserably the auburn head shook as everything she had

come to hope for seemed to be crumbling about her, “I don’t know what I feel from you any longer, I don’t know how you can deceive me as you do. I have been able to sense the dread in men as they were forced to be with me, always. Now everything is confused, my heart, my head---everything is so constant---never-ending.” Looking to the walls, she turned as if to follow the wisps of circling shadows, “why are they doing this to me?” The scream threatening to rip over her lips was contained within the clench of teeth as her fists pressed to temples, to the pounding which would surely make her head explode if it didn’t stop. “You have to make them stop; they have to stop!”

'Leave us! It is enough! Can’t you see what you are doing to her?' Commanded to the voices which she was sensitive to, the whispers which plagued her. *‘Angeline, please.’* Whispered as it seemed she no longer would respond to his spoken words, *'look at me, know that I would never deceive you, would never hurt you. Sweet Christ, I love you like no one before.'*

A soft sob escaped to the momentary reprieve of silence as it came to her, the banging of a constant drum against her senses stopped only to be replaced by a single voice, a longing decree, *'It is not me you want, it is not me you need.'* Angeline’s mind cried out to him even as the realization she could read his thoughts set her heart to pound furiously. *'This bond between us is so strong---too strong. Never have I been able to achieve such with any before. How can this be possible? Let me go, Nickolai, please, let me go before I fall in love with you and you break my heart. Let me go.'*

“There is no one but you.” Seeing little resolved to his pleads, Nickolai gathered her into his arms, forced her to confront him even as doubts to his fidelity crowded her mind as strong as the words of his ancients. “You have to listen to what I have to say!” Hissed as she fought to escape his grasp, “I did this to you!” Came in a shout, stilling her movements, “all those men, the ones who turned you away, who refused to touch you it was not because of you, little one, it was because of me.” Silence reigned as the steady pressure of his towering, powerful length pressed into her weakened one as his heartbeat pounded wildly into hers and if not for the haggard breaths still escaping her Nico would have sworn she turned to stone under his touch. “All those years ago when they began to call on you, when they became interested in you, I was there. I followed you from the age of twelve and made sure none would find you desirable; none would want you as I wanted you. I placed images inside their heads, images of you with not so desirable attributes. From the flop that sought only to have your father's lands, I reduced you to the most hideous of hags, warts and blackened teeth included; convincing him there was no lands or dowry to be had. To the dandy who did not deserve you, I placed a hump on your back, making you appear to him as nothing short of a freak, crooked and grotesque in sight and smell. You name any other, and I was there, I was always there. It was never you, my little one, you were always perfect. Graceful, patient, a light to any darkness. I could never bear the thought of another ever coming to claim your heart, your hand.”

The hand rose with a resonating slap to the closeness of his face, the palm stinging to the welt that rose across cheek before she staggered back from his confession. Wildly the head shook as she sought to cover her ears to hear such a horrible admission, as her head seemed to pound, and sickness rose thickly within her throat gagging her to the comprehension of his actions. “How could you?” Angeline could only shake her head to the words shared as the heel of her hand came to press against the pound of the temple, and she fought to understand why he would do such a thing? Why would he make her believe she was the one who caused such disgust? Why he sought to damage her confidence as he had? “Why would you?”

Reaching to her, Nico wasn’t surprised to see the disgust which greeted his attempt, “I never knew of your gift, Angeline, I never knew you experienced what they felt. If I had known I would have sent them to their destiny with the confusion I am capable of; wiped the memory of you away. I would never have intentionally hurt you, would never have made you come to believe you were anything less than perfection.” Came as he ventured a step to her retreat. "I only thought to keep you unto myself."

Moving deeper into the room away from his approach she went to where the piled clothing remained and staggered weakly to her knees amongst the creations as she was sure her legs could no longer carry her so heavily did his betrayal weigh upon her heart. Gathering the silks, satins, and velvets into her arms, she held them for silent moments as avoiding the concern which swamped her senses, the anger he directed to self in the betrayal she believed and forced herself to close her heart to his concerns. Burying her face in the material a soft sob escaped as his hands came to caress the heave of her shoulders, "so many years, Nickolai," the words came as she pressed tears and hair from her cheeks, "so many years I looked in my mirror and hated what I saw. Wondered what others loathed." The eyes could do little more than stare a little apprehensively onto his nearness; "do you have any idea what it is like to look in a mirror and hate what you see? To avoid the contact of others because of the self-loathing I felt?" She questioned softly.

Caressing the remaining tears from her cheeks, the wet strands as they clung to features, Nico avowed, "no, little one, that is why I am on my knees before you now, begging, hoping, for your forgiveness. I want nothing more than to take that pain from you, to let you know, feel, understand how beautiful you truly are." Seeing the dubious expression to his words, even now, he asked, "would I have been able to make love to you repeatedly throughout the night and day? Look at me, Angeline, feel what I am feeling, know that I only want you to love me as much as I love---need you."

Emerald searched the piercing blue as she opened her heart to him, sought to read his most profound thoughts; searched for the single beat of heart telling her of his cruel intent, "if you were there you would have realized none of those men meant anything to me. None thought to love me." And the face returned to the gathered material, pressed there as sobs heaved shoulders till the tears were a near painful thing and not the relief as they promised.

Gathering her into his arms, burying her against his strength Nickolai allowed the tears to come, allowed the moistness to seep into the very cloth of his shirt and smiled reluctantly as her fingers were felt to tightened into the shirt's ruffles holding him, drawing him tighter to her length, and at least for the moment, needing him. The cold dampened cheek as it sought the flesh of his neck and hung to him. When the tears ended with a hiccup, he drew the tortured features from their press to whisper, "I did it because I have always loved you, because you are my destiny."

Drawing away from his nearness as it seemed to beckon her Angeline pressed trembling fingers to the remains of tears and forced them from cheeks with the press of knuckles as her arms yearned to be back about his length, drawing needed strength from him, needing him if only for the assurance of all that he promised, "if you could send Martine in I should get dressed." Carefully the length of the robe came to be tugged over her exposed legs even as his eyes revered such flesh. Watching as his hand penetrated the fold of closing material, caressed and cupped the firm length beneath his palm, she managed, "please, Nickolai, don't. Not now."

A nod addressed her avoidance; the touch she shrugged away was removed without contest. When the door closed marking his exit, Angeline visibly staggered to his absence, *'I have always loved you,'* echoed within her head, the emotions which crushed him to her sadness still curled painfully about her heart.

Looking about the mess they had created Angeline slumped weakly to her bottom as she stared to the pulse of her reddened palm and paled in remembrance of the force in which she had assaulted him. Already she could hear the lectures from stepmother when she was sent home for such actions; already she could see the disappointment of father to such failings. For surely the Count of Illevante` would not stand for such insult from a mere wife, especially one with the blood of Belaveuta coursing her veins. Closing her eyes, she drew the throbbing hand to her breast to realize she felt mostly the need to find her husband, to be held in his arms, touched by his hands. “Nico!” Cried as on hands and knees she crawled to the massive mirror and stared to the woman before her. '*I have always loved you.*' Repeated and his turmoil settled at the back of her mind as he sought only to soothe her, ease her shattered emotions.

The halo of dampened, tousled curls framing face were raked back as Angeline struggled to her knees, then stood before the mirror. Daring the reflection to defy her; Angeline released the single clasp of her robe, and she stared to the naked length. Carefully she scrutinized every curve and hollow, the legs, calf, and flat of her belly. The narrowness of waist to rise of ribs and swell of breasts. Even the neck came to be caressed under the press of trembling hands realizing for the first time in twenty years the woman before her. '*Beckon to him.*' Whispered about her head as images of the hours they had spent in each other’s arms once again filled her, and she sought to find her husband, sought to convey her forgiveness to his heart. '*Two as one,*' beseeched as the words whirled endlessly about her head, '*beckon to him, he awaits your need of him.*'

Closing her eyes, she allowed the thickening air to swirl about her, felt the caress as it swept over her breasts, causing the pink flesh to harden and strain to its tease. Lower, it swept over her belly, the length of her thigh; to tease the deepest part of her. Enveloped her entire length with such an intensity she dropped to her knees as the touch continued along her neck, across her mouth and desire slammed within her, “Nico,” whispered softer than the most reverent of prayers as the body moved in rhythm to the ceaseless search. The whispered mouth to stroke, suckle and caress, but still, she was unfulfilled. '*I have always loved you*' came again to taunt as she laid breathlessly before the mirror, sweat and desire running from her body, gathering in the deepest hollows as the imprint of unseen hands moved over her flesh, and the release slammed again and again.

“Sweet Jesus.” Came in a gasp as a weak hand came to press

the length of hair back from her features and she stared nearly blindly to the woman who came to her bidding as the door opened to the summons. “Martine.” Was stated with obvious disappointment as her entire length prayed Nickolai would be behind the door, waiting for her to throw herself into his arms, beg him to touch her to take the constant need from her yet again. “I thought you to be the Count.”

Smiling gently, the woman managed as drawing the door to a close behind them, “he seemed quite determined when he passed me in the hall. Perhaps we should get you properly dressed, and you can go to him.” And the naked length was realized with a flame of blush.

“Perhaps that might be best.” Came as she realized she nearly walked out of her chamber stark naked. Wouldn’t that have been a lovely greeting to servants from their new Mistress?

Pressing hands along the length of peach silk as it seemed to cleave to rib then flow back gracefully about her thighs, Angeline smiled to the woman who watched her with a newfound gentleness in her knowing eyes, “you are breathtaking, Milady, I’m sure the Count will be most pleased to see you.” Martine managed, her smile deepening to see the tears of gratitude that misted the young woman’s eyes.

Turning from the praise, Angeline moved to the terrace doors where she was able to overlook the labyrinth of garden paths below, the steppingstones which all seemed to lead to lands she had yet to explore. For a moment she closed her eyes an allowed the salty breeze to envelop her, nearly calm her as the faint sounds of endless waves could be heard to roll into shore with unfailing rhythm, “do you know where I may find him, there is so much I don’t know about this place. So much, I need to know.”

“All will come in time, to be sure, Milady, however when

I have seen such determination in the Count Illevante` eyes before he can usually be found in his tool shed. He likes to tinker with Joseph when things are not going as planned." With a deep curtsy, the woman scurried to gather the needed help to set the room back to the right as it seemed a great battle had been fought among the clothing.

Searching among the garden paths confronting her with a slight touch of dismay; why had she not thought to ask for directions from Martine, Angeline paused to attempt to reach out to her husband. Closed her eyes and concentrated on the man who seemed to be a constant in her mind, and she turned toward the main path of the gardens. Winding her way through the many flowers which surrounded her, Angeline followed the steady pull of emotion which caressed her with infinite gentleness. The lead drew her through the gardens, to an ornate opening where only the hinges of a missing gate door remained, beyond servants' quarters where off-duty servants rose in curiosity to her venturing upon their domain and still further to a place old and seemingly cut out of the very rock which surrounded it.

Forcing down the natural reaction of rushing into the structure and throwing herself into his arms, Angeline entered the cool, torchlit confines to find herself surrounded by a vast array of woodworking tools. Coming upon the man, she found herself staring as his back was to her, bent to the instrument he pressed with long strokes over a length of wood. The sweat-soaked shirt clung to each muscle, cleaved to the strength as arms were watched to press and strain, the back to flex and ripple with each exertion. Waited for a few precious moments unnoticed by either man in silent awe until the voice stated in tease, "you should have noticed the rot of the gate before I was able to break it from the hinges, isn't that what I pay you to do?"

"Milord, I checked the gate only days ago, it was not

in disrepair. Perhaps if you weren't in such an agitated state of--" Nickolai looked up to the man's distraction, then over his shoulder to follow the man's pointed stare before he dropped into a respectful bow to the woman appearing at his master's unsuspecting back. Turning quickly about Nickolai couldn't help the smile of appreciation that came to his lips to find her before him, emerald eyes silently appraising the man before her; and she found her breath catch as every muscle, each hardened plain of his body accentuated under the cling of linen, shirtsleeves rolled up to elbows emphasizing the strength of forearm and hand.

"Angeline, allow me to introduce this drooling fool to you," Nicolai teased the woman whose unwavering intent appeared to awaken the most profound need to be with her, possess her, "Joseph is Illevante' carpenter and caretaker. A finer craftsman you will never find, Joseph, the Lady Illevante`."

Dropping into a bow, Joseph peered up to the woman and managed, "it is indeed a pleasure to make your acquaintance, Milady." Awkwardly he grasped to the hat Nickolai snatched off his head and pressed into the clutch of his chest, "welcome to Illevante`."

Smiling to the man's nervousness, Angeline couldn't help her appreciative laughter to the obvious friendship between the two as acknowledging, "thank you, Joseph, and I only hope I am not interrupting with my untimely visit, but I was hoping to steal the Count from you for a few moments." Then turning to her husband, a hesitant step ended the separation between them as her fingertips came to brush over the lingering welt of his cheek, "Martine told me you could usually be found here when things are not going your way. Tell me, Milord, do you pout?"

Caressing the line of her cheek under the cup of his palm he stepped closer to her length, swallowed thickly to the heat felt to rise within his body as her thighs were met by his own, "remind me to speak to Martine once we return home." His lips pressed to the ivory plain of the forehead as he managed in the softest of whispers, "where did you wish to steal me to?"

Turning an evil eye to Joseph who was heard to cough in a polite reminder to his existence, Nickolai gave last-minute details to the craftsman before gathering up discarded clothing and joining Angeline as she ventured from the dusty confines. Out along the paths which lead to the rocky shores below Nico explained as righting sleeve cuffs and brushing sawdust from his clothing, "Joseph is only the smallest of reasons I did what I did to have you, my love, do you not see how any man is instantly lost to your beauty and goodness." A hand pointed to the path leading toward shore; "this is the most used." He explained as Angeline ventured before him in continued silence, leaving him mindful of his pressing behavior as he sought only to regain her favor.

How was it, he mused in quiet follow, that such a mere slip of a thing could reduce him,
Count Nickolai Illevante`, to nothing more than a lovesick pup trailing after her as if in his first crush. He was the man whom at Court the ladies trailed after, wanted after, never the other way around. Never did he seek any favor it was always granted as if deserved from the many who persisted, but now, with a tinge of color coming under his collar he realized what those women must have felt like. He realized how it felt for them to attempt the simplest of his attentions, the softest of his touches. Fate could be cruel came in revelation as he followed in her wake.

Angeline continued along the well-worn path down to the pounding of shore forever aware of the towering protection Nickolai offered as even the smallest of branches or tiniest of stones were quickly brushed from her path. For long moments she allowed the wind to whip about her length and tangle hair from the style Martine had arranged, welcomed the salty freshness of the air to embrace her with a new contentedness as his insecurities came with a refreshing reassurance to the seemingly confident exterior of the man. Reaching down, she drew the slippers from feet then tugged away stockings as to press her toes into the lapping waters, "you'll freeze." Nico warned seeing the gooseflesh as it rose along her arms to the contact.

Looking over her shoulder to the distance he maintained, a soft smile was Nico's reward before her hands came to press the cold along her length. Her smile deepened as his jacket draped about her shoulders, and Angeline burrowed into its warmth. Moved into the strength of hands holding her, leading her back into his length. For silent moments the two remained; she carefully tucked under his chin his arms enfolding her, warming her to the fire he was capable of generating along her flesh by a mere touch; and he simply waiting. "Did you break the gate?" She asked breaking the silence between them.

With a rueful nod, "I was a little upset with myself, however, I do not 'pout', Milady." Was biting tease as it whispered over her sensitive ear, pleasing him to hear the laugh as it escaped her lips. "Have you managed to find it in your heart to forgive my selfishness?"

"I fear I will always forgive you too much." Responded as a reluctant smile came to his words. "You should have trusted in what was meant to be, Nickolai." Angeline managed to halt the search of lips as they sought the column of her silken throat beneath fall of hair, the press of teasing kisses to the flesh found with a single touch, "if you knew I was your destiny then you should have known nothing would have kept us apart; eventually I would have found you. I would have sensed you. These ancients which surround us would have allowed nothing less, at times they are near---relentless---in their quest to bring us together." Hands ventured beneath the fold of jacket splayed to the rise of rib; drawing her hard, close, to his towering length. "You don't think they have influenced us, do you, Nico, this constant need I have of you could it be from their interference and not my heart?"

"Nothing could be named so easily to explain the feelings I have for you, the constant need I have of being deep within your flesh. The longing within my heart to hear the words of love from you, to protect and cherish the love you will have for me." Nico whispered along sensitive skin sending sparks over the flesh and through her blood. Drawing her closer to him, he let his need be known his body tightened nearly painfully to the urgency to be with her. The mere brush of her bottom against his hardness causing a soft moan to escape his lips, “I could only hope you would want me as desperately as I wanted you, needed you.”

Rolling her head back to rest at the mantle of his chest she allowed the mouth to return in sweet assault to flesh as confessing, “there has been none before who have made me feel like this, has made me feel safe and protected. Loved and beautiful all in a single day, in a single touch.” Closing her smaller hand over the one seeking more of her flesh, she managed, “you won’t ever do anything like that again, will you, Nickolai?”

Turning her within his arms, he confronted the woman who took his breath, searched the perfection of her face with piercing eyes only to confess, “you are mine, Angeline, and I will do whatever necessary to keep me in your heart forever.”

“Forever.” She seemed to breathe as he bent to capture the sweetness of her lips, to delve into the recesses of mouth.

“I want you, Angeline.” Whispered against the caress of wind as it battled across her flesh and her consent was nothing more than a purr growing from the back of her throat.

Angeline's fingers ventured into the protected flesh of his nape where the hair kept it safe and warm. With gentle pressure, she welcomed the mouth as it battled over hers, tightened the hold of her arms drawing her closer, harder to the length craved, “please, Nico, you have teased me long enough. First with mind and now hand,” managed softly as his mouth moved to heave of breast and a knowing chuckle teased her. “I can’t think, I can’t breathe.”

Looking for a place of privacy, he swept her into his arms and carried her to an alcove located deep in the recesses of battered rock. Holding her to him the length of gown was quickly gathered over silken thighs as he hastily freed himself to be deep within her beckoning heat. Became lost in the tightness that immediately engulfed to the smoldering need. Pressed back along the slope of boulder Angeline drew him over her, coveted the perfection of his mouth unto her own and nearly cried to the emotion coming to fill her heart. Beginning to embrace her entire being as his emotions filled her as never before, as he allowed her to feel and experience the very need as it came to him heightening the desire already felt. Made her clutch him deeper, harder to the core of her passion, making her release a near torturous thing as it rose to engulf her. It seemed to spread across her soul in a blinding light of love and need as he too finally lost the strict control maintained and allowed the fury of release to swell then explode deep within her.

Cradling the raven head to her breast as breath was lost, she couldn't help but laugh out loud as his eyes rose to confront her, "Martine was quite proud of me when I left Illevante` nearly an hour ago. What would she think now?" Wild curls freed about her face from the wind were pressed back over her shoulders in uselessness to the gesture as the elements came to overtake her good intentions.

"I'm sure I will be the one to have her knowing eyes set on me with a vengeance." He bantered as he once again sought the warmth of her flesh, the softness of her mouth. "Have I thanked you for coming to find me, little one?" Nico whispered as he explored flesh with hand; ear with the softest of teasing nibbles before conquering the pulse of the throat causing her to nearly lift them both from the unexpected reaction of such a touch as her body arched suddenly into his.

"How could I have resisted such an invitation as the one you so urgently sent before you?" Quipped as her mouth searched his jaw, her teeth scraped in teasing boldness over the stubble that grew there in prickly touches — her lips to soothe the cheek in a healing caress.

Smiling wickedly to her reminder, he whispered into the throat, "what did you expect me to do when you turn me away so carelessly?"

"Yes, what do I expect?" Questioned as her laughter came softly, warmly to the nearness of his cheek, the touch of his lips.

"I'm sorry I slapped you, Nico; I have never reacted as such before. I swear it will never happen again and if you wish me to return to my parents, I will understand perfectly. Even though I never really listened to anything Antoinette tried to teach me about being a proper wife, I know one is not supposed to hit her husband."

"There is no reason to apologize, my love; it was what I deserved." And he pondered her words for silent moments before asking, "did you honestly believe I would send you back to Belaveuta only because of a slap?"

"It was quite a hard slap." She managed, unsure if he was once again teasing her or considering such options.

"Definitely, hard. Though I believe I have had far worse done to me in the past for far less reason." He once again found her mouth then lifted away to find her still and concentrated beneath his touch, her eyes nearly blank in the stare of such concentration, "what is it?"

Pressing her fingers over his lips, she focused on the urgency felt to vibrate through her, to the need of him from others as it came, "someone is coming for you." Hastily she pressed from his arms, attempted to draw the length of material over thighs as the resolve of the approaching men seemed to hover close by, "you should go, they need you."

Pressing his hands up under the fall of the skirt she fought to return to proper he caressed the exposed thigh whispering, "they can look all they wish; no one could need me as much I need you." Caressing the parting of her legs, Nico pressed through the fiery triangle to invade the depth of her desire; pleased to feel her hips churn unexpectedly toward his teasing, deepened the touch as it played over flesh cupped to the heat of her passion as she weakened against the contact. "Stay with me, Angeline, let me make love to you again. I don't think there will ever become a day I grow tired of touching you, making love to you."

Fighting to be from the deepening touches even as the essence of her desire pounded, seeking the release he teased her with. "Nico." Escaped in breathless wonder as she pressed into the unforgiving mantle of his chest; her fingers raked through his hair, needing the perfection of his mouth over hers. The pound of her desire pressing all urgency away as with a soft cry the release spread through her. Resting her forehead to the chest for silent moments, she fought to regain breath, as his hands seemed to be everywhere, yet, nowhere. As they were soft and caressing one moment then searching and demanding the next nearly making her forget once again that he was needed elsewhere, "please, Nico, they are very anxious to find you. Please go; it may be important."

With a moan to her resolve Nickolai came from the cradle of her arms, "come we will face them together, I am not letting you out of my sight until I have had my fill of you, to be sure." Waiting the moments it took for her to replace stockings and slippers she allowed the arm to encase her, nearly carry her to the ascent as it seemed her legs too weak to step on their own, her need to be held by him too great to deny any longer, "they would have waited." He teased to feel the hand as it brushed across his chest and clutch into the material of shirt for long moments, to the body which unknowingly sought his time and time again. Dragging her hard against his chest he conquered the sweetness of her mouth, invaded the warmth with tongue till he heard the soft whimper of her desire grow from the back of her throat and the body press with an urgent response to the invitation of his passion. '*No one would have dared to interrupt me there with you.*' He vowed to allow for only a moment the strict control he held over emotions to weaken to such need.

Stumbling back from his deliberate intent, she whispered with a teasing giggle, '*and they could have found us.*' As the hand seeming to be forever caressing her, stroking her through the material of gown in maddening tenderness was grasped. "Stop," she admonished to the rising burn along her flesh, "before they realize what we've been doing." To see the Captain of his Guard to be in conversation with another in his charge.

Raising an amused brow to her statement, he growled as

his mouth brushed teasingly over her gapping one, “as if they don’t already?” Once finding the Count in the approach of him, the Captain quickly dismissed the guard and advanced upon Nickolai with such determination even Angeline was suspect to his intention. Involuntarily she felt her hand tighten about the one clutching hers; sought to draw him back as if into her protection. An action causing Nickolai to lower his head to the growing smile and pleasure of such a selfless act toward his safety, when was the last time anyone had thought to protect him, had anyone cared enough even to react?

“Milord, please forgive my untimely interruption,” Captain Deleon came to drop before them in humbled attention, “the Crowned Prince has summoned you to Bodiam. He has requested your presence immediately; plans for the pending invasion to Plona have begun.”

Pondering the summons, Nickolai frowned as Angeline was felt to step closer to his sheltering length, the hem of her skirt caught in the breeze, wrapping about his legs as intimately as the arm which held her to him, “is there a messenger waiting?” He questioned quickly evaluating the situation before responding.

“Yes, Milord. I have sent the guards ahead to ready the garrison. Did you have further need of me?” The man responded, lifting his eyes to meet the concern of the Lady Angeline then to quick adverted them as it was seen his Count more concerned to the woman than his duty.

Nickolai signed thoughtfully before he looked to the woman beside him, the question of her expression to the message relayed; by the Gods would no one leave him alone? How could he leave her now; now when they were only beginning to build a relationship; a trust; a bond. He instructed his Captain, “advise the Prince to have proper accommodations made ready; Lady Illevante` will be joining me. We will be leaving immediately; he can expect our arrival within the week.” And with a wave, the man was dismissed.

Halting in his natural reaction to carry out any of his requests, Deleon questioned, "a week, Milord?" Unsure if he had heard the orders correctly.

Raising a brow in the surprise of the man's questioning Nickolai reiterated, "yes, a week. We will be traveling by carriage; with full Guard. See that you make the necessary preparations." Seeing the surprise to the means of travel, as it came to the Captain's features, Nickolai nodded to the silent question, and the man turned to carry out his orders.

Waiting the scant moments, it took for the Captain to disappear to orders, Angeline's dubious eyes confronted him with a show of worry as the fiery head was already shaking to such a response. "Nickolai, I can't accompany you; the Prince wishes to speak to you of battle strategies not for you to be distracted by a new wife. Even the Captain of your guard realizes this to be true." And she was pressed along as the massive arm circling her waist drawing her to home; to the summons of Martine as he instructed the woman to ready trunks with needed wear for court. "Nickolai." She protested for a final time, "think about this. I will be better off here, safe at Illevante` it would give me time to become better acquainted with my new home, or I could return to my father until you have completed the Prince's business. I have never liked being about large crowds, and I understand Bodiam is exceedingly crowded when the Royals arrive. We will be traveling by Belaveuta; you could leave me there in passing."

A smirk sounded to the suggestion as he moved to his dressing rooms and summoned his man, "I will have you safe at my side then with that stepbrother of yours. He may look stupid, but his mind is far stronger than most." Gathering her into his arms, Nico held her to his length before confessing, "I want you with me, little one; I fear I will never be able to sleep without you beside me." For a silent moment, he contemplated the woman before him, the pleasure he felt in her referring to Illevante` as her home, "please, Angeline, we'll only remain a couple of days. Please say you will come with me, be with me."

Feeling her heart melt once again toward this man, she

managed, "will I ever be able to say no to you?" Martine was heard to be muttering to herself and scavenging closets to the most appropriate wear.

"Simply indulge me, if only this time." He pressed his mouth in conquer over hers, "I will advise Antony to our departure, as I'm sure this will be a definite inconvenience to the careful scheduling, he insists I follow." And before he left the room, Nickolai cautioned Martine, "I expect her to be styled befittingly as Lady Illevante`, Martine, do not disappoint her or worse, me." With a smile he was gone escaping the exasperated grumblings to his question of her duty to Lord and Lady.

Seven

Attempting to draw the length of hair into some semblance of order, Angeline threw the hair combs into the depth of travel bag as she admitted with frustration, "I will look like nothing short of a serving wench you have picked up on the road. You could have at least allowed Martine to travel with us." Looking at the amusement of her husband, as he lounged on the floor of the carriage, surrounded by the many cushions and furs provided for the journey, she shook her head. Sweet Jesus did he always have to look so beautiful; she sighed, staring at his considerable length. The mass of sun-bronzed chest and strength of arms as they were exposed to her, for her, by her.

"If Martine traveled with us, would I be able to do this?" His palm closed over her hand, tugging her across his length, where he buried his hands into the errant fiery strands and held her to him. "No one will care how you style your hair, or what gown you are wearing. You are beautiful."

With a snort, she allowed the constant pull to his chest and rested her head to heart, caressed the expanse of flesh beneath adoring hands as managing, "if only that were true." As lifting her head, she drew the attention of his eyes. Eyes capable of making her forget all except to be with him like this forever, only to lower her stare as fears and insecurities came to plague her. "Nickolai, you know it's not too late to return me to Belaveuta. At least you won't have to worry about me becoming lost or doing something that could embarrass you." Angeline's fingertips continued to trace the scars crisscrossing his chest; tugging her lower lip in worry, she confessed, "Antoinette tried to teach me to be a lady, but I was never interested. I don't want you to be sorry for marrying me; to have others wonder to my shortcomings and ignorance of a life you were raised in." She followed a predominate vein, as it seemed to outline the muscle of his shoulder down the strength of the upper arm and then forearm, before finding the courage to confront his watchful eyes.

"It seems to me, my love, you learned what you needed to know to become my wife, and I would never be sorry for marrying you even if you managed the most embarrassing scenario on God's green earth." He chuckled to see the nervous repetition of her lip tugged by the clasp of teeth, the eyes that seemed to look everywhere but at him. "Besides, what could you possibly do that would embarrass me?"

Shrugging her shoulders, she managed softly, "anything, everything."

"Nonsense." He scoffed to such a notion, "you don't have an embarrassing bone in your body; trust me. I've tried to find one repeatedly."

His tease only caused her frown to deepen as she managed, "Nico, I'm serious. I've never been presented to Court; my father believed such a lifestyle frivolous and a waste of time."

"Little one, I don't believe you are worried about being presented to Court, or possibly doing something which would embarrass me. Tell me what is troubling you, let me find a way to ease your concerns." Caressing the tug of worry as it came to brow, he reminded, "you can easily block out all you don't wish to sense. I know you do it to me enough and the ancients when they become too persistent."

"Only when your thoughts are of battle and death, and the ancients are always insistent, always there." Nickolai forced Angeline to confront her concerns with his silent insistence. "I'm not ready to face the women in your life to know what they're feeling. To know what they're feeling about me. Women who believe you're still available. I was never very good at the competition; I've never had the confidence to confront a stranger. To confront the many women who have slept with my husband. And it's not as easy as simply blocking them out; it's the look in their eyes. The way they will approach you."

A soft chuckle escaped before Nickolai realized its release to her insecurities, *'had there ever been anyone before her*?' His hands flexed into the length of hair with the reassurance, "you have no competition, little one, and I haven't been available for a very long time." Came in response to the questions that were seen to darken her glorious eyes with suspicion. "And I wasn't your husband when I was with them. I was merely taking advantage of certain situations."

"Situations that have presented themselves quite frequently---" and the thought went unfinished as the very idea of him with another woman made her stomach twist painfully. "I don't think I'm strong enough for this, Nico."

"You know you have been the only one for a very long time." And the palm, filled with her hair, clenched ever so slightly, forcing her eyes to remain fixed on his. "Surely, you didn't expect me to be the virgin on our wedding night?"

Pulling up and away from the pressure, Angeline snapped to his ridiculous question, "I hardly thought you to be virgin, Milord! I only wonder if I will have to contend with your ex-lovers as they enlighten me to your endowments. Their witty little quips to your ardor that I will not be able to respond to." Settling upon his length, her thighs straddling his, Angeline pressed her hands into the muscle of his chest and held there as she inquired, "and if I am, how should I react; as the frightened virgin or knowing wife?" Her sarcasm thick to his avoidance of such questions.

Arching a dark brow to the agitation displayed to his circumventing the subject, Nico clarified, "I prefer the jealous naked wife. It's intriguing, don't you think, and that fire in your eyes is fascinating." Shifting his weight, Angeline found herself trapped beneath his pressing length, a thigh capturing her legs so she could do little more than struggle against his strength.

"Yes, I think the jealous wife has a preference. Naked, most definitely."

"I am hardly jealous, Milord!" Angeline gasped as he gathered her hands into a single one of his own and stretched them far over her head, so she could do little else than allow him his victory. "I am simply preparing myself for Milord's abundant conquests."

Releasing the ribbons of her bodice one by one, his lips followed the line of flesh as it became exposed. "If you continue to use such titles on me, Milady, I will have to be quite relentless in my pursuit of having my name gasp from your lips." As the final ribbon released, his hand pressed up under the flow to splay her ribs, to tease the sensitive breast before drawing the puckered flesh deep into his mouth. "You are my love, my life, my eternity, Angeline, never doubt your place by my side. Any before you have only been a blur of undistinguished faces, all are quite old and have forgotten me by this time."

"Yes, I'm sure they're all grandmothers by now." She exhaled, twisting her hands free of his grasp she came to press the raven strands of hair away as they seemed to fan across her belly, tease the sensitive breast lavished. Drawing his face to hers with the hard pull to hair, she swallowed over tears that came to thicken her throat, "no one will take you from me, will they, Nico?" Caressing the beauty of his face, Angeline implored, "promise me you will stay with me forever, that I will never have to know what it is like not to have you in my heart, my head. I know it's been you all these years coming to me, comforting me when I needed it most, and I never want to be from that for even a moment."

Nickolai realized the insecurity harbored to her lack of self-confidence, and he berated himself for placing her in such a state of mind. "No one or thing could ever take me from your heart, my love." He swore as gathering her close to his length, hard to his strength he promised, "you are mine, Angeline, as I am yours." Reaching up to the dress coat that hung from a hook, he drew the elegant material into his hands as searching its length; "which reminds me, I have something for you." He answered the question that came to dubious eyes.

The coat was thrown aside as he presented a small wooden box. Nico looked down at Angeline's silent watchfulness to explain, "I wanted to give this to you with the Queen Mother's blessing, but I think now is more appropriate." Opening the lid, Angeline looked from the nestled item as Nico shared its history, "this ring has been in my family for many generations--- passed from mother to son. Though none are sure to its origins, many believe it forged by the first of my ancients. My father gave this ring to my mother on the day they wed. She told me when he presented this endless band of gold to her, he vowed never to love or need another as he needed and loved her. He vowed to share his eternity with her. I vow this to you, my love, with my heart and soul." Carefully the golden band was slipped over her finger before his lips pressed to the bonding with heated reverence to the place she held in his heart, his soul. "You will always be the only woman I come to, the only woman I will ever love until I complete my eternity; this I pledge to you as my word of honor."

A soft sob to breath escaped to such a declaration as she wrapped her arms about his neck and drew him down to her mouth, "what am I going to do with you, Nico?" She whispered before capturing the perfection of his mouth with her own.
"I could think of one or two things." Teased as his hands pressed in a cup to her bottom, lifting her to his need. Held her tight as his mouth claimed her, teased her till Angeline's body strained in search of release, till the cry of his name left her lips.
Pressing adoring kisses to the hollow of her throat, down over the heave of breast till finally recapturing mouth, he sighed, "most definitely jealous wife." Only to be rewarded with an ineffective punch to his upper arm.

"I am not jealous!" She laughed as he closed his arms about her length and drew her once again over his chest. "You could at least pretend that hurt!"

"Oh, ow!" He moaned, laughing out loud to her silliness.

"Feeling better?"

"Much!" And she fell contently into his strength. "Now, about these grandmothers---" and with his growl of surrender, he allowed her to dress.

∞∞∞

With a final errant curl tucked, Angeline stepped from the carriage with the assistance of her husband. Passing him a disgusted look as he seemed to emerge perfectly groomed, she growled, "you are not supposed to look so perfect." As a tug came to the corset gripping tightly about her lungs, then to stomacher, which seemed to stray errantly to the left no matter how hard she attempted to adjust it.

Bringing her trembling fingers to his lips, Nico whispered, "was that compliment, wife?" And a teasing nibble went to the knuckles lavished before they were ushered into the great confides of the crumbling surroundings beyond. Nearly laughing out loud to the dubious brow raised in his direction, Nico promised, "once we complete introductions, I will make the necessary excuses and ask for the Queen to dismiss us for the evening." The Prince's guard bowed to their appearance then turned to announce their arrival to the many which gathered in the main room.

With a distracted nod to the plans he made, Angeline quickly searched about the decaying structure that came to enfold them. The stone walls had seen many attempts to repairs where tapestries hung in camouflage to the irreparable damage hidden. The wrought iron chandeliers were dripping the remains of wax to the stone floors below, barely missing the ton gathering below them. The disregard, for what was once a beautiful home, caused a frown to tug lips that should have only shown excitement to the many who gathered. '*Many*,' Angeline realized reinforcing the natural barriers about her mind in protection to the onslaught sure to bombard her. Her curious eyes looked about the castle's many ramparts and walkways where people mingled, along its hallways and great gathering room where even more stopped to stare. Too many pressed into the rooms unable to handle such capacity, and it was apparent the structure was rebelling to the abuse. It seemed to Angeline the castle had seen better days, even for one that the Royals continued to visit every autumn. Coming into the foyer of the main salon, she glanced down the flight of stairs before her and was surprised by the faces that rose to acknowledge Nicolai's name. "I don't believe they were expecting me." Murmured as a flutter of fans suddenly took flight from the females.

Women who hid their faces behind the ornate sweep, so their gossip would not be too obvious to the gathering nor the young wife at Illevante's side. "Nor have you been forgotten, husband." Was dour snap as a wave of desire, jealousy, and curiosity came in an overwhelming rush infiltrating her best effort to fight the quell.

Exhaling with waning determination and a tug from Nico's hand; they merged into the fold of the crowds. Became entrenched by those feigning disinterest: even as all eyes followed the woman Illevante` presented. Tightening her hand about Nico's, as women stepped forward in familiar greeting to her husband, Angeline could only stare in awe of the beauty they possessed. The utter sureness of the power such confidence mandated, and she felt herself pressing closer to her husband's side. "Nickolai, it has been far too long. Where in the world have you been hiding?" One seemed to purr as she drifted by only to find another who came to sweep her dark eyes possessively over his length before smiling to Angeline with a smirk of knowing.

Raising a dubious brow to his carefully crafted avoidance of the women who boldly approached him, Angeline mumbled, just loud enough for Nico to overhear, "perhaps I should be introduced to your bevy of Grandmother's; I may learn a few things."

Drawing her close as the Captain of the Guard made Illevante's presence known to the Prince, Nickolai claimed the small of her waist under his powerful touch and smiled down to her with a patient shake of his head. “There is nothing you need to learn from them, little one, and it has never been a bevy.” He reassured as their place in line was established, and they advanced progressively toward the dais of the Royal family.

Craning her neck about to see all that bustled about them, Angeline came to realize the men who seemed to take an interest in her appearance. At first, she stared back, quite amazed they lingered in their study of her, then self-consciously looked down to the gown worn and patted the style of hair for errant curls which may have escaped hat. Curiously, Angeline waited for them to turn away, as in the past, when their disgust would be more than evident. When they became more confident with her watchfulness, she nearly laughed out loud to the attention granted. When the hand at her waist clenched in possessiveness, she turned to find Nico's curious eyes trained on her. His brow lifted in question to the consideration she welcomed, “I'm beginning to enjoy myself.” Angeline teased to the frown Nickolai directed to the gathering of men who were quick to turn from his growing interest.

"Tread safely, my love; you do not wish to press my patience; someone’s life may be in danger." Dropping into a deep curtsy before the Prince and Queen Mother, Nickolai managed to growl, “never forget, I am a very jealous man where you are concerned.” And with his presentation of hand, Nickolai drew Angeline to her feet and presented her to the Royals.

∞∞∞

Within moments of her introductions, Angeline found herself separated from her husband as the Queen Mother came to draw her closer for inspection. The hand dry and bejeweled touched the beauty of Nickolai’s wife and obsession for silent moments, “so you are the one he would change history for.” She mused as the emerald eyes were forced up from the respective stare held to ground, "he took a great risk in asking for you. It has been many years that your two families have battled over lands, many years neither Illevante` or Belaveuta would take the advice of crown. Your father, though absent from my frequent summons, is a man held in high esteem. A man loyal to God and Crown, as it should be."

"Yes, my Queen." Managed to whisper over the nervousness felt to encase her entire body, the apparent curiosity of her as it was felt to penetrate Angeline's senses from all angles.

Smiling to the fretfulness as it emanated from the young woman, the Queen turned to her son to comment, "she's stunning, isn't she, Phillip? If I had known, I would have summoned her for Andrew. He's always had a fascination with redheads, hasn't he?" Returned to her ornate throne, the Queen addressed Nickolai, as she was aware of his constant watchfulness over the young wife. "She will be introduced to Catherine while you address your summoning."

Involuntarily Nickolai stepped forward to implore, "My Queen, forgive me, but we have been traveling long and would prefer to retire early this evening." His hand came in the slight separation to where Angeline remained. "I beg your indulgence, My Queen."

Motioning to a young woman, who stood closest to the Royal throne, the Queen smiled to her niece, "my sweet, Catherine, see that the Lady Illevante` appropriately attired for this evening's festivities. I do not find myself in an indulgent mood. Perhaps if you had arrived when summoned, indulgence would have been mine."

Coming from the Royals, Catherine turned to confront Angeline, "Lady Illevante` if you would please." Turning toward Nickolai, Angeline witnessed the strain in his features, the silent beckon to do as bid. "Count Illevante` shan't be more than an hour with this silly business of war; then, you shall have him all to yourself."

Nickolai's piercing eyes followed the hesitant retreat of his wife with a troubled expression. Instantly he realized his arrogance in thinking he could protect her from every scenario; was nothing more than ego. "Illevante`," and the beckon of his name caused Nickolai to return his attention to the Queen Mother, "you seem to forget, if not for my interference that child would not be your wife, and you would be sleeping alone this evening. Well," she paused dramatically, remembering the frequency in which he dallied with new partners; "you never really slept alone, did you?" Was biting retort, leaving Nickolai to do nothing more than apologize profusely. A silent look to his Captain sent the man off in follow of the young women. "Yes, well, your apology is accepted, and the Captain to the Royal Guard is in wait of you. This battle is significant to my son, Count; I expect you to do your best work."

Catherine smiled reassuringly to the woman at her side as they circled the gathering room upon returning to the festivities. Catherine assured Angeline's appropriate attire by a bevy of circling servants who seemed to materialize out of the very walls once they secreted to the privacy of Catherine's chambers. "It usually isn't this crowded." Came in explanation to the crowds surrounding them, the women lingering to stare in curiosity then turn in conspiring whispers while passing. "The Queen Mother usually doesn't travel to Bodiam, but Phillip insisted, and she rarely goes against Phillip's wishes. Of course, when the word was received, she would be in attendance, all had to attend, all expected invitation." And a silent "*oh*" passed Angeline's lips as her eyes couldn't help but travel over the pressing masses as the floor suddenly cleared and the music began. "Have you known the Count for very long?"

"Nearly all my life." Angeline responded, and she wondered to the answer that came so quickly from her, '*could merely a week be considered her entire life?*' "He has been a companion of sorts for many years." Angeline corrected as she caressed the ring on her finger in soothing touches. "It is not an easy relationship to explain, one day he was there, and I knew it would be right being his wife, being with him for always."

Catherine looked down at the ring, donning her own finger, and sighed wistfully, "I wish I could say the same of Mason Vincente`." Confessed and the sadness which came from the young woman caused Angeline to refocus her attention. "I have been wed to Mason Vincente` for nearly a month and have yet to meet him." Angeline could sense the fear surrounding her, the thin veneer containing panic even as Catherine's shoulders shrugged as if to infer indifference. "My father signed the marriage contract, and Master Vincente' went hunting. Poppa insisted I come to Bodiam if only to keep myself occupied. I swear I am driving him right out of his mind, I locked myself in my chambers and refused to eat for days and days. I have even thought to threaten to join a convent, though I know that would be quite impossible." Once again, the ring twisted anxiously. "It won't be quite so frightening once introduced, or at least I keep telling myself."

Placing her hand over the constant twisting of the ring, Angeline drew the woman's attention with a sincere touch, as promising, "you must not be afraid." Hoping to ease the fear rising thickly between them, "perhaps he is as concerned with the match as you are. After all, you are both strangers for the moment, are you not?"

A small, hopeful, smile was attempted as Catherine whispered, "I can only hope, Lady Illevante." As her great emerald eyes swept away from the concern of her new acquaintance, "one can only hope to love as you so obviously love the Count." As her name carried over the din of the music, the smile came again to light her beautiful features missing the instant surprise which came to Angeline's. *'Love?'* Angeline questioned, *'did she love him?'* "Marcus!" Catherine called, "you simply must dance with Marcus; he's wonderful!"

Angeline watched as the young man approached and smiled to the emotion held expressly for the woman beside her. Did Catherine not realize the depth of this man's devotion, Angeline wondered, as his eyes sought only Catherine's. He saw only her even as others called to gain his single-minded attentions, "thank you, but no. You go, I'm sure he'd much rather be with you." And Angeline watched the couple as they quickly joined the swirling masses.

Nickolai cast a glance to the Captain of the Royal Guard as he stood to observe the scrutiny of his battlefields. For silent, torturous hours, the Captain watched as Nico paced slowly before his carefully thought out strategies and waited for him to find the weaknesses.

Wearily a sigh escaped Nickolai to the surround of battle and the death coming with each plan. Restlessly he moved from one planned strategy to the other, in a moment's notice, he began to point out weaknesses to own and enemy. Rerouted troops to the most strategic forces either coming from blindsided reinforcements to where the most substantial gathering of forces should meet. Looking up to notated changes and the strategy put to record, Nickolai met the satisfaction of the Prince's guard, "I can do no more this evening." He admitted to the weariness such planning brought him. The scenes of death and destruction as each battle was played out in his head, "tell my Prince I will continue in the morning for the advance of the eastern front. Many strongholds will need to be enforced before victory will be his." And with a slight incline of his head in dismissal, Nickolai left the inner chambers to find the gathering had blossomed into an all-out affair with dancing, magicians, jugglers, and men.

Men, he noticed, gravitating toward the woman who was his wife. Sometime during his absence, he found she transformed from the innocent beauty that beckoned him with sweet caresses to that of a breathtaking woman of Court. The most lavish satin and brocade gown appeared to cleave to the very breath of her, the powdered and styled wig a towering concoction of feather and lace seemed to balance the width of the hoop as lace and ribbon accented every delicate fold of gown's skirt. '*Had he commissioned such a creation*?' Nico vaguely wondered as she took his breath.

"She's lovely, Count," the voice caused Nickolai to turn in the confrontation of the Queen Mother's nephew, Andrew, as he commented to charms of his wife. "You were wise to wait for this one to blossom, you can see she is far different from the others who have sought your favor and your bed. It is rare for such a jewel, much like my dearly departed Aunt's daughter, Catherine. Fire and emeralds. She has won the heart of every eligible bachelor at Bodiam, it best you keep those forever-observant eyes of yours on her. Least, you are using your strategies to get into your own bed."

Nodding in understanding to his words, Nickolai acquiesced graciously, "I take your words as a compliment, Prince Andrew, as I am always protective of what is rightfully mine." As it seemed having this man notice Angeline caused Nickolai's stomach to clench painfully to ramifications of the past. To the history shared on more than one drunken dare.

For silent moments both men stared to the woman who had the attention of no less than four men, "you know, of course, I had your usual suite readied." The knowing eyes looked to the smoldering ones of the Count beside him, "you always put on such an interesting show, Count." And with a laugh, Andrew stepped toward the many who beckoned him. "I hope you, nor she, will disappoint tonight."

Exhaling a slow, tortured breath to the exchange Nickolai moved into the festivities, ignoring those seeking his attention as he studied Angeline from across the room. Watched with growing interest as young nobles came to beckon her. Smiled to see Angeline's unmitigated joy as they pleaded for her to share a dance, sought to take her hand or press their attention to her unescorted appearance. Attentions, Nickolai realized she needed to receive if only for the mere fraction of a moment he would tolerate them. She needed to know how breathtaking she indeed was, how any man at any time would come to do her bidding all by the crook of her little finger.

∞∞∞

Angeline looked expectantly into the surround of the crowded room as the air was felt to gather in a warm caress about her length. The touch to venture over the column of her throat and touch her mind with intimate familiarity. Emerald eyes instantly turned from the attentions of others to seek him. Their eyes meeting briefly from across the crowded floor, and he couldn't help but smile to the absolute joy he found in her. *'You press my patience, wife.'* Angeline's teasing laughter came in gentle admonishment as one dared to press his advantage, even as her eyes always sought her husband's. *'Serves you right for leaving me alone all this time.'* She retaliated to his threat.

Deciding his patience had been exhausted, as another came to grasp her hand to press lingering kisses to the grasped knuckles. Nickolai came from his lean against marble post as it was apparent the noble would not release the touch even as she attempted to pull from the excessive attentions. "Milord," Angeline stated as Nico neared, "I fear you have raised the ire of my approaching husband; he has been most patient, but you have pushed him beyond limits."

The man who adorned her hand lingered on the band of gold as his heated gaze rose to confront her. "Husband? What fool would leave you alone for so long?" He scoffed as blocking the very venue of escape with the press of his body, a press, Angeline realized, was one liberty Nickolai would not allow without retaliation.

"This fool." Nico seemed to grumble in menacing intent as all eyes turned to Illevante` as he appeared behind their backs. "Gentlemen," came as Nico studied the hand which still held Angeline's captive, "I believe that is my wife you have your hands on."

"Count Illevante`." The man managed with hushed tones to Illevante's position in Court and battlefield. There were few men alive who dared to interfere where Illevante` ventured, so was the reputation which proceeded him to the young man who sought the hand of his wife. "Forgive me; I meant no disrespect." When, in fact, the young man was speechless to the idea of Nickolai Illevante` married to such an innocent creature. Granted, the Count always had his pick of the woman who frequented such gatherings, but they were women known for their interests. Women, one expected a man such as Illevante` to be attracted to, never was there a hint of commitment. Never a show of favoritism as in the light of day, the women who shared his bed would find herself on no more personal terms than a stranger met on the street. How was it that such possessiveness now emanated from the Count, such devotion to see the woman who nearly glowed in the attentions he granted her. "We were unaware that Count Illevante` had taken a wife."

"Then perhaps you were not paying attention." Was the dour snap as Nicholai's dark brow arched in question to the young man who pressed his patience and continued to remain before his wife.

Looking to the men, who seemed one moment flank him, then the next retreat in the realization of the danger provoked. The young noble felt his resolve to keep the beauty by his side diminish dramatically, "perhaps, please accept my congratulations." And a gracious bow came in an offer of his apology.

"You will excuse me." Slipping through their retreating backs, to where Nickolai's scowl of disproval was undeniable even as she bridged the distance between them and caressed the tug of his frown with a fingertip. "Where have you been hiding, it's been hours." Angeline managed as she drew Nico's wary eyes from the men who melted into the pressing crowd. "You must tell the Prince it's an ungodly hour to be working, especially when I need you."

"Do you?" His arm came to claim the dip of her waist, drawing her closer to his towering length, "and to think I was worried you were alone and unattended."

Flashing a quick smile over her shoulder to the departing men, she managed, "I was, but if not for you, this would not have been possible. I know how difficult allowing me such moments has been for you." Her emerald eyes rose to meet the blue ones, feeling as if she became lost in their depth. "One would think you were jealous."

Raising a brow in surprise to her comments, he insisted, "I want you to see yourself as I see you. The beauty and grace you possess as easily as most of us breathe." Nico caressed the powdered cheek before quickly pressing his lips to the beckon of her mouth.

Her fingertips traced the persistence of frown, "I believe I hear a waltz, husband, dance with me and break any aspirations these dandy's hold."

"Or, I could go over there and challenge them all to the liberties they dare with my wife, it has been quite a while I fought a duel for a good reason." He reminded as her fingers came into the protection of his palm and she tugged him impatiently toward the crowded floor. "You press me farther than anyone has ever dared before, wife."

Laughing at his seriousness, she couldn't help but remind, "and just think, husband, it has yet to be a month into our marriage." And with a joyous laugh, she welcomed the arms surrounding her in the lead of the dance.

Angeline allowed the music to encase them as she stared to the beauty of the man before her, the smile which came to curl his lips as her stare was unwavering — lifting her eyes she felt the slam of emotion as it came to flip her heart with the intensity only recently named for her. '*Love,*' and a sigh of contentment left her. She did love him, she realized with a warming glow, how else could she describe the emotions that slammed her every time he was near? The way her heart seemed to skip a beat if only to hear his voice, feel his touch. Sweet Jesus, she had loved him her entire life, from the first image he brought to her, to the first time he caressed her flesh, she loved him as none before or again.

"Little one," Nico began as the music ended, and still they remained within each other's arms, "if you continue to look at me like you are I will forget where I am and have those sweet thighs of yours wrapped about my hips with little regret to the consequence."

Blushing to his bold words, the lip came to be tugged if only to hold the laughter from escaping her, "we could always tell them it is a new dance." Angeline teased as she allowed him to lead her from the mingling crowds.

"The dance is not new, Milady, however, I'm afraid of the flops who would dare to lead you all with the telling of your beauty." And a forced expel of breath was his reward as her elbow contacted his ribs.

"You have little faith in me, Milord; you should realize you are the only one who makes me feel beautiful." Turning in his arms as they captured waist, Angeline leaned into the brace of his chest to whisper, "the only one who has ever made me feel anything at all."

Moving into the palm as it cupped her face, he managed, "if only I could put into words how much I need you, Angeline, how seeing you with such men only serves to weaken my heart."

Angeline contemplated grasping his hand and running from the gathering, running till they were safe and sound behind Illevante's walls. Far from the intrigue and suspicion of those that surrounded them now. "They are only boys playing at being men, Nico, all amusing but never taken seriously." Slipping into the capture of the arm as he drew her to his towering side, the tuck of shoulder as they were ushered into the dining room and seated along endless benches that lined the tables.

Slumping against Nickolai's shoulder, Angeline allowed his strength to support her and sighed as the Prince began another retelling to one of his father's historic battles. Meeting Nico's amused expression, Angeline couldn't help the smile as his lips curled ever so slightly to the press of her boredom, "if you don't wish to remain, why don't you return into the festivities?" He suggested in a whisper as the Prince continued, and the young and unattached scampered back to the dancing and entertainment. "There is no reason for you to sit here with me."

Pressing her hand into his under the protection of tabletop, she tugged to the engulfing strength as managing, "can't you come with me?" And ruefully, the raven head shook to such protocol his station held. "Will it be much longer?"

"Not too," he motioned to where the Queen sat sound asleep beside her son; "she'll wake soon and dismiss us. Until then, I must remain." Motioning to the Captain of his Guard, he instructed Angeline, "go with Deleon. Angeline, be sure to stay close to Deleon, allow him to do my bidding."

"Haven't I always?" She promised, surprised, and pleased when he wouldn't release her hand until he pressed a soft kiss to the beckon of her mouth. "Please hurry." And with the man following in her wake, Angeline left the room to the gathering of men.

∞∞∞

Lingering on the outskirts of the quickly thinning crowd, Angeline looked expectantly about as musicians began to gather up their belongings, and guests finally began to wander to their rooms. "Milady?" Deleon came from the obscurity of shadows as she attempted to leave the room unescorted. "The Count will join you here." He reminded, refusing the escape she sought. "He would expect you to be waiting for him."

A sigh of disgust escaped as she wished to avoid further pointless conversations and the men who pressed too much liberty and the growing absence of her husband. “Only a breath of fresh air, Captain, I shall be no more than a moment, I promise.”

“Then, I will accompany you.” He insisted, stepping in the direction of her escape.

“Of course, you could, but then who would tell the Count of my whereabouts?” Seeing the hesitation in his restraint, Angeline quickly stepped about him and up the staircase to the ramparts beyond. The coming dawn was a surprise to the hours which had passed, and she pressed a weary hand against the weight of concoction upon her head. With a sigh to impatience, she continued along the walk, inhaled the fresh air, and fought the need to seek Nico out as she did so often as of late.

“Has he abandoned you?” Came the knowing voice as she turned from the cannon bay to find a man before her. Was she so deep in thought she had managed to block out even the closeness of one such as he as his smirk of satisfaction was more than enough to flag his intent toward her? “He’s more than likely behind closed doors with my cousin; Phillip won’t make a move, militarily wise, without Illevante’ approving it. It becomes quite annoying.” And a ringed hand came to touch the sweetness of perfect features, caress the line of full lips as they came in tug in a nervous repetition to his insistence. “If I had known you were the prize to service of the Crown, I would have donned a sword myself.” Instantly Angeline could feel the jealousy and hate which came to the idea of Nickolai Illevante’ could sense the maliciousness to the concept of all that her husband held. “My aunt, your Queen, was correct; you are quite beautiful.”

Stepping back from the liberty this man believed he had with her, Angeline managed, “I believe I should find my husband.” And as she turned to be from the towering man, she felt a hand come to grasp her wrist. Hold her before him, “please do not do this.” Angeline pleaded to the danger he was instigating to the fear as it was felt to rise within her breast to unknown situations. How did women react to the attention of unwanted men, how did one escape attention without instigating an all-out battle to the death for her husband? “Nickolai Illevante` is not a very understanding husband." Angeline had little doubt her husband would do nothing less than call this man out for approaching her. A confrontation which would only be certain death for Nico, as the calling out of a member of the Royal family, would only mean a sentence of treason and death.

Pressing his hand up over the wrist captured, he conspired, "I could have my cousin keep him busy," smirking to the indignation of the suggestion, Andrew elaborated, "it is an advantage I frequently employ. I could keep him so busy you could forget you were married to him, or he to you."

Struggling against the hold moving in restraint to her upper arm, Angeline allowed a shaken breath to expel before managing, "I am sure the Prince would find your tactics of interest, especially when war is imminent. It is not a good time to have the Count distracted by the worries of a new wife."

∞∞∞

Nickolai finished the last of his wine as the Queen raised her head with a sudden snort to wakefulness. She looked about then came from her throne with little patience to the story her son shared. "Phillip, it is late! Dismiss these men; there is much work to see to in the morning."

Leaving the room to the relief of all who had remained behind the closed doors for nearly two additional hours Nickolai wandered about the deserted hall searching for this wife. Spying his Captain in the main foyer, he came to inquire to her presence, "she requested a breath of fresh air, Milord." He informed continuing to guard the staircase she ascended into the night.

"Very well, goodnight, Captain." And Nickolai made his way, following the torches that dotted his progress along the parapet. Only once, he glanced down over the towering walls and smiled to the reflection of the moon as it cast into the moat surrounding them. Briefly, he thought of taking Angeline out beyond the oppressive walls and making love to her under the moonlight; he could nearly see her naked flesh in his mind's eye when the whisper of rising fear calling to him caused him to falter if only to catch his bearings.

Coming about the last set of flaming torches Nickolai found his wife in conversation with Prince Andrew and swore silently. Of all the men to take notice of her, why would this man press an advantage? A man capable of having any woman, at any time. He was notorious for manipulating the situation to his best advantage, and Nickolai feared to the very core of his being he now wanted his wife. "My Prince," came in respect to the position held as Nickolai made his presence known to the man, "thank you." Nickolai's fist closed about Angeline's upper arm, drawing her inescapably to his side, holding her there as his troubled eyes met her lowered lashes. "I was looking everywhere for her; I thought perhaps she had become lost among the many twists and turns which mar these ancient walls. I instructed her to remain with guard, however---" Nearly painfully Angeline stumbled to the pressure used on her, stood on tiptoes to relieve the strength of the hold insisted upon, "it has been a trying time, but she is young, and I hope to break this spirit before it becomes impossible to control. Her father, though a formidable warrior, has spoiled this young one to the point of distraction."

Watching the two for silent moments a line of disgust set the Prince's features, before snapping, "yes, it would be best to keep one so young and ill-experienced close should she get into further trouble." Before reaction could come to her features, the man turned on a heel having little need of her.

Releasing the crushing hold, Nickolai instantly claimed the tremble of her shoulders under his hands, the anger that screamed silently at him, "do not say a word. Not a single word." '*that man is not someone I would want to have to come up against; he is far more dangerous than his lecherous practices reveal.*' And he led her with a firm tug to their suite of rooms.

∞∞∞

Silently Angeline allowed him to lead her to the second level where their rooms were situated. Dismissing the waiting servants with a wave of his aggravated hand, Nico closed the door, and they were alone. With a thought all light in the room extinguished, and a startled gasp left Angeline to his actions. Pressing his lips against her ear, Nico whispered, "ssh." Instantly searching the darkness for the telltale pinpoints of light that would penetrate the dark to give evidence of voyeurs. Satisfied they were alone, he released the hold, and allowed light to fill the room.

"What in the world!" Snapped as Angeline pulled from the crowding of his body, “Nico, how dare you blame me for this! To tell him I am impossible to control, spoiled! I did nothing wrong.” Rubbing her arms against the trembles taking her length, to the bruises felt to rise where he had held her, she endeavored to explain the situation he walked into, “I turned around and there he was, he wouldn’t let me go. I would have never ventured out there alone if I knew he was waiting, watching." Pacing the length of the room, Angeline admitted angrily, "I should have made myself more aware of the surroundings. I shouldn't have been trying to block out all of the emotions directed at me, so many--” The emotions flooding her in uncontrollable waves were fought. “They’re relentless, Nickolai, constantly seeking me out. So cruel and envious.”

Crossing the distance of the room, to draw her into his arms even as she fought in her anger, Nico pleaded, “listen to me this one time and say no more of this.” His finger came to cross her lips, forcing her silence. “I know what Andrew is capable of,” came in a heated whisper as he pressed his lips close to her ear, and she stilled her struggling, “and what characteristics he appreciates in a woman, and independence is not one of them. He likes them docile and stupid.”

The elaborate wig came from her head, and the linen holding her hair to bind was carefully released, as he continued, "if he thought, for only a moment, you were willing to accept his attentions and that he could somehow bend you to his will he would never leave you alone." Hearing the catch of her breath in growing fear to his explanations, Nico continued in a heated rush, "please forgive my ignorance to your differences, Angeline; it never occurred to me how much this would affect you, I should have kept you safe at Illevante` I should have realized how much such a gathering would hurt you." With Angeline's nod of understanding and look of '*I told you so*,' Nico acquiesced, "yes, I know, I should listen to you." And with her smile and his chuckle, he offered, "since I have dismissed your women, let me assist." Came as he released the ties which held the gown to her length, as the satin and brocade design was eased from about her shoulders, then lifted overhead and quickly thrown aside without a care. Going to her trunk, he gathered a wrap, then drew it over her shoulders. Crowding her close to his length, protecting her from possible prying eyes, he first removed the stuffed bolster from about her waist followed by panniers. The lacings which followed her spine were released, allowing the corset to come from her flesh. The chemise slid from her body with the release of lace as his hands followed the materials fall, and she stood in the drape of wrapper beckoning to him with glorious flesh and wondrous eyes. Smiling to her uncertainty of his actions, he felt her breath catch as his warming hands erased any markings marring her flesh. Whispered as the head came to the mantle of his chest and rested there for silent moments, "keep the robe tightly about you, little one, until you are safely in bed and draw the draperies to a close. I will join you shortly."

Waiting the few moments it took for him to undress then extinguish all but a few of the candles dotting the room Nickolai came to press into the darkened interior pleased as she instantly moved into the brace of his arms, burrowed herself against his strength as it came to surround her, listened to the words which filled her head, '*once Andrew has noticed you, little one, he does not give up easily. And I have been privy to paintings that have their own eyes and ears in such rooms. I will have no one so privileged as to witness your glorious flesh nor listen to the conversations we will share. You are not to say anything negative about the Royals not as long as we are within these walls, and there is the possibility someone may be listening.'* He caressed the line of mouth as she looked upon him, felt the tremble as it came to her length with the implication of his warnings, and he tucked her securely into the strength of his chest protecting her from any daring to defile the innocence held. Burying his face against the fire of her hair as it fanned pillow, he managed, "we will leave as soon as I can get away from my duties here. I will have you safe at Illevante' soon, my love, now sleep." With an unsure nod, a caress which worried over her temple, sleep came as she lay safe, protected in the surround of his arms.

With a disgusted snort to the display by Illevante', Andrew replaced the cork cylinders into the drilled openings giving him a clear view of the room beyond. Illevant's behavior tonight disappointed him, and he turned to take leave of the passage. "He's far too smitten by this one to allow us a proper show." He growled to the man who joined him with a woman tucked under the capture of gathering arm. "Though it would have been nice to see a good healthy fuck, wouldn't it?"

A knowing nod moved the new acquaintance's head as he grumbled, "she's got him wrapped tight about her little finger, she does." As his hand tighten about the waist of the woman who agreed to accompany them with giggling interest. "It does a man no good to fall under the spell of a woman, does it, my love?" Hissed over the throat sucked in deepening pressure till purplish bruises appeared in the wake of his search. Grasping her by the hips, she was drawn hard to his length as punishing hands traveled over her curves, cupped the fullness of her bottom with his palms, and shoved his need into the softness of her belly. "A woman must learn her place in a man's life, has to learn to be tamed and broken. Soon enough, Angeline will learn her place in this world."

Andrew watched the crude display with growing disgust to the boldness of the woman's actions, to the brazen display until realizing the young woman squirmed in defiance against such liberties. Pleaded softly with a whimpering of words to her freedom as the man lifted elaborate skirts and the slit of under-garments manipulated by a pressing, punishing hand. "Please, my Prince," she pleaded as the hands invaded the bodice of her gown. Pulling and ripping until he exposed the lush flesh to his torturous touch. A sudden cry, nearly a scream, escaped her as the mouth cruel and punishing drew her flesh deep into his mouth, a sound of pure greed growled over suckling lips, "do not allow him to do this. You know my father; he has always served your cousin loyally."

Coming to have her lean against his chest, Andrew touched the tears as they were seen to follow over the pale of her cheek, "your quite right, my dear, I can't allow him to do this. What would your father say?" Eyes clashed over her struggling head as his hands came to travel the column of the ivory throat; to palm her breasts. The flesh squeezed and weighed in appreciation to the continued resistance wrought from her, the nipples stroked with the pad of thumb as he contemplated the situation before him, "we need to do this, to the bed, young man! And your father can go to hell." He demanded as he drew her back until she tumbled to the bed beyond. "Yes, to the bed." Andrew laughed as a stiletto came from his stocking, and the lacing, which kept the young innocence from him, was quickly sliced, away. "Now, my beauty, if you scream I will slice your throat, if you attempt to get away from me, I will slice your throat, and if you attempt to tell anyone what happens here tonight, I will have your father disgraced. Do we have an understanding?" With the whimper of her understanding, the blade caressed the swell of her innocent flesh. "Perfect, now as for these clothes---"

Slack-jawed and nearly drooling to the scene before him, the younger man came to join Andrew on the bed. Holding down the woman's arms as the material was expertly sliced away and she laid naked on top of a pile of her shredded garments. "Sweet Christ, is she fuckable or what?" Andrew hissed, shoving his hand between the clench of thighs, forcing them open he pressed first two then three fingers deep into her. "Tight too." He laughed as he freed himself from the codpiece. "Get her wet for me!" The Prince demanded, and the young man buried his face in the object of Andrew's lust, his tongue dragging slowly over her innocence, dipping deep in the purity. "Is she as sweet as she looks?" He questioned once the head raised.

"Sweet as honey." Came in a laugh as lips licked off the remaining taste.

Pressing the knees back and wide apart caused him to smile to the pinkened flesh exposed to him, the tenderness and innocence he knew to be splayed before him. "Perfect, now hold those knees wide I want to see what I'm fucking!" And he plunged deeply into her as the young man availed self to the gasp of mouth. "Nothing like fucking a virgin after a long night of merrymaking." Long after the woman lost consciousness to the pain and the continued abuse of her innocence, Andrew signed. "A perfect ending to the perfect day." Dropping to the bed exhausted, he shoved the woman so he could lay without touching her soiled flesh, "get rid of her. Nothing worse than a weepy woman." Stretching contently, Andrew managed as the man drew the woman over his ample shoulder, "we will have to talk further about this sister of yours, Stephen. I am quite interested in knowing what Illevante` protects so vehemently."

"As am I, Milord," Stephen grinned to the man, "as am I."

Eight

The morning light burned through the scant opening of heavy velvet drapery as it searched her face for recognition to its rise. Moaning from the insistence, Angeline turned under the press of Nickolai's arm as it crossed her body in the hold to hip and snuggled closer to his length as it seemed even though the sun woke her the room's chill penetrated the confides. "Nico, the fire." Murmured only to be greeted with a snore of his contentedness. "Great!" Grumbled, shoving aside the drapery, she contemplated the furs lining the window openings. *'What good is having a man that can start a fire with his mind if he won't do it when you need one?'* and her thoughts only brought an appreciative chuckle from his sleeping form.

Coming from the cuddled length to quickly scamper across the rushes of the cold floor, she placed a fresh log to the smoldering ashes in the fireplace then returned to the promised warmth of her husband's length once the fire rose to engulf the wood. "It's freezing." She groaned, burrowing into the heavy quilts that surrounded them.

"It's very early, go back to sleep." Nickolai grumbled as drawing her back to his warmth he winced visibly as her cold feet were felt to seek the protection of his length, "Christ, you are freezing." An additional fur was gathered about her before he muttered something in satisfaction to her warmth then returned to his slumber.

Smiling to his mumbling as his head came to nestle against the spray of hair across the pillow, Angeline lay under the press of his massive arm for silent moments absorbing the heat of his body before turning with a yawn and stretch to face him. Watching him with a scrutinizing eye her lip pouted in determination without realizing the intent; "I never thought you to be an early riser; tell me what has awakened you so that I can slay it." Grumbled as he drew her inescapably against his length, hugged her tight as his hand splayed to the sweet temptation of her bottom.

"Only you." She teased allowing fingertips to trace the definition of his abdomen one muscle at a time, lazily she traveled the rise of ribs then crossed the mantle of the breast. Lifting her head, she pressed her lips to the battle scars which marred his perfection, adorned the scar-hardened flesh with mouth and tongue before she smiled to the sudden gasp to air, he took. "I'm sorry, did I disturb you?" Was asked with as much innocence as she could muster to the piercing eyes as they landed accusingly upon her attentions through the slit of lids.

For silent moments Nico contemplated the teasing touch of his wife and nearly allowed the smile to come in conquer over his face to her growing boldness, how bold, he wondered as she concentrated on the thin lines of scars which crossed his chest, would she become demanding of what she wanted from him. What she desired in their bed, to their lovemaking, it was a thought which already had his heart pounding in a quicker rhythm, his need hardening to the growing confidence. Turning his massive frame away from her broke the connection as he managed, "not in the least." Leaving her in a near sputtering speechlessness for moments, pressing herself over the mountain of his shoulder, Angeline bit his ear in retaliation of his teasing. "Can't you see I'm trying to sleep?" As he attempted to swat her away, much like an irritating bug. "You're becoming quite the nuisance, aren't you?"

"Nuisance!" Came in exasperation as she rolled over his length and landed in waiting arms, "you haven't seen nuisance yet, husband." Laughed as he drew her close, hard to his strength.

"No, I suppose I haven't, have I?" He agreed as rolling to his back the movement drew her across his chest, settled on top of his length she stared down to the amusement as it lit his eyes, the smile was it curled otherwise stern lips. "God, you're beautiful." Escaped as he framed her face within his hands. And even as warmth was seen to deepen the color of his appraising eyes, Angeline watched as a frown tugged to his lips, "I did this to you, didn't I?" Nico questioned as the bruising outline of his handprint was found to purple her upper arm.

Shrugging her shoulders as she looked down to the bruised tenderness, a teasing twinkle returned to her eyes, "it's far less painful than you not making love to me." Placing her hands at either side of his head on the pillow, Angeline lowered her head as she sought his mouth, as she ventured to press her tongue into the recesses she craved much to his surprise of her forwardness, "have I surprised you, husband." Whispered as his massive palms were felt to draw the silken wrapper up about her till it lighted her length and she shivered to the feel of flesh against flesh. Grasping her hips, he lifted her slightly from his body then guided her to take the ready hardness of his need. Slowly he lowered her over the length till he was deep within her warmth, and she instantly set the pace. She raised herself from his impalement only to conquer the delving length with harder strokes. Taking his hands into her own, she drew them to the need of her breast as the fiery head fell back, and the release which rose between them seemed to take the very heart from her. "Nico," she cried as she fought for the contact her body needed, sought the friction which would lead her to the release craved.

Without breaking the contact or rhythm of their bodies, Nickolai swept her under his length and allowed self the pleasure of feeling her body as it writhed under him, begged, and pleaded to the release she sought only from him. Pressing the pad of his thumb to the hardened nub of her desire he felt the instant reaction as the body tightened about his buried length, and she cried out to the sweetness of such torture till she reached the pinnacle, and she milked the last of his self-control in a mindless spiral leading them both back to earth only as his arms clasped tightly about her quivering length and he confessed his love to her once again in word and action.

Her hands pressed away the sweat as it came to his flesh, caressed the gentleness of his features as they stared down at her with such love and adoration it nearly caused her heart to burst to the emotion filling her own, '*Sweet Jesus how she loved being in his arms, loved everything he could do to her body with only a single touch.*' Searching the eyes, as they seemed to study her studying him, she suddenly wondered what their children would look like, '*did he want children?*' She wondered, realizing he never mentioned an heir as part of their agreement. Perhaps talking about starting a family was a bit too soon; maybe she should wait at least another week into their married life before making the man accept a more settled role as husband and father. For now, he could be a lover. A content sigh heaved the breast, '*lover*' how she liked that word. "How is it possible for you not to open your mouth and still say a thousand words all by the expressions coming to your face?" Nico teased nearly laughing out loud as a blush pinkened her cheeks, and no matter how he sought to bridge the barriers her mind had set, he found himself unable to read her thoughts. "I make you blush, Milady, just what are you thinking about?" The fiery head shook before she smiled then laughed nervously to all the silly thoughts running about her head, ideas she was too embarrassed to confess. How could she begin to speak of babies when she hadn't even told him of her love for him, would that be the best place to start? After all, their life together should develop in a series of steps, should it not? A slight frown tugged her smile as she contemplated the man above her for silent moments, how did you tell someone they were everything to her, she couldn't live or breathe without him beside her for always. How? Angeline wondered without sounding like a lovesick pup. What if it was too soon? What if he doubted the feelings or used them to his advantage once learning such a thing?

The mouth closed then opened again, and then she began hoping to explain in a logical, if not reasonable coherency, "Nico, do you remember last night when the Lady Catherine was asked to escort me about the room?" With his nod, Angeline tugged thoughtfully to her bottom lip before managing, "after the introductions, we were standing on the outskirts of the gathering, and she began to ask me questions about our relationship."

The raven head rose from its nestle at her breast, and he lifted his weight slightly to lessen the burden to her, "our relationship? To what interest could she have in us?" Forever suspicious to the Royal family, even one as seemingly innocent as Catherine Stewart appeared to be.

Shrugging her shoulders, Angeline remembered half-heartedly, "nothing of importance. How long we've known each other, things that strangers ask when unsure in conversation." Swallowing over the dryness which came to take her throat, she lowered her stare from his silent interest, "she began to speak of the man she's married to, a man she has yet to meet. I could feel how frightened she was, how does one accept such a thing? How could she be expected to give herself to a stranger?" Wondered out loud as his dark brow rose in thoughtful contemplation to their circumstance.

"How have you accepted it, little one?" Nico managed to see the sadness as it touched her eyes, the hands, as they seemed to caress and stroke him with preoccupied thought. "Is it not the same with you, how do you give so much of yourself to me?"

Raising her eyes from the study of his mouth, of the flesh explored the muscles traced, and she answered, "but you have known me always, haven't you? Whenever I needed someone to escape to, you were the one I ran to; yours was the haven that kept my sanity. Even before we physically touched you had given me such wonders, shown me such peace, how could I not know you? How could I not--" and the two words seemed to lodge somewhere at the back of her throat. '*Coward!*' Conscious spat to the hesitation of her sentence, '*tell him what you feel, tell him how you love him as none before or again. Tell him you have always loved him, waited with bated breath for the day he would come into your life.'*

With a moan Angeline shoved him away and attempted to escape the entrapment of his length as his arms enfolded her, draw her back to him, back into the warmth of the bed, "my love, what are you trying to tell me?" Settling her into the protection of his length as it came to encase her, silently Nico watched as she struggled with her thoughts and fought to hide in the crook of his shoulder as he beseeched, "Angeline?" Feeling as if his entire length waited with bated breath for the final two words to come from her. "How could you not? What?"

The fiery head shook as one moment she was attempting to bury her face in the crook of his shoulder, "it's not important. Just a silly notion." And the next moment, she struggled from the embrace of his arms, the feel of thighs as they cradled her hard and warm against her bottom. "I'm sure you have far more important things to worry about then what I'm thinking."

Palming the back of her head Nico drew the features from their hiding place to confront him, "sweetheart, I have never seen you so flustered before, and I know you have no qualms in telling me exactly what you are thinking so this must be very important to you or you wouldn't be having such a hard time telling me."

"Because you'll think I'm stupid and foolish. Because it may be too soon, yet I feel as if I'm already years too late." She struggled to be from the clasp of his thighs, to be from the touch of his warmth. "Because you'll be able to break my heart that much easier when you no longer require me when you find another to take my place."

Tightening his arms about her waist, Nico held her fast to his length, refused to relinquish the crushing hold even as she was seen to wince to the building pressure about her, "say the words, Angeline; I need you to say the words."

"Nico, you're hurting me." Whimpered as his arms drew her even closer, the flex crushing her, making it nearly impos-

sible to breathe. "Nico, please."
"Say the words, Angeline; all you have to do is say the words." And his voice seemed to be forced as he nearly hissed in his insistence of confession. "Please say the words; if there is nothing, I ever ask of you again, I ask you to do this for me now. Tell me; you love me!"

"I love you." Gasped, as the room about them seemed to explode in a rush of heat and wind. "How could I not love you?" Questioned as Angeline buried herself into his protection as the air was felt to race across her body, trace her spine in a flash of pleasure-pain, causing her to gasp to the emotion to the breathlessness, and she clung closer to him as her hair whipped about and joined them as one. As the heat of the room invaded her flesh and raced her veins. Looking down at the ring which adorned her hand, she gasped to see the gold as it nearly glowed to the fire racing its endless circle, and when she looked to Nickolai, she could only see the love and adoration in his piercing eyes.

Returning her face to nestle against the protection of his body she stared upon the emotion as it traced her husband's cheek, a single tear raced features to drip from line of the jaw down to land upon her lips, "it is done, you are mine." Announced with a shuttered breath of emotion, "to cherish and protect till the end of my life, Angeline, know there will never be another to take your place, another to hold my heart. I love you; you are mine for an eternity."

"I have been yours since the first moment you touched me nearly seven years ago." Angeline promised as drawing his mouth to hers she suckled the tremble of his lips, brought him hard to her length as it seemed Nickolai Illevante` became lost to the woman who held his heart.

Nine

"Go!" Angeline ordered as she groaned to the weight which lift from her, "you're crushing me anyway." Teased as Nico pressed himself from the bed with the reluctance of leaving the invite of her tempting flesh. "Deleon is beginning to think I have you bewitched, and the Prince is becoming quite annoyed to your lingering absences." She informed as pulling the heavy blankets up about her length grateful to curl into a tight ball and allow her limbs a moment of respite.

"Very well, but I expect to find you right here when I get back." Teased as he came to lean over her already sleepy head, gently he pressed the strands back from her features before pressing a lingering kiss to her content smile. "And about the Grandmother's, little one," with her brow rising questionably Nico assured, "you could teach them a few things."

Giggling as eyes fought to remain open, Angeline murmured, "I'm glad I was able to please you, husband."

Pressing his lips to the crease of her brow, he reassured, "very pleased." Before quickly dressing and leaving her to the sleep she so obviously needed.

"Nico?" She called as the door opened, halting his escape.

"Yes, little one?" He asked, securing the door before the Captain would be privy to their conversation.

"I love you." She stated as snuggling deeper into the pillows and blankets.

"I know, little one, I have always known." Opening the

chamber door, Nickolai addressed his Captain, who remained on Guard, "Deleon," he instructed, "you are to stay with Angeline until I return. No one beyond myself will enter the room, and if she decides to venture beyond this room, you are not to leave her alone beyond these chamber walls, do you understand me?" With his nod, Nickolai began to walk away, then turned to confront the man, "are you married, Deleon?" Nickolai questioned the man he trusted with his life yet knew very little about personally.

"No, Count, I am not."

"Ah," and the raven head nodded in thoughtful contemplation, "you need to find yourself a good woman, one who is capable of driving you completely out of your mind. I highly recommend married life, Deleon, highly recommend it."

"Yes, Count." And the man couldn't help the grin that came to part his otherwise emotionless features to the recommendation of Count. Armand Deleon had served his Count for many years, rising slowly and steadily through the ranks to that of Captain. Early in his service, the Count recognized his ability in leading and training men. He was found to show courage and loyalty under the most challenging circumstances and being under the command of one such as Nickolai Illevante` the young man quickly gave the Count his loyalty and courage. From the first time Armand was on the battlefield shoulder to shoulder with Nickolai, he knew there would never be any question to the man's military experience. War came naturally to some men; it was one of the uncanny abilities that Nickolai held, master of swordplay, and strategy each battle likened to a game of chess. A game carefully thought out and scrutinized before the very first pawn was sacrificed. "Count!" He called before the man had the chance to quit the hall.

Armand ventured the few steps that separated them and bowed to the man with the murmur, "I heard what happened to the Lady Angeline on the ramparts last night. It was not her fault, Milord; I should have remained with her as you instructed. If you are to punish anyone, please let it be me who takes your disappointment. She is still innocent to the workings of men, the deceit some are capable of."

The cape hanging about Nickolai's shoulders came to be shoved away displaying the heavy leather and metal that crossed his chest, the sword as it laid in wait of use where his hand went to the hilt with a lingering touch, "you would draw the brunt of my punishment to yourself instead of the Lady Angeline?" He questioned oddly pleased to such a revelation.

"Aye, Milord, she never expected Prince Andrew to be awaiting such easy prey. I should have stayed with her as instructed." Armand repeated lowering himself to a kneel before his scowling features, waiting, accepting the inevitable power of his first blow. Deleon had seen the fierceness in which the Count had executed those who dared to defile what was rightfully his, and he knew no one or thing would ever come to hurt the woman he had claimed as a wife — the woman who so obviously held his heart within her innocent hands.

Feeling the smile that grew to his loyalty to wife Nickolai informed, "to your feet, Armand, I appreciate your protection toward Lady Angeline, and no one has suffered from my punishment, least of all the Lady Angeline." Clasping the man about the shoulder with his massive hand, he assured, "we will all use last night as a learning experience as it is true, we have never had reason to protect a woman as we do this one. However, going forward, if you are commanded to protect and remain with her, and you disregard those orders in the slightest, you will receive the brunt of my punishment."

Opening the door to chambers sometime in the early afternoon Angeline smiled to the man she found guarding any attempts of escape, barring her exit from the room, "I am to be captive in these chambers, Captain?" She questioned the scowl of disproval as it came to her attempts to step about his massive barrier.

"No, Milady, however, it may be best if you were to wait here for the Count to return." And his body seemed to inch closer to her, forcing Angeline to step hesitantly back into the room no matter what her determination was. "It is not a wise thing for you to attempt to wander these halls unescorted."

Raising her chin in undeterred purpose, Angeline placed her sweetest smiles to face as she suggested, "perhaps you would feel safer if you were to accompany me, we could walk about the gardens. The weather is changing so quickly I would hate to waste the last of the warm days hidden behind these walls. Besides, I have heard that the gardens of Bodiam are magnificent, wouldn't you like to explore them?" and with a conspiring whisper she shared, "something about this place has to be magnificent." Only to meet he reluctant smile which came to threaten the corners of his mouth, "besides, I seem to remember you having an interest in the gardens at Belaveuta with my woman."

Armand studied the woman before him, the deep emerald eyes, as they remained steadfast in her study and wait of his reaction to such a reminder, the smile that gave evidence to the slightest of a dimple in her left cheek. No wonder his Count recommended marriage. "I never stood a chance, did I?" Armand grumbled as he pointed the way. "Milady, a walk about the gardens. Then we shall return here, directly."

"Directly, Captain Deleon." Instantly Angeline drew her wool wrapper about her shoulders before linking her arm through that of the Guard, "now you must simply tell me all about your time with the Count." She began as they strolled through the many paths that lined the gardens of Bodiam.

∞∞∞

Coming to a lingering pause at the very center of the remains of what was surely a magnificent rose garden in full sea-son, Angeline cast a guarded look to the man at her side, could sense the protectiveness and caution he used with every step. "The Count as a great deal of faith in you, Captain Deleon." She cast her gaze to the lingering blooms before her, "he is not one who trusts willingly, is he?"

Slowly the dark head shook as he forced the expression of pride then surprise from his features, "no, Milady, there are very few whom he places his trust. The Count has always guarded his solitude as a prize. The few who know him intimately believe it the curse of his family, others whisper to the mystery of his being, the things he is capable of."

"Do you understand the things he is capable of?" She ventured, sensing only a deep loyalty to those that he served.

"I believe the Count as a remarkable gift to war, a master strategist he constantly realizes the moves and defenses of others, and it has forced him into a self-solitude." Presenting his arm once again, he waited a moment for the woman to link hers through his before leading them back to her chamber, "if you will allow me to speak honestly, Milady." He ventured to the woman beside him.

"Of course, Captain, if we are not to have honesty between us, how can I trust you with my life?" Her eyes came to greet his humbled ones for a mere moment before Angeline cast her gaze to the path before them.

"I was at first slightly apprehensive when you came into his life. I did not believe he needed such a distraction from the service of Prince, you are, after all, Belaveuta." He started slowly not surprised by the emerald eyes that peered quickly up to his confession, "there are many who covet all that he has, all that he has acquired through service to Crown, even those that say they are loyal to the Crowned Prince resent all that he instills as trust upon Illevante` but now I can see you will be good for him. You will bring him the contentedness he has long searched for, the reason to go on fighting for God and country, as it seemed he was beginning to lose his directive. He was starting to lose his way. It is a hard thing for a man to come to terms with his loneliness; to believe in a whispered curse for generations."

Frowning to his observations, Angeline couldn't help the slight paling as it came to cheek, "do you think any will attempt to hurt him for what he has achieved? Do you think such jealousies could run so deep?"

Shrugging his massive shoulders, he looked down to the woman whose head came to the mid-point of his chest, witnessed the fear as it rose in concerned eyes, and he could only assure, "that is what he has us for, is it not, Milady?"

Nodding thoughtfully to such an observation Angeline smiled as it was apparent the man was attempting to pay her a compliment, "thank you, Captain." Was managed as she found herself before chamber doors.

Holding her back, he opened the doors and inspected the rooms beyond; allowing her entry when the safety of the room was confirmed, he managed, "it was my pleasure, Milady." And with a bow, the door came to be closed between them.

Looking to the door for long moments as it closed between them Angeline couldn't help but frown to the concerns and foreboding which plagued the man to her interference in his Count's life. Could it be possible for Nickolai to need her so in his life, for her to be here to take such loneliness from him? Shaking her head as the women of the night before were remembered she put it off to that of his Captain as it was now apparent, he accepted and nearly welcomed her into life at Illevante`. Tugging her bottom lip into the clasp of teeth, she vaguely wondered to her place in Illevante`, to her position as Nickolai's wife. Feeling the softest of caresses as it came to her throat, Angeline smiled to the instant reassurance given before turning into the coolness of the room and quickly went about drawing the logs in the hearth to full flame.

As the warmth settled about the room, Angeline realized

the evening had arrived, and still her husband had not returned. Twice she contemplated venturing from the chamber to seek Nico's whereabouts and twice she stopped before the closed door when apprehension came like a cold trickle to her spine causing her to turn once again to the solitude of the room behind her. She couldn't lie to herself; she honestly had no desire to be in the circle of any who petitioned for her company last night, she was wary of false attentions and curious questioning, the fake smiles which hid the trueness of the emotion radiating from them — flopping herself into one of the deepest chairs she wished to return to Illevante` and begin her married life. It seemed as if they had not been given a single day to themselves since they shared their vows. All she wished for was to start taking care of her own home, being a proper wife and hopefully mother to Nicholai's children. With a happy sigh, she sought her husband and with little concentration realized his preoccupied thoughts to war and death, causing her to quickly back away from his feelings.

∞∞∞

Some hours later, Angeline opened the chamber doors to find Deleon before her, "yes, Milady?" He questioned to see the indecision that came to mar her brow.

Tugging on her lower lip, she could hear the musician from below, the laughter and happiness of the gathering, "it sounds as if they are having a wonderful time, does it not?"

Turning to the floating sounds as they encroached on the upper floor to the castle, he nodded with realization, "yes, Milady, did you wish to join them? I could escort you to the gathering."

Wrinkling her nose to the unappealing idea of joining the gathering below the fiery head shook against his offer, "thank you, but I believe it is best I remain here at least until Nico returns. I would much rather be on his arm when I have to be with these strangers." Angeline reflected surprised by the smile that came begrudgingly to the man's lips. "Do I amuse you, Captain?" She questioned curiously to his smile.

"No, of course not, Milady. I only find it interesting that someone who could have the company of any would rather be alone, here in this room, until your husband is by your side."

"It is an odd thing, isn't it?" She conceded to his observation, only to admit shyly, "but he makes me feel safe."

"That is a good thing, Milady."

"Yes, an excellent thing; however, Deleon, with all my good intentions, I am still bored to tears." She groaned to the hours which still loomed before her. "I was wondering, perhaps, do you play chess?" Pointing to the readied game board before the fireplace she suggested, hopefully, "I don't know how much longer the Count is going to be, but we could keep the door open till he returns."

Armand stared over her shoulder to the game pieces beyond, then back to the woman who smiled hopefully to his hesitation, "I haven't played in years, you probably won't get much of a challenge from me. And I doubt the Count would appreciate me in your chambers, even with the doors open."

Waving off any of his hesitations with a flit of her wrist, Angeline beckoned, "any challenge at all will be most welcome." Stepping back from the doorway she allowed the man to enter the chamber beyond. "Have you supped, yet, Captain, I could always send for food or something to drink? Perhaps some wine," and the decanter was brought forth from the corner of the room. "A servant brought this up last night but neither the Count nor myself have shared in it. I must confess I have never been a very capable drinker."

He watched as she carefully readied two silver goblets for them, "No, Milady, I am fine, thank you." And he settled before the warming fire once she had taken her place at the table.

"I'm sure the Count won't mind if we have just a little." And a sip was taken from the heavy goblet.

∞∞∞

Nickolai pressed his hand through the length of hair, drawing it from his face with a weary sigh. The palm then rubbed to the fatigue as it tightened at the base of his skull. Alone he walked the seemingly endless corridors of Bodiam, and although it was not a large castle, it seemed it was taking him forever to return to his chambers once excused from the Prince and the attentions he had given to his planned attacks on Plona in the months to follow. For hours Nickolai redefined the defenses which lay weak to Prince Phillip's advances and for longer hours he listened to the Prince continually detail his strategic plans of gaining Plona through bribery and coercion. He suspected such talks between his Ministers would last at least another six months until it became necessary to show greater and greater shows of force. So, in all telling, Nickolai realized with little interest, the actual battle was nearly a year away, a fight he knew he would be expected to be a willing participant. The mirrored darkness of window gave him the evidence he only suspected at; he had been gone from Angeline for the better part of the day and only once had he even suspected she searched for him with concern to his absence.

So, when he neared his chambers, he was a little surprised to find the doors wide open and her sweet laughter coming in the wake of a masculine voice. "---so then the Count charges up this hill only to find a wagon full of naked---" The blue eyes confronted the Captain with curiosity to where this story was leading only to find the man stand suddenly, so suddenly his chair fell backward with a loud clatter to his rising. "Count Illevante'!" Was stated as he clumsily righted the chair and backed toward the doorway. "Goodnight, Milady, thank you again for the wine and game."

Watching the man with surprise to his reaction, Angeline sighed as replacing the chessmen to board, "you intimidate your men far too much, my love." And a sweet smile came in his direction. "He told me he couldn't play chess very well, but we had a wonderful game." Finishing the last of the wine from her goblet, she inquired, "have you finished your work with the Prince?"

Watching as she seemed to have to hold to the table as a sudden sway caused her to stumble from the position, Nico asked, "just how much wine did you share with my Captain, Angeline?" And the decanter was spied to be nearly empty.

Scrubbing her hand over the numbness of nose she promised emphatically, "I had only a couple of sips, Armand refused to have any more than a single one. You really should teach your men how to drink, it's deplorable."

"Armand?" He questioned the familiarity borne between the two in the hours of his preoccupation. "Since when has the Captain of my Guard been addressed as Armand, especially by you?" The mouth opened as if to answer then promptly shut as her shoulders shrugged without an answer. "Is that all you have to say for yourself?"

"No," plopping down in the chair as Angeline was sure her legs were no longer steady enough to allow her to walk the slight separation between them, she managed, "Armand and I have had the most enjoyable conversation, he told me some of the funniest stories about you. Things I'm sure you would never, ever tell me."

"Did he now?" Coming to kneel before the chair she occupied he looked up to see the emerald eyes intent on his, "Angeline, do you think it wise to invite a man into your chambers while I am otherwise unavailable?"

After a thoughtful moment, the fiery head nodded in agreement, "no and I would never do anything like that, you know I wouldn't. Besides, you would know if I were doing something wrong, just as I can sense what you are feeling." Her hand came to caress his cheek, trace the perfection of his mouth with a fingertip, "it makes me feel very safe, even when you aren't near."

Lowering his eyes for only a moment, so she would not witness the pleasure her confession brought him, he asked with renewed sternness, "what about Deleon?"

"Armand Deleon?" She questioned feeling as if her head was becoming increasingly more massive every moment he insisted on talking to her. "But he isn't a man, my love; he's the Captain to your Guard. He has sworn to protect me, he wants to keep me safe, but only you make me feel safe."

Attempting to keep the smile from spreading across his face he watched as she propped her elbow on the table and sought to rest her cheek to the positioned hand only to have it repeatedly slide from the position, "Angeline, he is still a man, and you are far too trusting and innocent to be alone with any man. Not to mention being one of the most beautiful women I have ever seen, do you still not realize how every man you look at is instantly under your spell?"

Sliding into his arms as her own came to enclose his shoulders she explained logically, "you are the only man to find me beautiful, Milord, the only one to bear my touch as all others are under your spell. Besides, you left me alone for hours and hours; I had to talk to someone. Armand was quite accommodating; he is one of the few to stay in my company without disgust showing." The length of hair was caressed with gentle touches as she witnessed his tugging frown, "have I upset you, Nico?" She questioned as she touched her lips to the corner of his perfect mouth.

"Sweetheart, I thought you realized how beautiful you are, how desirable from last night." His lips pressed to the concentration of her frowning brow.

"It's all right, Nico, I know you're making them think I'm beautiful even though I'm not," and the tears thickened her voice to confession, "you do it because you truly do love me, I realize that now, but never fear, my love, Armand was the perfect gentleman and I was the perfect hostess. And I," a finger came to stab at her chest repeatedly as she pressed unsteadily away from the brace of his chest to confront him, "am not that innocent anymore." A crooked grin spread across her face, "you should know that." Her hand scrubbed across the numbness of features again as it seemed to spread from nose to cheeks. "Though I do have to admit you are far more beautiful than Armand and I would have preferred getting you drunk, instead." A giggle came to tickle along his neck as her head fell against his throat and held there for silent moments, "I love you so much, Nico." The arms slipped from their hold, and he had to grasp her before she fell.

Holding her silently to his length for long moments, he gathered his heartbreaking emotions which seemed to mist his eyes before being able to confront the woman who lay asleep in his arms. Would it be worth arguing with her further, he already guessed to the stubbornness, but how was he to convince her she was beyond the mere beauty his meager vocabulary was capable of, with a sigh he realized no matter how much he argued his point she would always believe he was placing such thoughts into the men's heads. Gathering her quickly into his arms, he went to the door and opened the barrier to face the Captain who turned to his appearance with a paling expression. "Deleon, just how much did she drink?"

"I thought it to be only two goblets, Milord; I didn't think it would have such an effect on her." And the Captain couldn't help the smile which came to lips to see her sound asleep in cuddle to her husband's chest, "she did mention that she was not a very capable drinker."

"Not very capable at all it would appear, goodnight, Captain." And the doors closed to the man's worry.

Quickly undressing her once in the draped protection of the bed Nickolai couldn't help but laugh as she reached out for him a single time murmured her love once again then turned away with a snore. "Goodnight, my love."

Angeline woke slowly with the realization she was no longer at the chess table, but was in fact in bed, naked. "Sweet Jesus!" Hissed over lips as she turned to the side of the bed Nickolai preferred, only to find it vacant. "You have to think, you silly twit!" The idea of forcing her brain to do anything more than throb caused the bed to heave and spin precariously beneath her. "Oh, sweet Jesus, what have I done?"

Closing her eyes, as it seemed to help ease the pound of her head, Angeline tried to remember what happened only hours before. "*Could she have allowed the man to take her to bed*?" And nausea, which rose thick in her throat, was quickly fought, as she knew that couldn't be possible. "*How could she have allowed such a thing; they were simply having a game of chess?*" And you drank more than you have ever drunk before in your life. So, anything could be possible, couldn't it? Sweet Jesus, where is your husband? Came scolding in a voice surprisingly sounding like that of Antoinette's. How else could her conscious sound if not like that of her stepmother, was wondered with a groan. "Nickolai?" She questioned, attempting to raise her head from the pillows. Surely, he had returned to the chambers by now, how long had he been gone, did he return while the Captain was still here? '*Did he kill him*?' The thought could only force a groan from lips, as she seemed to have the weight of the world balancing between the pulse of her temples.

Nearly jumping out of the bed as he threw open the drape, she greeted Nickolai with troubled eyes as the sun was seen to flood the room beyond, "ah, so you've decided to return to the land of the living." Nico teased coming to settle beside her staring silence. "So, are you hungry?" And the very idea of eating set her stomach to twist painfully, with a rueful shake of her head he suggested, "then perhaps a cup of ale, it will help to settle that stomach and ease your headache."

"No." Reaching out to stop his leave, she managed to croak, "how?"

"How, what, my love?"

"How did I get into bed," clutching the blankets to her

nakedness she nearly whispered, "without any clothes?"

Settling back at her side, he asked, "why don't you tell me?" And his hand came to press the strands of errant hair back over her forehead; "don't you remember what happened?"

Slowly the head shook as she returned to the pillow and allowed her eyes to close with a soft sound of pain. "Nico, please tell me you are the one who put me to bed and removed all of my clothes. Tell me I haven't done something to disgrace myself."

Arching a dark brow to her worried confession, he managed, "what do you think?"

"I think I'm going to be sick if you don't tell me that you did this." She insisted grasping his hand under the press of her smaller on, "please, Nico, don't tease me, I can't remember anything that happened."

"Not even the stories Deleon told you?"

"Stories?" She questioned opening a single eye to barely more than a slit to confront him to such questions. "Stories of whom?"

"What about telling me you would be the most accommodating of wife's; you promised to see to my every need and never question any of the decisions I make. Promised you would never get drunk again and promised never to invite a man into our chambers again, unless, of course, you wanted me to kill them." Nico pressed nearly laughing out loud to the cringe, which came to take her suffering features.

"I said that?" was nearly moaned in growing determination to never have another glass of wine again in her entire life.

"No, but you did tell me I was beautiful and that you loved me." Pressing his lips to the concentration of her forehead, Nico eased her worry, "of course I was the one to put you to bed, little one, do you think anyone else would have done so and lived?" With a relieved sigh, the head shook, and she settled into the cushion of the pillows. "I was planning on leaving here sometime today, do you think you'll be up to traveling soon? I have but one more piece of business to address with the Prince and then we will make ready."

"If it means leaving this place and going home," Angeline attempted to lift her head but only responded to the attempt with a groan as managing, "I will be ready whenever you are, husband." And with his press of lips to her own, he left her to the silence her head so wished.

∞∞∞

Casting the last of turkey leg out the carriage window Nickolai wiped the grease from his fingers and lips before confronting her still and silent staring, "are you feeling any better?" He asked as sipping from the skin of red wine.

Simply smelling the liquid even after the many days of their travel caused her stomach to revolt as she cast a deadly eye in his direction, "I don't ever want another sip of wine in my life." She proclaimed as adjusting the cushion behind her head, so the constant bouncing and jerking didn't seem like a relentless assault on her brain.

"I don't know; I think this is a liken alternative to traveling with you; at least you're not bombarding me with a thousand different questions, and I have learned to enjoy watching you sleep." Recapping the skin, he placed it back to the prepared basket that the Royals had sent them off with, "and Deleon did tell me it was only two goblets of wine. I'll have to remember that in the future, when I need a little peace."

Flinging the cushion from behind her head, it hit him squarely in the face, and the expression of surprise coming to his features caused her to laugh out loud much to the cringe of her head. "I'll give you peace." Growled as she threw herself into his arms.

Quickly trapping her within his arms, he drew her down onto his lap where she seemed to cuddle there for silent moments. "You know, wife, this abuse to my person has got to stop. Punching, pushing, elbowing me in the ribs, slapping, throwing things into my face, next thing I know you'll be kicking me under the table. Perhaps I should start to work on crushing this independence just what would my father think of me bringing such an ill-mannered Countess to Illevante`; he's rolling thunder across the heavens to be sure."

"Ill-mannered---" Stilling under the teasing she held his words for silent moments as realizing his words, "did you call me Countess?" And the raven head nodded to her question, "but only---"

"I have petitioned the Prince to sanctify such a document. After meeting you Phillip has deemed you worthy of such position and so has granted me the permission of making you Countess Illevante`, that is of course if you wish it to be."

"That will make our children---"
Instantly the objection to such a subject was closed off to her with the simple answer, "if there are to be children, they will be of titled descent." Nico finished for her as caressing the brow that suddenly creased in question, "yes, little one?"

Coming up from his cradle of arms, Angeline settled on the cushion beside him with the realization of his objections to family, "you don't want me to have our children." Tears instantly came to blur her vision to have such an essential part of their marriage decided without consulting her. "Our baby, Nico?"

Caressing the crease of the brow as his palm came to frame her features, he managed sternly, "I don't believe this is the time to discuss such a thing. We will wait until Illevante` is reached and we are behind private doors; it will only be a few more hours."

"I don't believe I wish to wait." Came as she pressed away from the caressing hands, "this is just as fine a place to discuss this as our home, just answer my question, do you want me to have our children?"

"No, little one, I would prefer not to have children. I know what it was like at Illevante` as a child, I know the scorn and mistrust to my legacy." Nico answered the sadness that confronted him, "it was never a decision to be discussed; it was something I knew from a very young age. Why do you think I never pursued Belaveuta as part of your dowry?"

"But what if I want a baby?" Angeline questioned suddenly feeling very much out of his life, very much out of the understanding that brought about such determination, "what if I become pregnant?" Blue eyes held hers for silent moments before the emerald widened to such thoughts, "what have you done to prevent such a thing? Tell me, Nickolai." She demanded as involuntarily her hand pressed to the sanctity of womb. "What have you done to me?"

"There is an herb when added to food helps in the prevention of conception. I have requested Martine to place it among your breakfast fruits which you enjoy in the bath, and I have been adding such during the last few days." He answered her honestly even as it became apparent she was withdrawing from him physically, as well as mentally. "Little one, if you would only listen to what I have said. If you would understand what my childhood was like."

Moving to the opposite cushion she stared out the window for long moments before managing, "we would be able to see to our child's happiness, Nickolai, we would be there together to see that the mistakes of the past would not come to haunt our child. As you so continuously protect me so we would protect the child."

"It is not always that easy, little one; there are always rumors and cruelty. You must know this is true having similar differences as a child. You even admitted to me how terrified your father was of the prosecutors which come to investigate such differences, can you imagine a child with your power to read feelings and mine to start fires if another were only to think the wrong thing they would set the villages on fire."

"Nothing is ever easy, Nico, no matter how we try, we all make mistakes. That is why we could only love and cherish our children and let them know we are there always for them. We would be there to teach them between right and wrong; to learn to accept and control their gift. As it is, you're not even giving us a chance to try." Tears and sweat were pressed away with a brusque hand as she met his eyes to implore, "if your ancients have not brought us together to love each other and our children, then what are doing together? To allow the Illevante's name to die with us, is that what you want?"

Hanging his head from the insistence of her questioning; to reasons he could not share with her. Nickolai could only shake his head and shrug shoulders, "the ancients will let us know the reasons for us being together soon enough. For now, all I know is you are my future."

Gasping in exasperation, Angeline snapped, "what future, Nico? How can I be your future if I am not allowed to bring our child into the world?" With a blink, the building tears gained freedom, and she turned from his silence, turned from his beckon of mind, of hand. "Don't, please." Pleaded as she felt the desperation of his heart, the understanding of such a decision beckon her.

"You can't close yourself to me, Angeline," Nico warned as she sought to ignore the constant of his intimacies with his mind, "you know what it would be like if we were without each other, the darkness, the chasm felt when I merely closed myself from you for a moment."

Refusing to address him for long moments she stared out the window, contemplating all that he had shared with her, all that was taken from her, "I have learned to overcome many things in my young life, Nickolai, and if learning to live without you is one of those things I will have to cope with then so be it." She retaliated to what he believed to be a threat of her leaving him. "I could always find someone who would love me, need me, as I thought you did."

Feeling his jaw clench to the words; the idea of another ever being allowed the privilege of such a woman, he stated, "you would never find another who loves or needs you as much as I, and you know you would never survive without me. Even though you won't admit it, not even to yourself, at this moment, but you know this to be true. We need each other far more than either of us realizes."

Casting her eyes to him the words, "it would appear your ancients believe quite otherwise; it is you who needs me not the other way around."

"You told me you loved me; are you going to tell me now that because I refuse to give you a child, you will simply leave without thought without care to the emotion between us?"

"I never thought to love like this," came as she diverted her face from his, fought to breathe over the strangulation of her own emotions, "in only a matter of days you have become everything to me, I thought I understood what kind of man you were. Kind and gentle, patient, and loving. And to think I felt sorry for Lady Catherine, married to a man she didn't know." In vain, she fought to tamp the anger as it grew, tried to restrain the fury as his sureness of position was nearly goading her into admission. What a fool she had been to believe he would be the perfect husband as he had projected himself to be; if she weren't so angry, she would have screamed to the betrayal felt toward his selfishness. "All I know of you is what you want me to know what you manage to pretend time and time again. Not the real you, not the selfish, conniving man you are. First, you twist the thoughts of my callers, making them think me too disgusting even to touch, and then you manipulate me into a barren shell, and you think nothing of it. I won't live like this, and I certainly won't love like this." Reaching up the door which separated her from the driver was opened, "driver, stop the carriage! I'm getting out." The vehicle was felt to slow, and the Guard following came to circle the vehicle, curious to the unplanned stop.

Flinging open the door Angeline was from the confides and walking along the road repeatedly looking over her shoulder waiting, wondering how long it would take for him to come after her. Force her to return to the carriage. "Milady," Deleon was the first to react as she was seen to be muttering to herself and walking quite quickly away from the stilled vehicle, "Milady, please." He beckoned as he dismounted and went after her. "We are many miles from Illevante', and it is not safe for you to be walking. Please return to the carriage," looking over his shoulder he found the Count to be slowly advancing on the two, "please, Milady, I'm sure whatever happened it is all a misunderstanding." Gently his hand grasped her shoulder in hopes of retaining her till the Count could reclaim her.

"Misunderstanding?" She snapped, turning to find Nickolai coming in their direction; "I will never get back into a carriage with him! Never!" Quickly Angeline inched herself behind the massive strength of the Captain hoping in some small way he would protect her from the anger of her approaching husband even as she knew it to be futile as all were unfailingly loyal to him.

"Deleon, get your hands off of my wife!" Nickolai snapped as coming to stand before her cowering stature. "So, you will never get in a carriage with me again, will you?" The fiery head nodded as eyes blazed about the massive body which continued to protect her, "very well, leave her." In a moment the silence settled till even the very birds paused, as the air seemed to thicken and gather. Angeline was sure all could hear the heart which suddenly stopped beating within her chest as Nickolai asked, "is there a problem, gentlemen?" Turning to the Guard that surrounded them as the air suddenly whipped about the trees leaving them in the wake of their scattering leaves, "I said leave her." And with a slight bow in her direction, Nico returned to the carriage. "Deleon, unless you wish to confront my dissatisfaction, I would suggest you get your ass on that animal and move out of here."

Setting back into the vehicle, Nickolai flexed the hands that trembled uncontrollably before clenching them into tight fights, "go!" He shouted, causing the driver to jump to the order. Instantly the horses were brought into line, and with a slap of rein over the rump, they started at a slow trot. Watching her figure till it was little more than a speck in the distance Nickolai reached up to rap at the driver's window to instruct, "stop over the next ridge."

∞∞∞

Angeline held the hair back from her face as the wind only continued to build, and the clouds were seen to gather slowly over her head. The shoulders braced with determination as the carriage was seen to disappear over the next ridge and she was alone. Expectantly emerald eyes looked to the left and right before deciding on a direction to follow. "Leave me on the road without the least bit of protection will you!" Bellowed as she looked up to the patter of raindrops as they began to hit the dusty road in a growing rhythm, the lightning as it seemed to split the sky in its fury. "Perfect! Just perfect, Nico, what will you do next cause an earthquake?" And cautiously she eyed the ground at her feet.

∞∞∞

Coming from the carriage, he looked about the men who gathered silently and couldn't help the smile which grew to their foreboding of leaving their Lady alone on the road, unattended. "Don't worry; she's more than capable of protecting herself simply by opening her mouth." Motioning to one of the guards to dismount he quickly explained to the hooded expression Deleon continued to scrutinize him in, "go on to Illevante', I will see to the Countess, it's time for the two of us to have a long talk, in private." Swinging up onto the mount, he managed, "if we don't kill each other first."

Ten

Shoes in hand and stockings draped over shoulders, Angeline found him as she came over the next ridge settled on the grass his back resting against a rotten tree stump safe in the umbrella of leaves overhead. Only slowing her stride for a matter of contemplative seconds she continued without a word, forced herself to pass his watchfulness without so much as a look in his direction, "I could offer you a ride to the next town, there's an Inn you could take lodgings at if you wish." Called after her. "It appears as if you've become slightly dampened in your journey." The shoulders straightened in deepening determination as her stride quickened; "I was speaking to you."

Lowering her head, Angeline stopped at the crest of the slight incline to whisper, "I don't wish to speak to you." Feeling the insistence that she speak to him, the constant pressure of his attempts to invade her thoughts, she hissed *'go to hell, Illevante, how's that for a conversation!'* And the strands of wet hair clinging to her cheeks and neck were pressed back with undaunted fortitude even as his laughter was felt to ripple up her spine, *'I knew you would break my heart.'* Escaped to the pain staring at him brought her. *'Now, leave me alone; I don't wish to speak to you.'* And the words came to touch over the frown confronting her.

"Ah, but you have." Managed the voice startling her to find him astride a great black beast as he came to scoop her up onto the saddle before him, "don't fight me, little one, I always get what I want, whenever I want it. You should know that much about me by now." He smiled to feel her slump against his chest; her head tucked under his chin as she settled into the brace of his thighs, and his heavy cape gathered about her length. "Are you warm enough?"

"You didn't have to make it rain." His arm came in grasp about her waist, and he held her tight to his length, close to his warmth a warmth Angeline desperately fought to reject as it seemed to seep into her very veins, press upon her heart as a direct assault to the wall she fought to keep in barrier against him. Tight against his strength, she tried not to inhale the masculine scent of him; clean and wild like the woods as it was dragged deep into her lungs. A smell she knew she would always associate with him; how could another man ever smell so wonderful?

Involuntarily she felt her hand close over the arm which entrapped her, felt the fingers caress slowly of the thickness of muscle from his forearm to upper arm then back again in growing need of his touch. *'His touch!'* Conscious scolded, '*what need do you have of his touch when he denies you the one thing you truly wish to share with him? A child of your own, the blending of your two loves into a single being.*' The thoughts only brought the fight back into her length as she struggled uselessly against the encasing arm, "wiggle all you wish, little one, it is only making the ride that much more interesting. You know how much I love it when that tempting backside of yours moves." He couldn't help but chuckle to the hiss of breath escaping her to the words, the length that suddenly became stone still in his arms with the fury of his teasing.

"Let go of me." Angeline hissed, looking over her shoulder to the closeness of his face. The features which caused her heart to take a funny leap to look into his piercing eyes. The perfection of his mouth even if he did have the evilest of smirks on his lips. "Why are you doing this? Why don't you just let me go?"

"Because I love you because you're right, I will not live without you." He answered only to feel the jab of her elbow penetrate the folds of clothing and contact his ribs, "I thought we discussed you're abusing me once all ready."

“I wasn’t listening.” Spat as she attempted to repeat her aim only to find him ready for her this time, trapping her arms close to his body and held them there for the remainder of their ride.

“Then perhaps it’s time I teach you a lesson or two about being a proper wife.” Came in biting retort, “as it seems we have the bedding part down to a science we need to work on your temperament as Countess Illevante` and what your responsibilities are.” Nickolai stole only the quickest of glances to her as she became ridged under his press, the heat of her cheeks nearly glowing as it seemed he had found another of her weakness. “Ah, I will take that complacency as agreement.”

“You can take my complacency and shove it---” With a scream to the utter hopelessness of her situation, Angeline retched herself from his enclosing arms to slide from the saddle of his thighs. For a moment, the two stared at each other, one of surprise and one of waning patience before Angeline quickly scrambled from his sad expression and into the woods beyond.

A weary sigh heaved his chest as he stared for long moments to the point of her disappearance. Did she honestly believe she could escape him; did she honestly think he would allow her to be free of him quite so easily? “What is this fascination women have with babies anyway?” Nico wondered out loud before contemplating his next moves. Should he go after her, gather her up before him, or should he allow her to believe she had thwarted him at least for the moment? He knew they were only a few miles from Belaveuta` it would take her an hour or two, but she would make the journey quickly with her present demeanor. Perhaps he should follow, allowing her to believe the escape possible only to crush such beliefs at the last possible moment. With a muttering of profanities coming over lips, he steered the restless mount in the direction of his guard.

With a growl to the expressions greeting him to his solitary return, he ordered without answering a single question to their concerns, “go back and follow the road to Belaveuta, you are to remain unseen unless trouble befalls your Countess.” Two of his best men were pointed to, "I am putting her safety completely in your hands, don't disappoint me."

∞∞∞

Angeline looked over her shoulder; sure, at any moment, the black mount would come crashing through the woods, and once again, she would find herself scooped up before his furious length. For every step she took, it seemed the anger first coming to crowd her like an ominous cloud was fading in the distance. Soon all that was left were the distant feelings of those neared. With a frown, Angeline concentrated on her husband only to find she could not reach him, and it was apparent he did not attempt to contact her. "Teach me a lesson, will you?" She smirked as familiar landmarks came to her, and Angeline realized she had traveled the few miles to Belaveuta in record time.

Lifting the filthy, ragged hem of her skirts as she crossed the shallowest point of a stream before venturing onto her homelands, she swore silently to herself as she reached once again for Nickolai, and he completely blocked her from his feelings. "To Hell with you!" She yelled over her shoulder only moments before one of her father's guards came at breakneck speeds to her trespass on the lands.

"Lady Angeline!" He gasped, drawing the animal to such a stop that he reared in fright with the shouted name in surprise and horror to her appearance. Swinging down from his mount, he instantly offered her the animal and proceeded to walk beside her as they returned to the Baron's Keep.

∞∞∞

Ushered to her former rooms with a stern expression from father and crestfallen disappointment from her stepmother. Angeline paced in her room once properly bathed and attended to by her women. Alone she waited for the appearance of her father, or worse, stepmother. Spinning about as the door opened without so much as a knock, she opened her mouth in protest only to bite her tongue as her father stood in the door's frame his disappointment more than evident on the expression of his brooding face. "Angeline." Managed to escape him with a bone-weary sound as the door closed behind his entrance, and he waited the moment it took for the woman to cross the distance between them and fling herself into his arms. "What have you done, my little flame?"

The fiery head could only shake as it buried against his neck, and her shoulders rose in a shrug to the heartbreak she felt to such a situation, "he won't let me have a baby, Father, he refuses to have a family. How do I live without a child of my own, how could he make such a decision without even consulting me first?" The words rushed forward as tears were quick to follow.

Caressing the length of the braid as it traveled her back, Anton could only hold her closer as he whispered, "you should have stayed with him and came to a decision, either way, you are his wife now, my love, at his side is where you belong." With such words, Anton only felt her arms tighten about his neck, and the sobs increased in quite an unladylike fashion. "Angeline," whispered as he felt the heartbreak within her, "little flame, you are no longer a child to run away when things are not going as you choose. You are wife to Count Illevante`; you have to abide by his decisions."

"He left me on the road, Father, and told me I had a horrible temperament. That I was not a proper wife!" Again, the sobs returned with a wail to the anger of his disproval of her, and she didn't know which was more heartbreaking: Nico's betrayal or her father's disappointment. "I've tried to be a good wife, Father, honestly. I've done everything he's asked of me---everything." Came in reinforcement to the brow, which rose in question to her beliefs. "I've tried!" Came in her reiteration of the doubt seen to cross her father's dubious expression.

"You have never done everything anyone has asked of

you; how could you start now? Surely the man has not been able to tame you in a less than a month?" Though he was teasing, he realized how sensitive she was to such a falling out with Illevante' and drew her back into the security of his arms. Holding her near for long silent moments, Anton resolved her tears by promising, "very well, you will remain here until things settle down between the two of you, and then you can discuss such a thing civilly." Gently he drew her from his shoulder, confronted the torture of her features as Angeline continued to have a continuous stream of tears from her face, "has he been good to you, my love, patient and tender?" He probed not knowing how to learn what he wanted without offending her or embarrassing himself.

"Until this morning, Nico has been wonderful, Father," the lip was tugged in the resolve not to cry again quite so soon, "he presented me to the Prince and has had the necessary papers filed to make me his Countess." The golden band, which encircled her hand, was presented to the father; "he gave me this with the promise to always love me."

"And?" Anton prompted, waiting for the terrible news she was building up.

"And---I've fallen in love with him, Father." Roughly the tears were pressed from her cooling cheeks as she averted the surprised expression greeting him, "I could not seem to help myself, Father, it's as if I have always loved him. I have always been waiting for him."

"There is no need for you to explain to me, daughter; if I didn't wish for you to find such with him, I would never have allowed you to leave, never allowed you to ventured into such a marriage. Your husband has been in love with you for far too long to allow you to escape him, has he told you of the years he has been coming to this keep under the guise of a pauper? The years he has watched over you and protected you?" Touching the beauty of her features, he questioned, "I have never known a man to love as this one loves you, needs you. No, I fear he will not allow you to escape him so easily."

"Why didn't you ever tell me, Father, how could you have known?" She searched the patience of his loving eyes, raising a brow only as the realization was seen to dawn in her own eyes, "I always thought it was Mother."

"I have only allowed you to think what I wished." He explained with little reason, "it was easier to have your mother show you control, I knew the fears my parents had endured in watching me grow. I thought it best if you thought, once your mother had passed away, that you were alone that such gifts. If you believed you were alone, you would become more reserved in your isolation. You have to believe me when I say I never meant to hurt or betray you, my little flame, only to keep you safe." A loving hand came to touch the wonder of the expression greeting him, "I assume you have told him everything he needs to know of you?" The head nodded solemnly, "and what did he have to say to such confessions."

"He already sensed that I was different from the others." Angeline managed not willing to share Nickolai's secrets with anyone, not even her father. "And he thinks I'm beautiful, Father, and he loves me, or at least he confesses this to me whenever I need it most."

"And because of this, you ran away from him?" Anton teased to the irony of the conversation.

"No!" Angeline wailed, and the tears began anew, "because he doesn't want to have a family. It's as if he knows we will never have a future together as if Illevante' is so cursed with death and lore that our child would not survive."

Nodding to the understanding of Illevante', Anton asked, "have you thought perhaps your husband is afraid of what others have always said about Illevante.' Have you thought that perhaps he is merely attempting to protect you and this child? There have been many rumors to the Illevante ` keep, many who have breached such walls have not returned to tell of it, the few who have they say are mad. They say they heard voices, voices willing them to death from the very walls. Others speak of the Illevante ` blood; they say they do not die; they are cursed to forever wander Illevante` in the form of a shadow; always two are taken upon death."

“Do you believe such rumor and superstition?” Angeline questioned the parent with building determination to prove him wrong.

Shaking his graying head, Anton lowered his eyes from the demand of daughter, “if I ever thought such to be true, do you think I would have sent my only daughter into such a place? To condemn you to madness, even death?”

“Exactly!” Angeline goaded, knowing he had no other opinion to boast without placing her own life in jeopardy. “Rumor and superstition, how can one expect to base a life on such?” Stepping back from his waning determination, Angeline paced furiously before his silently watching stance, “nothing but ignorant people spouting tales to what they do not understand. Illevante` is wondrous, Father. Such beauty and harmony I have never known, and I above all others would know of such malicious voices, would I not?”

“Of course, you would, Angeline, but that still does not make the decision the Count has made any easier for him, nor you, to accept obviously.”

“Nickolai has to understand I would protect the child, father; I would love it above all else.” She implored to the argument she consistently fought during the last few hours of her life, “it will be as how you raised me, how you protected and trained me to guard myself, my thoughts, the thoughts from others!”

“Alas, my little flame, it is not as easy as you would assume; there is a constant worry and sleepless nights that come with that worry. To see a stranger on your lands and your first thought is to hide what you love above all else, to live with a constant fear that whomever that stranger is, they have come to judge what you cannot explain.” With a heavy sigh, Anton managed, “sometimes love is not always enough.” And with a final touch to the heat of her cheek, he turned to leave the room, “once you are more composed, I will have a guard assembled to return you to Illevante`; after this discussion, it is obvious that is where you belong." And before new tears could come to sway him, Anton turned and left her alone in the room.

Nickolai closed his eyes as the gentle search for him was felt to touch over his senses. Holding the barrier which would allow Angeline to penetrate his deepest feelings, Nickolai knew the torment she would endure by such a restriction, but he could not give in to her demands, at least not so easily. "Does she know you're here?" Anton inquired as he came to rejoin the man who paced his library.

The raven head shook with troubling thoughts; "she doesn't know where I am for the moment." Nico answered not willing to share the complexities of their relationship, even with one so close to his wife. "Though I'm not sure how long I can keep such from her." He admitted reluctantly, "has she indicated what her next actions would be?"

"She can be a bit stubborn once she sets her mind to something; I'm afraid it one of the characters she has inherited from her mother." Anton attempted to keep all bias from the confrontation with the man he questioned for he knew the trust between him and his son in law was still a new thing to contend with, something neither was quite sure how to do after the many years of hatred that stood between them, "she loves you, Count, would bowing to her request be such a horrible thing?"

An ironic snort of laughter left Nickolai's stern mouth as he confessed miserably, "having my child grow within her would not be a horrible thing, it would only complete the happiness Angeline has already brought me. However, the child would be cursed, just as I am, just as I have always been." Turning from the man, he stalked off in the direction of the guestroom, where Anton agreed to house him for the evening.

∞∞∞

Nickolai closed his eyes as he settled fully clothed upon the massive bed, a weary sigh escaped him to the storm of emotions his marriage had turned into in only a matter of hours. '*Angeline,*' whispered and instantly, he sought the softness of her flesh, followed the line of her body with his hand. '*I ache for you, wife, I need you here beside me.*'

Moaning in her sleep, Angeline fitfully turned in her dreams and sat up abruptly from the call of her name, the plea that came to her in a heart-wrenching need. The caress to her length as it was felt to yearn with a burning need. Instantly she sought him with her mind, concentrated so hard on reaching him her brow was creased, and her neck ached to such study. '*Nico, please don't do this to me. Please let me sleep.*'

∞∞∞

Remaining in her room as instructed by father, Angeline turned from the view of the gardens below as the latch lifted, and her father came to confront her, "Antoinette has planned a dinner gathering for this evening, and you will be expected to attend. Your woman will be up shortly to assist with your dressing. There is plenty for you to decide on from your remains in the closet." With her silent nod to understanding, Angeline returned to her vigil, and the father left the room carefully, closing and locking the door behind him.

∞∞∞

The ribbon holding the emerald pendant about her neck was tugged at absentmindedly as Angeline feigned her way through a meal, she had no interest in partaking. Suffering through the endless meal and then secreting herself into the shadows of the gathering room as others danced. It surprised Angeline to see the many which crowded the polished wooden floor as she hardly remembered a time when such parties were held in her home. It was even more surprising to see how happy and well attended Antoinette seemed under the gentle attentions of her husband. The woman positively glowed as Anton never left her side, as he was continually smiling and complimenting her to the many details overseen in her preparation of such a well-received evening. An Angeline envied her, envied the life and love that she had, the child she already raised, and the man who smiled at every word which sputtered from her lips.

Angeline sought the solace of Nickolai's thoughts, felt her chin tremble to the fresh onslaught of emotion as it came with his avoidance. Sighing to the heartbreak Angeline turned to search the gathering for father and stepmother as she wished to bid them a good night, she didn't know how much longer she could stand to be from Nico without losing her mind. Without casting the last of her dignity aside and beg him to take her back. Could she live without having his child, could she live without any child? Once again, the tears were felt to rise with the newest wave of heartbreak. How could she ever live without him?

'Little one,' whispered as the touch came to the column of her throat, as the warmth of air caressed her in sweet teasing, *'I would never break your heart, and you could never live without me. Come to me, little one; I need you.'* The words crowding her head caused her to pause, making her wonder if the connection they shared had only grown in the hours of their separation in the degree of her desperation.

The touch came to caress her length, penetrate her very soul as desire stirred suddenly to life, and all thought to anything else, but being with him filled her. Eyes closed as her breath was felt to deepen and the touch to intensify, *'now, little one, feel it now.'* The release flushed her body in a wave of heat, causing her to gasp to the power he could generate within her.

A staggered step brought her back against marble post as quickly scanning the milling crowds; her eyes found the imposing figure across the distance of the room. *'No,'* her heart cried, *'you are not supposed to be here. You must give me time, time to come to terms with your demands. Time to know if I still love you.'*

'You will always love me.' Immediately she was mesmerized by the man as he advanced on her; shouldering his way through the press, *'you will always need me,'* the raven hair thick and loose across massive shoulders became lost in length as the velvet black cape worn seemed to blend perfectly, his piercing eyes to study her without fail once emerald eyes found him. How could she not have sensed him sooner, how could he be here and still she did not know it? For a fleeting moment, her heart seemed to soar that he was here; he would take away the pain and isolation which had settled upon her. *'Yes, how could it be otherwise,'* she wondered, *'how could you ever not love this man, not need him?'* "Nico," seemed to whimper as he was only inches before her. Towering over her, she had no escape past the power of him, the strength that surrounded without even a touch, "oh, Nico." Whispered as his lips touched the sadness of her mouth, the lines of a frown that creased her brow. And she knew that she would never want to escape him, would never want to be far from the emotion and warmth he brought to her. "I don't want to argue with you anymore, Nico, I can't." Her hands came in splay to the hardness of his chest, and she knew there was no worry to others wondering to their open display for his towering length sheltered her from any daring to linger in their inquisitiveness. Her hands clenched into the material of tunic, drawing him closer; harder to her need, "please," whispered to feel the mouth hot and wet on her throat as need of him swept her like a flame.

"There will be no more arguing, no more time or separation between us. You love me; we belong together, not sleeping in separate beds dreaming of what it is like when we are together." Coming from the sweetness of her flesh, he caressed the tremble of her mouth, pressed the pad of thumb over the temptation known to lie there, "come with me from this place, little one." His hand came to frame the perfection of her features as a soft nod moved her head, and she instantly found herself safe in the shelter of his shoulder, his arm claiming waist as he led her through the many that gathered about. "We will go somewhere private, where we can talk, we need to talk."

Allowing herself to be cradled to his strength Angeline simply fell into the fold of his protection and sighed with relief to know he was there with her, to be able to feel the gentle easing of his thoughts as they touched hers, "I never thought you would come for me, that you would change your mind."

Leading her from Belaveuta, he remained silent for long moments before correcting her, "I have not changed my mind, little one." In an instant, he drew her up onto the saddle before him as if she was nothing more than a child with the effort, "however, I will not spend another night without you beside me."

Instantly the struggle for freedom began as his cold, calculating words touched her, causing the pain of a breaking heart to fill her once again, "then you should not have come for me, Nico, you have wasted your time. I will not lay with you; I can't."

"You will and shall." He stated as drawing her hard against his chest he hissed in to her ear, kicking the horse into motion and the miles seemed to fly by them in nothing less than a blur, "don't make me drag you into an Inn like some common serving wench who hasn't yet learned her place in life. You are my wife, Angeline, my love, don't make me do something we'll both regret in the morning."

The heated retort died on Angeline's lips as a building loomed before them, and the sign dangled as in confirmation over her head. 'Inn' was all she was able to read before she turned once again to her husband. "You are truly forcing me to sleep with you here, aren't you?" She asked, sliding from the height of horse to be from his cradling thighs, "and I thought there was an ounce of dignity in you somewhere." Brushing out the skirts of their many wrinkles, she cast him one of her most disgusted expressions, "thank you for the ride, Count Illevante`. It may be best if you were to leave now, surely my father will be sending someone to find me."

Swinging down from the mount Nico grasped her upper arm aggravating the bruises which already marred her flesh, "no one is coming for you, little one, and as far as your father rescuing you, who do you think suggested such a meeting in the first place?" He goaded as he led Angeline into the nearly deserted establishment, "we will remain here as long as it is necessary to have these differences between us clarified. Until you realize your place beside me as a wife."

Struggling from the crushing hold, she managed to spat, "you have been quite clear in your wishes, Milord, I hardly believe there is anything left to speak of." Dragging her to the planked bar, he demanded a room and threw a handful of coins to the proprietor who handed him a key no matter how desperately she fought to be from his lead. "You would allow him a key?" Angeline shrieked as the man continued with the mundane chore of washing mugs without looking in her direction.

"It's what he paid for, isn't it?" He asked, looking into the eyes of the Count who seemed to wish someone to defy his wishes toward this woman. "Seems to me you should simply accept your lot in life, it would be less painful; there are few who escape Count Illevante` once he has a notion of having you."

The hold about her arm became nothing less than crushing as she spat, "just how many have you had a notion of having, husband?" With a teeth-clenching scream, Angeline found herself dragged along.

"Far more than you could comprehend, wife," Nico growled, as he forced her up a flight of stairs and down a hallway to a room in the far corner of the building where he fumbled for a moment with the lock before shoving her into the chambers before him. Once the securely fastening the door behind them, Nickolai turned to confront the woman who stood in the center of the room; arms folded tightly across chest her breathing nearly haggard as he allowed the smallest of smiles to escape him to her demeanor. "You can't hate me as much as you express if you're still jealous over my past conquests."

"Too many for me to comprehend?" Screamed over the furor of her rage, the audacity of him in handling her as he had. "Too Many!" Was repeated as she bolted for the locked door only to have him there, before her as if anticipating her next move, instantly she pressed herself from the cling of his arms, the touch of his length as it pressed into her own. "Perhaps it's the many bastards you have sired; that is why you do not need a legitimate child. Perhaps this is why you have no true need for me." Tugging the lower lip between teeth, Angeline bit down hard and held the tug till the sweet coppery taste of blood filled her mouth.

"Think whatever you wish, I have never been able to stop you before." Spat as he confronted her for silent moments, stared to the pale stricken face before him, and he wanted nothing more than to go to her. Make her believe in him, return to the few precious hours when she was soft and loving in his arms, trusting him as no one had ever done before in his life.

"I want to go home." Came with far more pain than wanted to be expressed, "I hate this nonsense, the ridiculousness of this situation! I am a wife; I want to be mother --- nothing you say or attempt to say will convince me differently. Tis all I have ever wanted in life."

Removing the cape from about his shoulders, Nico swung it to the back of the chair. All the while, he watched her, studied her study of him. Fought to infiltrate the barriers of her mind, barriers which were far too intense and complicated for him to press aside at will. With an oath to her stubbornness, then placed his sword next to the hearth before telling her, "I will take you to Illevante` when it is time." Carefully the cuffs of this tunic came to be rolled up till they were placed just above his elbows.

"That is not my home," came softly, painfully. "It will never be a home; it will only be your Keep."

"It will always be your home," Nico stated as kneeling before the fireplace; willing the flames to grow about the bark, he found himself wondering how to approach this woman without it ending in a battle of wills. How could he put aside all that he had willed all for the happiness of this one woman? "Do you honestly believe I would allow any woman to carry my child if I don't allow the only woman I have ever loved to do so?" A furtive glance passed over his shoulder to address the silence of the room. "Christ, Angeline, why are you so stubborn about this?" Came in exasperation and near desperation to understand this need within her, "why is this so important to you?"

Raising her hands in utter defeat to such single-mindedness, Angeline gasped, "why am I so stubborn? I have given you everything you have wanted without a fight, without thought to consequence of self, and the one thing I ask of you, you refuse!"

"And just what have you given without such consequence?" He asked with a knowing smirk.

"Myself, my love! Willingly I have given time and time again, lest you forget, husband, we have been enemies longer than we have married."

"I forget nothing, wife," came in a low, dangerous voice, causing Angeline to involuntarily step back even though he made no move to advance on her. "And lest you forget, I have been your enemy for longer than you have been mine." For lack of anything better to do he absentmindedly tossed twigs into the growing fire before continuing, "for the last seven years I have been watching over you, making sure that no harm would come to anyone in your family every time they ventured onto Illevante'. Don't you think I could have ridden into Belaveuta and claimed it, as well as you, as my own? Your father had grown tired of battle years ago and has allowed an incompetent to command his forces. Your stepbrother isn't capable of leading a pack of mules let alone a garrison of warriors. Everything I have done, while contending with your family's persistent need to command my lands, I have done for you." Brushing the remains of wood from hands, he lifted his head and confronted her silence, "during such years I have grown to love you like no one before and never doubt how much I cherish the love you have given me. The willingness and courage you have shown in coming to me time and time again, you are the one true warrior of Belaveuta; of this, I have no doubt."

For long torturous moments, Angeline stared to the presentation of his back the material of shirt as it was stretched taut across the definition of muscle as she felt her heart weaken to the words he spoke, the emotion placed behind them. "You wanted me to love and accept you as much as you love and accept me, that is why you have done everything as such. That is why you couldn't simply have stormed into my life and taken me as a prisoner; you couldn't have taken me in any other way than what you have---in love, in gentleness." Angeline ventured to realize the actual depth of his conviction to her, to his need of her. "I fell into love with you so many years ago, Nico, I don't know where you end, and I begin. Even before I saw you, or knew who you were, I loved you, wanted you, knew it would be right to be with you." Sounded with far more pain than wanted as Angeline took a hesitant step to his presented back as she wished for nothing more than to touch him, to have him realize the importance of her need and as if her feet had a mind of their own she slowly closed the distance separating them, gently touched the slump of his shoulder beneath fingertips. "How can you say you know me like none before without realizing how important a family is to me, how much I want to bring our child into this world." She dared, willing to stop the wild pound of her heart, forcing the breath to return to her instead of the gasps as it now did. "If you won't allow me to have our child then let me find some---"

And before she could finish the sentence, she gasped to the expression he cast over his shoulder to her. "No one will live long enough to give you such a child, Angeline, have no doubt I will never allow another to touch you. Never."

Nearly stamping her foot to his stubbornness Angeline beseeched, "all I have ever wanted was to bring my---our---children into this world, to love and cherish them, to let them know how wonderful it feels to be loved. A child should always know that they have someone to care for them, someone who will understand anything---everything. To know that they would never be left alone or frightened to their place in this world."

Rising slowly, he confronted her statement with a touch of sadness, "and what if our children are left alone and frightened in this world?" He watched as the eyes shimmered to building emotion, the defiance of such a suggestion, how he longed to breach the distance between them and caress the slight tremble as it came to her chin. "Why isn't being with me enough, why can't you simply be my wife, Countess to Illevante` and not a mother?" Nickolai felt his shoulders slump slightly to the loss of yet another battle to her will. "You know I would do anything for you, ask me anything, but this, wife, and I will grant it."

"I am no wife, and without this, I do not need anything more." Whispered as she staggered to the encompassing sadness he emanated, "a wife infers a sense of family and caring for a home where that family gathers in security, in love. I have neither; you have taken everything from me."

"You are my wife," Nico repeated to his growing agitation to her stubbornness.

"I am nothing more than a convenience for you, a finely dressed chattel expected to perform whenever and wherever necessary as long as it pleases you." The emerald eyes rose to the bitterness as it seeped into her blood, attacked her heart, "tell me does it make you proud to be above me, bending me to your will, the victorious Count Illevante` has once again conquered, has won Belaveuta not by the sword but by his cock!"

"And it is a cock that you crave, *Countess*!" Came in biting retort to how easily she dismissed the moments they spent in each other's arms. "You are my wife; you are expected to service me in any way that I deem necessary. You are mine, Angeline, always."

"Then, you have made a whore into a Countess." She spat clawing to the ring that circled her finger it was flung across the room to land at his feet with a deafening chime, as it seemed to circle endlessly before settling. "Give this to someone you can truly share such words with, for those words meant nothing when you said them. We are husband and wife, not husband, and possession."

Nickolai felt the heat of the room escalate about him, as the fire in hearth grew to menacing proportions to hear such words from her. "You are the one I have spoken the words with; there will never be another who will hear such; there will never be another to wear this ring. And you have always been considered wife, never a possession, never taken for granted." Reaching down to retrieve the ring it came to be placed on the very tip of his smallest finger and was held there with snug sureness before he crossed the room that lay between them and had to reflect the beautiful babies they would have miraculous babies, he ventured to the power of the parents. He briefly wondered if Martine would live through the bringing up of yet another Illevante`. With a heavy sigh, his raven head shook to her damn obstinacy. "From the first moment I laid eyes on you, little one, I knew I would do anything within my power to make you happy. I would make any sacrifice to keep you in my life." Gently he caressed the heat of her cheek, pressed his thumb over the tremble of lips wanting if nothing else to take the pain from her eyes.

A sob escaped Angeline as she forced her eyes to meet his; "you don't have to sacrifice anything to bring our children into the world. All you have to do is love them, be patient with them." Reaching in the distance between them, Nickolai captured her mouth under his own, waited the moment it took for her to take the additional step to forge the separation of their bodies, "I know that I'm not the type of wife most men want. I never listened to my stepmother when she attempted to instill such virtues upon me. I don't know how to care for Illevante`, how to order about servants nor do I know how to cook, clean or sew but I do want to make you happy, Nico, I want so many things for you." The tears were felt to touch his lips as she fought to continue, "if you only give me a chance, I won't make you sorry for allowing me to have our baby. It will be a wondrous miracle. And I promise to work at being the wife you need, and I will attempt to hold my temperament."

Watching as a single more tear escaped her lashes and trailed along her cheek, Nickolai could do little else than gather her into his arms, carry her against the cradle of his massive chest, "there has never been a woman in my life who has cried as much as you." He reflected in awe of the emotions that she was able to display continuously. "I'm not sure if it's a good thing or not. How do you expect me to cope with a pregnant woman if you're like this already?" Laying her to the bed, he pressed his lips to the moistness of her cheeks, then crease of the brow before capturing her mouth, "you are my wife in every sense of the word, little one, and I would have you no other way than how you are, then who you are. You are my life, Angeline, the reason I can go on, the reason I want to go on. There is no pride; no conquer, only my love and devotion to you." Grasping her hand, the ring was returned to its proper resting-place as he vowed, "my service to the crown calls me away quite frequently during the year, I will not always be there to oversee the raising of our children. Most of the responsibility will land on you."

"Children? So, we can plan on having more than one, yes?" Reaching up, she threw her arms about his neck and allowed the raven length to surround her as tears of joy were felt to escape, "thank you, Nico, thank you so much."

Settling beside her on the narrow bed, he drew her close to his length as he was able to cuddle her and know he had made her happy, "you caught that children part, didn't you?" He teased as the fiery head lifted and nodded contently. "Just how many of these babies are you planning to bring into this world?"

Pressing the remains of tears away, she stated firmly, "six."

"Six?" He questioned. "Is that a definite number?"

"I thought six to be a good solid number; however, if you would like more, I'm sure I can arrange more." A sudden frown came to her encompassing joy, "you must promise that you will love me even if I get fat and grumpy."

"Ah, I knew there was a catch." He teased, drawing her completely over his length, "fat and grumpy, huh?" And his hand came to press over the swell of her backside, "is it feasible for you to get any grumpier than today?"

"Very feasible." She laughed, releasing the buttons along the front of his tunic, "and don't forget the fat part. That's very important to a pregnant woman, though you must never tell me when I am getting so." Teasingly her lips pressed to the bronze of muscle, suckled along the mantle of flesh, as it became available to her. "Promise me, Nico." Slowly she worked the shirt from the waistband and pressed it away as the buttons along the front of his trousers came to be released. Fingers moved inside the band, easing the material down over hips till she freed the hardness of his erection, and his breath inhaled in a noticeable gasp. Smiling, she allowed her mouth to trace the coarse hair as it led her lower along his torso.

"Ah, yes, a promise." The head rose from the stomach where soft teasing kisses were pressed down his belly, "the fat and round part." And a moment of silence filled the distance as her hand cupped his hardness, "just how fat and round are you planning on getting. You know I like to stretch out in bed, you may take up too much space."

"Nico!" Growled as her lips came to tease over the very tip of his erection, her tongue to trace over the flesh before drawing it deep into her mouth, only to repeat the action faster and deeper until she felt his hands clutch into her hair and hold her to the tortuous action for moments longer.

Drawing her down into the tangle of blankets, he caressed the joy as it came to her face and promised, "I will love you even if you become a pumpkin." And before Angeline could think of a retort to such an exclamation, he was deep within her warmth, burying himself in the tightness that beckoned to him. “I will love and cherish every child you will give me, little one, all six to sixty of them.” He smiled to see the hesitation in her expression. “I will take this to be happiness.” Pressed into the silence.

“Most definite happiness, my love.” Angeline agreed, pressing up and into the strength of his arms. "You won't ever regret this, Nico, I swear!"

“But you’re crying again.” Came with a groan as he attempted to understand her constant tears.

“Can I not cry when I’m happy?” She questioned as pressing her tears and nose against the sleeve of his shirt.

“You’re happy?” He questioned, and with her nod, he managed, “good, now shut up and let me enjoy this for a little while longer.” Feeling the body as it moved up to meet his growing thrusts. “and, little one, as for giving yourself to me willingly? You threw yourself at me.” And before she could retaliate, he captured her mouth under his, his tongue quickly seeking hers till the body beneath him as felt to surge to the culminating heat of her growing release.

Eleven

'You have promised her a child!' Came in accusation to his pledge, *'a child is not possible until you fulfill the legacy.'* The words seemed to swirl in anger about Nickolai's pacing length as he pondered all that they berated. *'You should have never promised such an impossible and impracticable thing.'*

Looking up to the merging and blending of shadows as they surrounded him in the torchlight Nickolai could manage nothing more than, "what would you have me tell her, you brought me to her only for your own gains. That what her future holds is nothing but thousands of endless nights? She is not the willing woman you thought her to be; she is strong and independent. Why should I torture her for no reason it is soon enough that the foretelling of the prophecy will begin, it is soon enough she will learn of her future."

'Such creation will have to be terminated if it is so conceived.' Another joined in. *'It would not be fair for it to be left orphaned and alone.'*

"No!" Nickolai bellowed against the voices, the decisions he had no choice in, "you will not harm her or our child. No one or thing will ever hurt my son; he will remain safe with me no matter what the determination. If he does not join me in the shadows, I will provide for him here until the end of his days."

'There will be others for you to raise.' Offered in the console of compromise. *'She will keep her promise to the children. She will keep her promise to her sons; not now, not in this current world.'*

Feeling the emotion as it came to thicken throat, as the vision blurred to their intent, Nickolai threatened, “if a single child comes from her body before it is ready, we will leave this place and too hell with your prophecy. To hell with all of you, you can remain as you are for all of eternity. And when it is time, I too will join you for my eternity.”

A caressing hand came to his features, a flutter of touch to the crease of the brow; '*you sound as if you admire her.*' Whispered, causing him to follow the touch, yearn for the love lost for so many years.

“Do you find that so impossible, do you think I lie when I confess my love to her?” Nico asked as he attempted to follow the images. "I have vowed my life to her and will do whatever necessary to keep her onto me.”

'*You weren’t to fall in love with her, Nico.*' And the gentleness of the voice, the concern it held caused him to yearn for the wisdom and caring known to come with such. ‘*You know of such consequence.*'

“Your warnings are already years too late; she is the woman who holds my heart, and I will do whatever necessary to protect her. To end this prophecy without sacrificing her.”

Watching as two shadows seemed to merge into one the voices echoed, '*you have given her our ring, the ring was to be a sacred bonding. When the words are shared, for eternity, you will be joined. Two of Illevante` are always taken; the curse will sacrifice two.”*

"Do you think I don’t know the power of the ring, she is my wife, and we will remain joined until death as the vow states,” Nico shouted to the cave walls surrounding him.

'*There will be no death, Nico, you will wander as we. You will become a part of the legend which surrounds Illevante’.*' Coming to the wall, his hands pressed to the cold of the stone, reached for the elusive shadows which gathered about him, '*you will condemn your son to live without a parent; you will condemn him to this. The prophecy has begun. Two as one.*'

Searching the circling shadows, he sought the familiarity

of the parent as he implored, “Mother, you know I would have never given your ring to just anyone. With this woman, I will fulfill our legacy; I will release Illevante’ ancients. My sons will be allowed to choose a life beyond these walls; they will be free of Illevante’.”

Angeline sat on the crest of the hill overlooking the training fields below as Nickolai and Armand worked with the newest of recruits to her husband’s garrison. Watched as he shed usual leather and chain protection to his chest as the lessons for the day began, and she found it hard to pull her stare from the breadth of Nickolai's naked arms, the muscle as it glistened in raw strength and power from his exertions. For hours she sat, her knees drawn up tight under chin arms hugged about calves, the heavy fur cape tugged tight about her warding off the constant wind and cold from the ocean beyond, watching as one after another came in charge of her husband. As one after another was easily swatted away as if they were nothing more than schoolboys playing with sticks instead of the metal they wielded. It was true; her husband did have a gift of war. Even one who had no inkling to such mastery could see how easily her husband defended himself, could see how he barely had to exert himself to send lesser men flying from their feet, all with the slight flick of his sword, or movement of his stance. She could only hope, no pray, when the Prince sent for him such talents did not fail him.

Rising with the heard dismissal from the Count, Angeline quickly made her way back to Illevante’ wanting to be waiting for his return.

Since the day they had returned from the Inn, she had pushed herself to be the perfect wife for him. Angeline rose early each morning to oversee the preparation of morning meals, the readying of his clothing, and the general monitoring of Illevante' as needed. At first, Nickolai waited for her to scamper from the bed as she thought him to be still sleeping, and as the days passed and she did not return to their bed he followed her to the kitchens to watch as the cook began instructing in the simplest of recipes. When completing cooking lessons, another who oversaw the cleaning of Illevante' started her instruction by pointing out different areas requiring special attention and then the everyday cleaning. Later, when he returned from training or touring the lands, they would settle in his library, where he would oversee the correspondence. Diligently she would labor over menus and schedules for the following day. Often amused by her persistence, Nico would lose all track of time as he stared at her. Wondering to a time she would grow weary of such mundane chores, only to find in the days and weeks which followed Angeline quickly settled into a strict routine. A routine that incorporated servants into the easy lure of her loyalty, it was soon found they would question his orders to the running of the house without confirmation from their Countess. And she was the woman who confessed to him that she was not what a man would want as a wife, what more he wondered could he ask of her. "˜What more?" Came in nudging reminder to the time as it quickly slipped through his opened hand.

For long moments Nickolai stared up to the woman who turned and walked away from him, felt his eyes fuse to the figure that held his heart, and it wasn't until Deleon touched his shoulder that he realized the man was talking to him. "Forgive me, Captain." Came with a touch of embarrassment as the man was seen to follow his line of stare.

"There is nothing to forgive, Milord." Armand couldn't help but notice the slight smile that came to the man's otherwise stern mouth. Could see the appreciation of such a woman as it lit the Count's hooded eyes, "I was saying I will see to the final administrations if you wished to retire. It has been a long day, and winter will be quickly settling in."

With a thoughtful nod, Nickolai realized the only thing

he wanted was the feel of his wife in his arms, the touch of her lips under his. Quickly he recounted orders and weaknesses he wished worked on before excusing himself from the quickly tiring group. The Prince had sent him twenty recruits of the rawest of talents; it was nearly embarrassing to see how inexperienced they were when such a battle loomed before them as the one Plona promised to be. Deleon was an excellent trainer, but Nickolai knew it would take far more patience then Deleon or even himself had to get these men battle-ready and courageous enough to face an enemy. It would take time, and unfortunately, he knew he would never have enough of it.

∞∞∞

Entering the center gathering room, Nico looked expectedly about hoping, as it had become Angeline's habit in the last few weeks, she would meet him as he walked in the door. She would very nearly run down the stairs and into his arms, so it was with a touch of disappointment that he found the house quiet and void of her presence.

Handing off his weapons and discarded cape to an approaching servant, Nickolai grumbled to hunger then moved deeper into the room to stand before the massive hearth as a fire was found to be burning hotly in its depth. As chasing the chill from his length, he became aware of the gentle tugging of insistence as Angeline beckoned him.

Looking up and about the room, he growled softly to the games she played to the images which filled his head. Stamping up the flight of stairs to her dressing rooms, he flung open the doors only to the find the room beyond empty, "Angeline!" He bellowed as crossing the distance to where her hidden bathing chamber were located. Throwing aside the tapestries, Nico strode into steamy heat only to come to a halt, as she was found naked beneath the fall of water.

"I was wondering what was taking you so long." Looking

over her shoulder to his appearance, she teased, “I thought perhaps you would like to bathe after your training lessons.” Pointing to the towels and soaps, as well as the array of foods placed about the tub’s rim, she goaded, “of course if you’d rather eat---” And laughed as he stepped into the water clothes and all.

Breathlessness caught the laugh as the determination of his features caused Angeline's entire body to respond, in the strength of his massive arms her naked length was brought up hard to the leather and metal of his armor as it still protected his chest, the leather of trousers and boots as they chafed tender flesh. “Nico,” whispered as her arms circled his neck, and he drew her up to the readiness of his need as she caressed the strength of his arms under the search of her hands, “I love you.”

“Angeline,” whispered as his mouth found hers and the gentleness of her name was gone. Holding her hard, fast to his length, his hands marveled in the perfection of her softness as it molded to him, the breasts as they crushed to the mantle of his chest. Her hands as they caressed the length of hair from his forehead, back over shoulders as her eyes held his in unabashed emotion.

“Sweet Jesus, little one, do you have to be so willing.” Nico’s laughter seemed to fill the room as a blush was seen to cap her cheeks, and she instantly buried her face in the crook of his neck.

Lifting her head from the neck she sought sanctuary in; her arms tightened about his breadth as she searched the stillness about them. The silence as it seemed the air was gathering, the heat increasing, “something isn’t right.” Angeline managed only seconds before the waters about them began to boil, and the air grew thick, making it nearly impossible for her to breath, “Nico?” Angeline screamed as shadows swirled, and the thunderous sound of 'No!' vibrated till the very walls about them trembled and threatened to collapse. “Sweet Jesus, what is wrong? What have I done?”

Lifting her up and out of the waters as they rolled to a steaming bubbling temperature Nickolai drew himself from the intent of the ancients as they made their disproval common knowledge, "are you all right?" Nico questioned covering her naked length with his own, drew her hard into his protection as he bellowed to the encompassing worry of her safety, "did they hurt you? Are you burnt?" To see the palpable fear in her eyes, the flesh as it was bright red from the scalding waters, he repeated, "are you hurt?"

Attempting to catch her breath Angeline shook her head as she burrowed deeper into the strength of his arms, clung to the breadth of shoulders even as Nico could feel the trembles as they racked her length, "why did they do this to me, what have I done?"

Placing her back to arms distance, he pressed the wet strands of hair from her features, caressed the features as terrified eyes stared upon him in question and fear, "I believe you have conceived our first son."

Her breath came as a staggering gasp as her hands slipped weakly from the contact maintained at his shoulders. "Conceived?" Angeline questioned, and her hands came protectively about the place where their child would grow, "how could they know?"

"How couldn't they?" Nico countered as carefully inspecting her flesh, relieved to see he had removed her from the heat in time. "I'm afraid his conception was not quite in the timeline they had hoped."

"His?" She questioned, still not realizing what was attempted to be explained to her so surprised she was by his confession, "you're serious, aren't you?"

"Yes," and he caressed the wonder which came to take her expression, "I'm afraid they will all be sons. There has never been a female child born to Illevante`."

"Six boys." Angeline gasped, cuddling closer to his length pressing into the strength of his arms as furtive glances went to the surrounding walls. "Will they try to hurt the baby, Nico?" Her eyes met his to the realizations of fear and protectiveness coming to well deep within her. Ruefully rumors from her father haunted, could it have been such ancients which had sent others from here in madness? Could they invoke such uncertainty to her place as they had done to others who had displeased them?

"No, little one, they are simply angry with me for encouraging this, for allowing it to happen before agreed upon." Pulling off the sodden boots, he rose from the wet of the floor and drew her up into his arms, carried her from the bath to the dressing rooms beyond. "They would never do anything to hurt you or the baby, I swear this to you, Angeline. They know that we will leave this place if they were to try. They know that I will take you and the baby far from here, far where they could never venture."

"You would leave your home for us?" Angeline questioned as he wrapped her in thick towels and scrubbed the dampness from her flesh.

Lifting her face to confront him, Nico reminded, "did I not say I would sacrifice anything to have you in my life, to keep you happy?" His lips pressed to the concentration of her brow, "you are my love, Angeline, this child our future. There was never a question of what I would do for either of you."

∞∞∞

Nickolai turned over in the massive bed, his arm instantly searching for her length to hold close to him, caress even as he slept. "Angeline?" He questioned, candles were set to light as he came from bedcovers in search of her, "where did you run off to?"

Sensing the quietness of the house which surrounded him, Nickolai instantly became concerned with her whereabouts. Dressing quickly, he came from the room with the leather tunic barely across his shoulders as racing the stairs; he mentally searched for her, '*Angeline.*' His heart cried out as the doors to the back terrace were flung open, and he stepped out into the night. For long moments he stood catching the breath that had been robbed from him the moment he woke to find her gone.

Quickly his eyes adjusted to the night which settled about him; the moon though no more than a crescent gave an eerie glow to the figure which stood in the garden's center. The white of her robe nearly iridescent as she stood still, fearful to the strength of emotion as it came to her, "sweetheart, it's the middle of the night. You'll catch your death out here." Nico admonished as coming to drape his arms about her waist and drawing Angeline close to his length, aware of the eyes wide and fearful confronting him as he joined her. "Sweetheart, what is wrong?"

Cuddling to his length, Angeline closed her hands over his as they came to the swell of her belly. "I've been trying to sense him, Nico, and I can't. It's has been nearly two months, what if you are wrong. What if I'm not pregnant, what if they won't let me have a child. It's what they did to your mother. Martine told me she was only allowed a single child. How could they manipulate our lives as such?"

"Sweetheart, you have already missed two of your monthly flows, have you not?" Ruefully the fiery head nodded to his words, "and I have already begun to see a few other changes in you," and the hands came up to cup the new fullness of her breasts, "definite changes." He teased, returning his palm in splay over her belly, "give him a little time soon he will be as demanding on you as I am." Gently his lips came to press into the column of throat, suckle there will growing intent. "There is nothing to worry about, little one; you will be fine. He will be as perfect as everything you do for him."

Placing her hand over his, Angeline held to him for silent moments before pressing, "you would tell me if you knew something was wrong, wouldn't you, Nico? If there were something wrong with the baby, you wouldn't keep it a secret from me, would you? If they have taken him from me, you would tell me; you wouldn't let me keep hoping." The head shook to such questioning, "I know I sound like a hysterical pregnant woman, but I have this feeling something is going to happen. Nearly an expectation as if all been too wonderful these last few months."

"Everything has been so because you have made it so." Drawing her up into his arms, Nico cradled her close to his chest, held her there for silent moments as he confronted the hopefulness of her brilliant eyes; "let me take you back to bed, it is very late, and you need your rest. My son needs his rest."

Shaking her head, Angeline held to the breadth of shoulders, "no, Nico, here. Make love to me here where they can't reach us. Where I can't hear their words." Her head nestled to the crook of the shoulder as he drew her closer, harder to his length, "only the two of us." Struggling out of his arms, she grasped his hand and led him deeper into the winding paths, further into the darkness where even the scant moon could not follow. "Make love to me, Nico, while there is just the two of us."

Struggling to remove Nico's tunic, her trembling fingers pressed the material back over his shoulders, reveled in the strength of his length as her robe was removed and laid to the grasses beneath them. Drawing him to her, Angeline caressed the power and wonder of the man she loved as none other and pleaded with her mouth and hand in an endless search over his body. "Please." Whispered as her mouth sought his ear, "don't let them take you from me, Nico, don't leave me!" Cried as all control was lost to the release slamming over her to the man deep within her, "don't let them take you." Repeated as tears streamed her face, and he cradled her to his length, promising to be with her always.

∞∞∞

Curled against Nico's side on the overstuffed leather sofa which occupied an entire wall in the library, Angeline attempted to remain interested in the book she had clutched in the brace of her hands. Closing the book, she placed it aside as she sought to concentrate on the gentle nudging to senses, "are you hungry?" She asked, turning about she came on her knees to confront him. Looking up from the book, he was reading his brow rose to the question, "are you hungry?" The raven head shook as he marked his place and put the book aside. "I could have sworn it was you."

Smiling to her vexation, Nico pointed to the slight swell of her belly, "perhaps it is him."

"Do you think?" She wondered, closing her arms about her waist, "maybe it is him." Angeline laughed as tugging Nico along by the hand, "come, my son has finally made a demand on me, and it is one that I can easily rectify." Leading him through the Keep down the stairs to where the kitchens where located. She rummaged about cluttered cupboards till the main table displayed cheese, bread, fruits, and pastries. A half of cold chicken, as well as an assortment of vegetables that finished the final selections.

Pulling the remaining leg from the chicken he watched as she went from item to item filling the plate till it nearly overflowed, "do you think you have enough?" Nico questioned as he peeled an apple for her then continued to slice it into quarters.

Munching on a raw carrot, Angeline stated, "he's hungry." Taking the chicken leg from his hand, she bit into the tasty flesh before pressing her greasy lips against Nickolai's, who could only laugh to the joy seen to light her eyes.

∞∞∞

The fur cape came to be gathered tighter about her length as she stood above the training field, watching the garrison for long moments. The blanket of snow falling in deeper and deeper inches about her feet was contemplated for silent moments as she had to blink away the flakes as they landed on lashes. Angeline knew she should return to Illevante` before Nickolai caught her, she couldn't help but be fascinated by his skill and training. Training even she was able to see in the men who only six months ago could barely get out of their way, let alone nearly beat her husband's best men. "Count." Deleon nudged him as he was the first to spy the solitary figure lingering on the crest above, "I fear we have a visitor."

Turning from the sparring of recruit, he cast a look in the direction his Captain pointed to and swore in a muttering of choice words under his breath, "how she doesn't catch her death out here is beyond my understanding." Directing a stern reprimand to the woman, he swore, *'Angeline, what are you thinking to be out here in this weather?'*

Nearly blanching to the anger felt from husband, a reassuring hand came to caress the swell of her son, "he's far too protective, little one." Teased feeling the hardness of her belly strain and press to the child's understanding. "We best return to Illevante` before he sends his troops after us."

∞∞∞

Sitting to the left of him at the dining table, Angeline barely lifted her eyes from her plate as Nickolai continued to converse with Armand and two of the other seasoned guards of his garrison as their company at the dining table became routine in the last months. Their talk frequently straying to the rising unrest in Plona and the smaller skirmishes which other Keeps were addressing. Only occasionally would a question be directed to her as she had little to say to such talk of war or the implication if Illevante` should be called into such battles.

Finishing with the final course, Angeline quickly excused herself from the table, leaving the conversation behind as she sought company in the kitchens with the cooks and servants who were quick to take her mind from death and the games of grown men. "Countess," one of the serving women ventured as at the summons of the Count, and a second decanter of wine was readied, "the Count is requesting you join him at the table."

Placing aside the needlework she was attempting with the help of cook, Angeline inquired sheepishly, “has Nickolai dismissed the Captain and his men?” With the woman’s rueful nod, a frown tugged to her lips, “he’s going to be furious; he caught me at the training square watching him again.” Angeline couldn’t help the smile to hear their reluctant chuckles to her woeful confession, “alas, it’s lecture time, ladies.”

Martine smirked before she shared, “ah, so that’s why the Count ordered me to hide your heavy cloaks.” The quick click of Angeline's tongue in disapproval was the woman’s reward, “he’s right, you have to be more careful. The weather will be turning soon, and then you can wander all you like.”

“You’re as bad as he.” Angeline teased before returning to the dining room to find her husband alone at the massive table already the book opened before him.

Slowly Nico sipped from the goblet of wine the servant refilled and barely looked in her direction as he pointed to the chair closest to him, a final page finished before he sighed heavily, marked his page then looked to her, “we need to talk, wife.” Came with as much oppression as he could muster to the continued risks she insisted upon taking. With a stern expression, Nico gathered a handful of walnuts and began to crush them within the press of his palm as he stole a quick guarded glance to her anticipation.

Sinking weakly into the chair, she adjusted the flowing folds of material about the growing bulk and attempted to smile to the sternness of his expression, “you’re going to scold me again, aren’t you?” Angeline asked, stealing the nutmeat from the walnuts he cracked as quickly as he could open them. “You saw me watching you from the hill again. I thought Deleon could be trusted.”

Raising a dark brow to the statement, “Deleon can be trusted; you, however, are an entirely other matter.” Nico managed sternly, “I do not mean to scold you as if you are an errant child, Angeline; however, if you continue to throw every caution to the wind, how am I to proceed? How many times do I have to remind you it is not safe for you to be walking about in such weather? What if you fall, you could hurt yourself or the baby? As much as you refuse to believe it, I can't be everywhere, and you know how intensive this time is with the recruits. I have to be sure they're ready for battle, if the Prince is going to call us it will be soon." Casting a glance in her direction, he grumbled, "and my Captain has been more occupied with your safety than that of his garrison; he's getting downright weepy. It makes me wonder who the pregnant one is some days."

Nodding ruefully to the same preaching she had received nearly a half a dozen times in the last two weeks, Angeline attempted not to laugh outright to the vexation which came to his features. "I know, Nico, but lately, you're gone hours at a time, and I do so enjoy watching you train." The lower lip came to be tugged in hopeful intent to ease his worry, "I promise not to venture so far from Illevante` in the future."

"No, you will not venture from Illevante` at all. At least until the weather turns warm or the baby is born, do you understand." He warned, "I have already advised Martine to my wishes."

"But neither is due for another three months, Nico, how can you expect me to stay cooped up in the house for all that time. Hiding my cloaks? Don't you think that rather extreme?" Rising with a groan from the chair with Nico's assistance, she paced before his passive reaction to her objection. If not for the hesitation in the continued cracking of walnuts within his hands, she would have sworn he ignored her, "what if the Prince calls you to duty, am I to stay in the house all by myself till you return. You promised to be here for the delivery."

Nico was chewing slowly to the nutmeat then swallowing thickly to the warming wine as he watched her pacing for silent moments. He had to hold back the smile to see how her hands pressed into the strain of her back as she nearly waddled back and forth under the pressing weight of his child. Scraping the weight of chair back into the path of her walk, he stood before her as admonishing, "listen to me, little pumpkin, you will do as I say to ensure the safety of yourself and my son. Do you understand me?"

"Your son?" Pressing his hands to the insistent kicking and movement of the mentioned son, she smirked, "such possession from a man who I had to blackmail into having a child." And she smiled to see the wonder and joy as he felt the constant movement beneath his touch, "he already knows you." She whispered as the hands splayed over her flesh, as he bent to press his lips to the sweet swell of her body, "and what did you call me? Did I hear the word pumpkin from your lips?"

Catching her hands before she could box his ears, Nico teased, "it's not like I called you fat or grumpy." He defended as returning to the chair and drawing her onto his lap, "and didn't we discuss abusing me?"

"I wasn't listening," Angeline growled as settling into the brace of his thighs she sighed as he captured her close to his length with one hand as the other returned to his book. For long moments she attempted to read the pages, tried to follow the military prose of the storyline only to find her eyes too heavy. Nickolai looked down to see she slept, safe in the protection of his arms. Drawing her closer to his length, he allowed his hand to caress the swell of his child with a loving touch. "All has been made ready for you, son; there will never be a day you are not protected. A day that you will forget the love of your mother and my devotion to your well-being."

Achieving the final incline, Nickolai came to overlook the surrounding lands below, the rumble of the ocean as it erupted with a spray of mist about him as he stared to the beauty of the properties, "the entire household is looking for you. You have Martine, quite worried about your location." Kneeling beside Angeline, he stared into the eyes confronting him with a touch of guilt. "Why are you hiding from her?"

Shrugging her shoulders miserably, Angeline confessed, "Martine wants me to stay abed as if something is wrong with me. I am perfectly fine; I haven't felt this good in months." Doggedly she tugged to lower lip before forcing herself to return her stare to that of the ocean beyond as she realized his motives for finding her, "if you've come to take me back to bed, I am not going."

Fighting the amusement threatening a smile to his face, Nico settled with the surrender at her back, drew her into the protection of his length as he stated, "Martine is only worried about you wandering off; say to a rocky cliff overlooking the ocean." Teased as his hands came to caress the hardness of their child, "he could come any day, what if I couldn't find you in time? What would you do then?"

Closing her hands over the searching ones she managed, "he is quite content where he is right now, at least for a little while longer, and you always know exactly where I am. Don't think you can frighten me into staying home; I waited weeks for the weather to change and be allowed out of the Keeps walls."

Chuckling to her words he simply drew her closer to his length, deeper into the protection of his arms as he realized the plateau she had decided to settle upon, "though I was hoping you would find this place one day, I never anticipated the idea of you being nine months pregnant when you decided to climb up here. How did you manage this all by yourself?"

"I can be quite determined when needed." Snuggling into the comfort of his chest, the strength of arms surrounding her, the whisper, "thank you for showing it to me so many years ago, you don't know how happy it always made me. I always thought it nothing more than a fairy tale castle." Smiling to the memories, Angeline confessed, "though I never saw your face, I always imaged you to be a beautiful prince forever a prisoner in its Keep."

"No fairy tales, and I am only a Count." Pressing his lips into the crown of the nestled head, Nico whispered, "it was always my quest to make you happy."

Twisting about so she could face him Angeline touched the perfection of his features, the mouth she constantly craved to confess, "you have always made me happy, Nico," and tears were seen to well within her glorious eyes, gather there till a single blink allowed them freedom, "I know you didn't want to have this baby---I know I forced you---"

Palming the twisted features within his hands, he pressed the tears away with the pad of his thumbs as the raven head shook to dispel such beliefs, "don't, don't even try to remind me of what an idiot I was. To think I would never want to have our child, that I would never want to feel him growing within you. I know now that you were right; it is up to us to protect him from any harm. You must know, I would do anything in my power to keep him safe for always, Angeline, always."

Nodding as a shaken breath exhaled, she managed grudgingly, "Nico, you remember when I said he was content for a while longer?" With his nod, he suddenly paled to the implication of her question, his eyes instantly dropped to the protruding belly, "I don't believe he's as content."

Scrambling to his feet, Nico drew her up to her own as asking, "are you telling me your pains have started now? Up here?" With her nod, the word "Angeline!" Bellowed out and about the countryside till even the birds halted in their song to the disturbance. "Can you walk?"

"I'm perfectly fine; deliveries can take hours, sometimes days. We will be fine as long as we take it slow." She reassured grateful for the arm coming to encase her waist in support as the growing pain quickly drained her of the needed energy to walk down the winding path.

Taking the lead, Nico attempted to keep one eye on the path and the other on her as it seemed the easy trail followed up was nothing less than a treacherous cliffhanger at every turn, "and you wonder why Martine wants you to stay abed?"

"Nico, stop yelling at me and keep walking." Stopping suddenly, Angeline leaned weakly to a nearby tree, slapping away his assistance as he attempted to learn of the reason, "my water just broke, forgive me for taking a moment to rest." Snapped to his mumbling to the time they were wasting. "Now stop it, you're making our son anxious."

"I'm making him anxious! He's contemplating being born on a mountainside, and I'm making him anxious?" Nico's head shook to the irony of the situation, to the predicaments she always managed to provoke.

"I didn't provoke this!" Angeline barked; her anxiousness was growing to match that of her husband. "Did I know he was going to become discontented at this moment?"

"Why do you think I've been preaching at you for the last six months, for my health?"

Shrugging her shoulders, Angeline retorted, "what else, you always seemed to feel better after doing so." Listening to the string of expletives as they came over Nico's lips, she retorted, "and stop saying such things he doesn't like the tone of voice you're using with me."

"He doesn't like my tone of voice?" Stopping his pacing abruptly to the statement Nico told her with no uncertain terms, "if I'm carrying our son from this mountain anytime within the next few hours neither of you is going to like the tone of voice I'm using. I had no intention of being anywhere near his delivery. I've already picked out a lovely space to pace in the library."

The amusement quickly left her features to his plans, "you don't want to be with me when he's born?" Came with far more pity instead of the anger she intended.

"You'll have enough adoring servants about you, so there's no reason to be concerned with my presence in the room, I would probably only be in the way."

"But I don't want people there that adore me; I want you." And the brow which rose to her statement caused her to shout, "you know what I mean!" Her hand pressed to the perspiration that dotted her forehead as she attempted to lift the weight of hair from her back and shoulders.

Recognizing something he could assist her with, Nico

ripped a strip of leather from his tunic and drew draw the hair up into a thick tail and quickly tied it off as he told her, "there are enough people to take care of you, love, people who will know what they are doing in such a situation. I have experienced a great deal in my life, but assisting in birth is not one of them, and it is not something I wish to experience at this moment."

Turning toward him, she managed softly, "but you're my family, Nico, I have no one else but you."

Signing miserably to the presentation of pleading eyes and trembling chin the raven head could only shake to the battle he knew he had lost even before it had begun, "thank heaven I don't have to meet you on a battlefield, one look and I'd be lost to be sure." Disgusted by his weakness he promised, "if you want me there, I will be there."

"We would both appreciate it." Came with a quick gasp of breath as another pain came quickly to follow the last, the strain to her back increasing as she had the natural urge to press into the insistence of such. "Oh," came with a deep exhale of breath, "they are definitely getting stronger."

Sensing Angeline's deepening pain and worry, Nico sought to ease her to take her mind away from such until safely returned to Illevante'. "I take it your worries about not sensing him have diminished over the last months?"

Nodding, she allowed the arm to once again encircle her in hopes of hastening their descent, "ever since the night he let me know he was hungry, I have been able to sense him, his likes and dislikes." And a smile came to her lips though reluctantly, "he isn't pleased when we were making love, though it does usually put him to sleep." She shared with a giggle to see the expression Nico granted her.

"Better him than you," growled to the confession, "why didn't you tell me?"

"Because you would have been even more aware he was there and wouldn't have made love to me." Grasping his hand, she held to him for only a moment as managing in strained conversation, "could we stop for only a moment." The path stretching before them seem to yawn unending in its lead to Illevante'. '*What was she thinking to walk up here*!' "Maybe next time, you should have a flight of stairs put up here."

"Stairs? Would it be easier for you with the stairs?" Progressing a few feet down the path, he located a fallen tree and led her to it. "Give me a few minutes; I don't know if this is going to work." Angeline looked down to her feet as the very ground beneath her was felt to rumble then heave. The dirt about them to shift as a small tornado grew from the very spot she sat.

The wind gathered till a precision point was achieved, and as if carving the ground, Nickolai directed where to begin work. In only moments a flight of stairs was carved into the dirt before her, "why didn't you think of this twenty minutes ago." Angeline wondered as hand in hand they descended the stairs as they appeared before them.

He mumbled a few select words under his breath then turned to address the darkening skies, "it will be dark soon. Martine will have the entire Keep out looking for us."

Pointing to the torches which were progressing up the path, Angeline managed as joining him on the final rise before the wind lost its strength, and Nico willed the earth to cover any evidence of his craft, "she already has."

∞∞∞

The Count's Guard escorted Angeline from the remaining incline to the safety of the Keep where Martine waited with white-knuckled anticipation, "Countess!" Gasped as Martine witnessed the state she returned in, "what in the name of all that is holy happened?" A scathing look of accusation passed over her shoulder to the Count, who followed in their wake.

Patting the hand which engulfed her own in leading assistance, Angeline assured, "I'm perfectly fine, Martine, only the baby has decided it's time for him to join the rest of the world, and my water broke on the way down." Casting an amused expression to her husband, she conspired with the woman, "I fear we have scared the Count nearly to death; Nico was certain he would be carrying the baby before we left the mountain." Leaving the procession of Guards at the chamber doors, Angeline was grateful for the thick warm robe tugged about her shoulders once removing the gown and cloak. "I would like to take a bath, Martine, could you have the necessary things laid out for me."

"Yes, Countess."

Coming from his dressing room to hear her request, Nico wondered, "do you think it's wise at such a time."

"It's fine, Nico, the worse to happen is I'll give birth in the tub." A teasing smile was directed toward him, "care to join me?"

"Angeline!" Bellowed as he stalked after her escape into the bathing room.

"Nickolai!" Retaliated as she attempted to slip into the steaming waters without falling face first.

Throwing his hands into the air with total surrender, he slipped into the waters then helped her to settle onto the marble bench, "you know you are probably one of the most stubborn women I have ever met in my entire life."

Nodding, she pointed to space beside her and forced him to sit. "I know, but you love me anyway," teased as she instructed him to rub the tenderness of her lower back as the pains seemed to increase as each wave of pressure built within her.

"It's my only weakness." Gently he massaged the strain of her back, allowed his hands to radiate the heat which would ease the growing pain, "feel better?" With a content sign and nod, she sagged weakly to his length. Pointing to the toiletries Martine left at the tub's rim, he instructed, "hand me your comb."

Carefully the leather strip was removed from hair as he combed through the length till all snarls disappeared, and she was nearly asleep in her lean against him. Carefully plaiting the hair down her back as she rested in the brace of thighs, '*Nico?*' Whimpered as she rallied to the building pain. '*I am here.*' Taking the hands as they came to caress her shoulders with the reassurance of his presence, she brought them to their son, allowed his warm touch to ease her, "perhaps we should allow Martine to see to you, little one?" Nico stressed as her body was felt to press and breath to quicken to the building pains.

"You will stay with me?" Angeline asked, clutching her hands about the easing ones, holding to him as the breath seemed to escape her, and the child's urgency was felt to sweep her. "He's so close, so determined, Nico, please stay with me."

Drawing her into his arms, he lifted her from the water to the bedroom where Martine, as well as a bevy of servants, seemed to be waiting with breath held expectation to the event, "I'll be back in a moment, I swear." He promised as water pooled about his feet from the wet trousers worn. "I'm only going to change my clothes, and I'll be right back."

Reluctantly she allowed him to escape the room for his dressing quarters as Martine was quick to pull a cropped dressing coat about her quickly dried length and ease her worried expression with a loving touch. "It will be soon, Countess, soon." Allowing the woman to clutch her hand as another contraction came to ravage her length.

Nodding in agreement, Angeline looked to the path Nico had followed and allowed short pants of breath to escape as the pain grew to match her anxiety. "Nico!" Cried pitifully, causing him to rush from the dressing room and gather her close to his length. "Let's get you to bed, little one." Laying back against his chest as Nico propped himself behind her, Angeline nearly sighed as his hands returned with an easing heat to her tortured spine, "that feels so good." She relaxed against the brace of the chest as she sought his comfort "he's so strong, Nico, so determined."

"What else could he be, little one." He promised as he looked over Angeline's cradled head to that of Martine, who could do little else than wait as the hours continued to slip by, and the pains grew in pressure.

Sleeping because exhaustion claimed her Angeline woke with a start as another pain came, “he’s coming,” she cried as Nickolai allowed her to grasp his hands and crush him to the intensity. Allowed the small, tired body to use his in resistance to the final pushes.

“Countess!” Martine cried as a final scream pushed forth the child into the hands of the waiting servant. Already wailing to the injustice of plight as emerald eyes opened and stared at the gathering that searched for imperfections upon the tiny pink length. “It’s a girl!”

“Impossible!” Nickolai gasped to the announcement, and he came quickly to open the covering draped about the tiny body. “There has never been a female born to Illevante`. You must be mistaken.” Fingers found and instantly traced the circle with an arrow positioned diagonally upwards at the base of her skull, given the evidence needed to her gifts as an Illevante`. Already the raven hair covered the marking as Nickolai whispered against the dampened cheek of his wife, “you are far more remarkable than you can believe.”

“Count,” Martine reprimanded sternly, “I would like to think I know a little girl when I see one. She is a beautiful daughter, Count.” Martine reassured, as his blue eyes never left that of the tiny screaming bundle in the trusted servant’s hands.

"Of course, she is, do you not see her mother!" Pressing his lips to the forehead of Angeline’s, he whispered, hoping to hide the tears which were felt to thicken in his eyes, “She’s perfect, little one, a perfect miracle to be sure.”

“Bring her to me, Nico,” Angeline whispered, her throat raw and voice exhausted, “let me hold her.” A motion of his hand brought forth the tiny swathed bundle on the arm of a servant. With Nico's help, Angeline drew herself up into a sitting position as Martine continued to clean and pack the ripping of her flesh. “She’s wondrous, is she not, Nico?”

“Truly, my love.” He managed still in awe of the child,

even as his heart nearly broke to the implication of the female child in the scheme of his family's prophecy.

Lifting her eyes from the perfection of child Angeline studied her silent husband for silent moments before inquiring, “you’re not disappointed in her, are you, Nico?” Was questioned to see the absolute disbelief as it still adorned his staring eyes.

Slowly the raven head shook as his knuckles came to caress the infant’s cheek, palm the raven hair as it crowned her head, “how could something so perfect be a disappointment to any man, my love?”

Cuddling the tiny length to her breast, Angeline whispered, "the ancients were wrong, Nico, do you think they could be wrong about the prophecies they torment with."

"I don't know, my love, I wish I could tell you they were wrong, that they are wrong about everything."

∞∞∞

Welcoming the warmth of blankets over her length Angeline managed now that they were alone, “I know you were expecting a son, and now you’ll have to get used to two crying females in your life.”

“I’m only now beginning to fathom the idea of having to contend with men seeking her company as urgently as they seek her mother’s.” He teased settling beside her on the bed, drawing her carefully into the protection of his length where his arm came to enfold her to his body, “she is perfect, Angeline, what more could I possibly hope for?” With a wearying smile, Angeline settled contently against him, allowing the sleep her body needed to embrace her.

Captain Deleon cautiously opened the doors to the

master's chamber to see the man as he remained on the bed, his wife cradled to the protection of his length. Soundly he entered the room as the woman slept as the child held in his Count's arms. "Count," he began as coming to the bedside with the Count's beckon, "please forgive me. I would like to send word to the village that all is well with the Countess and the infant; with your permission, of course." His eyes looked down to the cradled infant and smiled to the contentedness of the child, "she is a fine little girl, Milord."

Blue eyes came from the cradle of his daughter to reassure, "she is perfect, Captain." Gently easing Angeline to the piled pillows beyond, he came to place the infant beside her before coming from the draped confides. "As soon as the Countess has regained her strength, I will have a meeting with you, Captain. It is of the utmost importance to me, and I want you to decide before we meet if you are willing to see to the safety of the Countess above all others." Nickolai drew him from the bed even as objections were seen to rise into his eyes that the man would ever doubt his loyalty to the family he served, "do not answer me now, only know that this will be a feat that will seem to span more than a single lifetime." Ushering the man from the room, he closed the door firmly on the confusion found there before returning to the whimper of his wakening daughter.

"You would trust him?" Martine questioned as she appeared from the shadows as the infant's demands grew with agitation.

"I know he will keep her safe; he is in love with her. He has been since the beginning and I have no choice. Do you not see now with a daughter there is no reason for Angeline not to complete the prophecy and Angeline to return to me? When it is time two of Illevante` will be cursed, the child will be with me." Turning toward the bed as the infant began to fuss into wakefulness, he watched his wife and daughter for silent moments before stating, "see to her needs, Martine, I don't wish to have Angeline woken just yet. She needs her strength for the days to come."

Drawing the infant into her arms, “she’s a hungry one, to be sure.” Martine teased, smiling proudly to the baby within her arms, “I will summon a wet nurse for the babe to feed while the Countess is resting, little Sophie from the kitchens gave birth only a few months ago she will be more than happy to help.”

“Martine, no.” Came as Angeline's head lifted from the pillows, “I will see to her needs.” Gingerly she pulled herself up, and the simple movement was seen to weaken her significantly, “I will be fine.” She admonished to the concern of her husband, as his worries came to blanket her with objection. “I can’t lay here forever and do nothing; she needs me.”

“You could wait until you have regained your strength.” Nickolai admonished gently, coming to arrange the pillows about her back, helping her into a more comfortable position before returning the child into her arms.

“I want to see to her every need, Nico.” She reprimanded gently as if she already fought time; the so precious moments, she would have with her. With Martine’s gentle instruction, the child was soon suckling hungrily at her breast, and Angeline passed a proud smile to her forever watchful husband, “have you thought of a name?”

“You seem to be handling everything perfectly; I thought that was also one of the many things you had already taken care of.” He answered, coming to settle on the bed beside her. "Of the many things we discussed to this day, naming never seemed to come up."

“That was the easiest part I was going to name him after you.” A loving smile was given to the child, “Nickolai is a bit too strong for a little girl to carry all of her days, however, if you didn't mind, I would like to name her Nicole, after her father.” She announced, “little Nici, would be fine till she is old enough to hate me for calling her such.”

Palming the raven head of spiky hair as it seemed to stick straight out from all angles on her tiny head Nickolai agreed, “Nici it shall be.”

∞∞∞

Nickolai threw the parchment down to the clutter of his desk as he read the simple message, "arriving soon; Andrew will be coming to offer congratulations to the birth of your daughter. You will find enclosed a contract of marriage for your daughter. Phillip." '*Contract of marriage,*' Nico spat casting a disgusted look to the message which had arrived only weeks after the birth of his child, Nici wasn't even six weeks old, and already she was engaged to a man he had yet to meet. Explaining this contract is not a conversation he wished to share with his wife---ever: came with realized intent.

∞∞∞

"You should be resting; there's no reason to push yourself so hard, you'll have more than your hands full of her soon enough." Nico reprimanded looking up from the sleeping baby in his arms to find Angeline at his shoulder; "she's sleeping just fine."

Touching the innocent cheek, she reached down to first press a kiss to the infant's head then to her husband's cheek, "what of you, while I lay abed all day, you are the one seeing to everyone's needs. You wake every time she cries and remain with me through every feeding; you'll be far more exhausted than I to be sure." Teased as draping her arms about the breadth of his shoulders, she whispered, "I knew you would be a wonderful father, that's why I love you so." In the firelight, Angeline saw the worry in his eyes, the hooded expression as it came to such confession, "what is it, my love, are you not happy?"

"I don't think there has been a time when I have been happier, or more in love with you, or our daughter." He rose from the chair occupied to return the sleeping child to her cradle, "I never even suspected what pride could be until I watched her come from your body, and I held her in my arms." Capturing Angeline's hand, Nico drew her back to their bed, where he cradled her in his arms as she snuggled contently beside him.

Caressing the stern line of his jaw under her fingertips as the oppression of his emotions was enough to make her pause to the happiness he confessed to, "but still something is not right. Something has you worried; if it's me I assure you I have never felt better, and Nicole is perfect. Have you ever seen a more beautiful baby?"

Smiling to her nervous rambling, Nico reassured, "no, there has never been one more beautiful." Caressing the troubled crease of brow he began hesitantly, "Angeline, I need to ask you a question---" seeing the glorious eyes raise to him Nico faltered for a moment to his direction, to the inevitable future they would hold, "if there ever came a time when we would be apart do you think you would fall out of love with me? Will there ever come a time when you wouldn't need me?"

Clutching his waist, worry came to the battle looming before them, "you have been with me always, Nico, a thousand years could pass, and still I would love you, I would need you. As long as I could sense you, feel you within me, I would always have you. Are these worries of separation because of that ridiculous quest Prince Phillip is pursuing in Plona? Do you think you will be called for help soon?" Not trusting himself to answer, he nodded as pressing a kiss to the worried plain of her forehead, "I will love you always, Nico."

A critical eye read briefly over the marriage contract before him, the land and titled position coming to his daughter upon reaching the age of seventeen. Lifting his line of scrutiny from the parchment to the man and boy before him, Nikolai stated, "apparently it is your contention to become adjoined to the Illevante` Keep by any means possible." Nickolai nearly sneered to Baron Stephano as he sat with quiet smugness to the ultimatum the crowned prince placed before Illevante`.

Allowing the smallest of smiles to come from the thin line of his mouth Michael Stephano managed softly, "it is my contention to honor the decree set before us from the Crowned Prince Phillip, and as a father, with five sons' it is also my duty to see that all have marriages which will benefit. As I'm sure, it would also be your contention. Daniel is my firstborn, destined to inherit the Stephano holdings and title. I assure you, Count; your daughter will want for naught with such a match as theirs."

Easing his shoulders to the tension which seemed to make him ready to break something, anything, Nickolai set his sights on the boy beside the Baron, "you will have quite a wait for her, she is no more than a few weeks old."

Raising his eyes and forcing them to confront the massive man who remained behind the width of desk, Daniel managed with all of the sureness a ten-year-old could muster to his place in life, "it is a wait worth anticipating, Count Illevante`, once we join our families we will be a mighty force against any attempting to wrong us." Nodding to the sincerity of the boy, Nickolai placed the quill to ink and scratched his signature across the parchment. He was wondering briefly to himself how he would explain to Angeline what he had just done without first consulting her.

The Count Nickolai Illevante` sat behind his massive black mahogany desk, waiting as his most trusted Captain entered at his bidding. "Captain, please come and sit." The chair placed before desk was pointed to and the marriage contract for his daughter was placed securely to safe, "I don't have much time to explain as I so wished, all I can tell you is men are approaching Illevante` as we speak. Men who have come to see me dead on this night." Nickolai reached into the top drawer of his desk and withdrew a packet of papers he had been fastidiously working on since the first day of his marriage. "These men are coming here under the veil of bringing congratulations and gifts for my daughter from the Prince. I want you to arrange with the Guard to make sure none of them leave my keep alive. I don't care what happens or how you do it; all I want is for you to avenge what will happen to my family on this night."

Standing Nickolai came about the massive piece of furniture to pace before the man's stunned silence, "I know your first reaction will be to kill them yourself, but I want---" he thought better to the circumstance, "I need you to stay with the Countess. Above all else, I need you to see that she is brought safely from these walls." Pressing the packet of papers into the silent man's hands; "these are for the Countess once you have her safely from here. When you leave the Keep you must take her down to the beach, along the outcropping of the rocks there is a cave. Within that cave, you will find a secured door," the key as ancient as Illevante ` was placed within his capable hands, "you will bring the Countess before this door, once inside you are to leave her and wait on the beach. In the morning, when it is safe, there will be a carriage waiting your departure."

Armand listened silently to all the man shared with him to the mysterious knowledge he possessed even to his death, "Milord, let me see to your safety now, let me take you as well as your family away from here. I have men, trusted men, who will see that these blackhearts never lay a hand on you. I will keep you safe as I always have."

Rising from the lean against desk, Nickolai cursed the emotion he felt growing, the helplessness when all he wished was to escape all that threatened him and his family. "You have always been a good, trusted friend, Armand, but there is something that I need to finish. Something that must begin, all I need is your word that you will stay with the Countess. That you will keep her safe until she can return to me."

Carefully the packet was placed into the fold of his doublet, patted with reassurance to its safety, "you keep mentioning for me to stay with the Countess, but what of the baby? Will you have me take the infant, Nici, also?"

Fighting the thickening of his throat, Nickolai reluctantly shook his head, "no, the child will not live through the night." And with the spoken words, Nickolai strode from the room, leaving the man to wonder to all the working of his Count's world.

∞∞∞

Cradled in the strength of his massive hands, Nici seemed to stare with wondrous green eyes to that of her father, her tiny fingers wrapped tightly about a single of his. "I will keep you safe, Nici, don't be afraid. I will always be there for you." He swore as tears traced Nickolai's cheeks, "you have to know this one thing to be true; I love you. I may have vowed never to allow my child to be born, but now be with you in my arms, in my heart, I love you as I have never loved before. You make me proud to look down at you and know that out of the love of your mother, you have come." Pressing his lips to the powder-soft plain of the forehead, Nickolai allowed the touch to hold for long moments before returning the infant to cradle. Securing the door to nursery behind him, he was greeted by a servant who rushed to tell him the Prince's guard had arrived; the guests were waiting.

∞∞∞

A final tug went to the snugness about her waist as Angeline groaned to the extra effort Martine took in closing the corset about her length, "I'm as fat as a pig!" Came with exasperation to the torture, "nothing is ever going to fit me again."

"Then, I will have more dresses made for you." Came in

tease as Nickolai entered her dressing room to find it in quite a state of disarray, "you don't have to dress for this arrival, little one, put on your best dressing gown and prop yourself amongst a pile of pillows. Nothing more is expected of you; you are, after all, the new mother."

Looking over her shoulder to his approach, a look of utter disdain was his reward, "as if I'd allow that beast into my chambers!" Hissed before another gasp of air came from her. Allowing the final knots to be completed, she waited as the gown was tugged over her head then adjusted about her length. "I don't even know why Phillip would send him; you would think for all you do he would come himself."

Caressing the heat of her cheek, he explained once again, "Phillip is quite preoccupied with Plona, he isn't thinking straight. This stretch of land has become nothing less than an obsession for him. I have heard he is pulling men into his service that have had no previous experience, using nothing short of blackmail to recruit them."

"Nevertheless, none of his encounters would have been victories if not for you and your planning." Managed as she slipped on shoes and turned to confront him, "do I look like a pumpkin?"

Slowly Nickolai allowed his eyes to caress the woman before him; the beauty and grace possessed more than enough to stop his heart, "my love, you are breathtaking." His eyes landed pointedly on the expanse of the exposed breast, "Martine, isn't there something we can do about the neckline?" Chuckling to his worries and the instant blush that came to cap the Countess's cheek, she artfully tucked a length of lacy linen into the neckline, "perhaps we should commission a few dresses with collars up to here." Her chin was teased.

"Nico!" Gasped as grasping his arm, she forced him from the dressing rooms down to the main gathering room where their guests were instructed to wait. "You know it's only because of Nici. I'm like this."

"Ah, only one more incentive to bring the rest of my

children to me." Tickled over her ear as he captured her waist under his arm and tugged her along the many hallways. Stopping before the entrance to the gathering room, Nickolai drew Angeline into his arms, captured her to his length for silent moments as he stared to the woman before him. "Little one," he managed as framing the questionable expression within the palms of his hands, "I want you to know how happy you have made me, how I have never ---" the voice caught to the emotion building within him to the worry which clouded her eyes to the overwhelming love he emanated toward her, "---loved like this before. I love you, Angeline Illevante`. I will love you forever. I must know you believe this; I must know you will keep Nicole and me in your heart for always. Promise me." His mouth crushed over hers, his arms tightened into a near punishing hold as he wanted nothing more than to never enter the room beyond or the destiny unfolding about them.

Slowly Angeline raised her hands to caress the face so close to her own as the kiss came to a lingering end, as the tears which clouded his eyes cause her own emotion to rise. Her senses sought the smallest of disturbances, which would explain such a declaration as the one stated, "you are my life, Nico, our daughter my soul how could I not hold you both unto my heart. I will love you; I will keep you forever."

Entering the gathering room, instantly a hush befell the room as Prince Andrew, as well as her brother, Stephen confronted her. "Stephen!" Gasped as Angeline immediately cleaved to the protection of her husband's side, "brother, I was not expecting you as part of the Prince's guard." Forcing herself to leave Nickolai's side, Angeline came to embrace Stephen, press her lips to the cool of his cheek. "It is so good to see you; it's been far too long." Turning to Andrew, a proper greeting went to the silent man who stared with only the smallest of nods in recognition. "Prince, you honor Illevante` with your visit, I was not aware that you were acquainted with my brother." Directing an enigmatic smile to the silence of sibling, Angeline pressed, "apparently father has changed his ideals toward court life."

"Your brother and I, Countess, have come to an instant companionship once learning we shared similar interests." The man's eyes were seen to slowly sweep over her length, causing Angeline to feel the discomfort of the room surrounding her. "We have, how you would say, shared--- passions." And a knowing chuckle passed between the two men.

Lowering her eyes from the inspection; the menacing intent of their emotions, Angeline managed as retreating she return to the sanctuary of Nickolai's side, "I'm sure father is most pleased with your endeavors, Stephen." Absentmindedly she tugged to the hand which claimed her waist, pressed closer to the security of Nickolai if only for reassurance to her safety. "I had planned to visit Belaveuta as soon as Nicole was strong enough for such travels, I know father has been very anxious to see his granddaughter."

"I'm sure he's most anxious," Stephen grumbled as he turned from her seemingly knowing eyes.

∞∞∞

The evening seemed endless, as Nickolai was in constant pre-occupation with the visitors before them and their conversations were pointless and inconsequential. Angeline could sense her husband's agitation and only wished to question him, as it was apparent the men before her though civil appeared to be preoccupied to a shared scheming, though she decided after attempting to sense their emotions found they were only anxious and confusing in how quickly they swung from one thought to another.

Acknowledging Martine's appearance in the door's frame, Angeline rose to the needs of her daughter. "Please excuse me." Relieved with the excuse to leave the room, she even smiled as the door to the sitting-room opened, and Stephen entered.

"I heard she is beautiful." Stephen commented, crossing the slight distance between them. Critically his dark eyes looked down to the raven-haired bundle in her mother's arms the cherub mouth as it was found to be suckling hungrily at the perfect pinkened flesh as he pressed the covering from the infant's head, "at least she has your eyes." Stephen grunted as he settled beside his sister in the silence of the moments raging between them. "Have the woman take her; I need to speak to you." He commanded, motioning Martine forward with an aggravated motion of his hand.

Placing Nicole into the trusted woman's arms when the feeding was completed, a quick kiss was pressed to her sleepy forehead as Angeline turned back to confront her brother, "Stephen, I am so happy that you are here, I never thought to see you in Illevante'."

Scoffing to her feigned joy at seeing him, Stephen was quick to sneer, "nor will you ever think to see me here again." Rising from the settee Stephen towered over the crowding worry of her features as he enlightened Angeline to reasoning behind his visit, "I have come to take you from this place, from this man. It is time for this farce of a marriage to come to an end; for Father to realize the mistake he has made in conspiring with the devil."

Emerald eyes stared for silent moments as if trying to discover if he had indeed lost the last of his sense in confessing such to her, in believing she would be a willing party to this scenario, "you are gravely mistaken if you believe I will leave with you. I love Nickolai, and I refuse to have you do anything you will be sorry for later." Fearful eyes were cast upon the man as he towered above her seat, and with a single thought of returning to the safety of Nico's presence, she sought her husband with her mind only to find him closed to her, '*Nico?*' Cried to the fear as it escalated within her, '*what is happening? Where are you?*'

"Already plans are in the works, little sister." Sneered as his hand came to caress the paling of her cheek down over the column of her throat where the fingers tightened in threat to any resistance she may attempt, tightening till she clawed to the fingers pressing into her flesh, "already the Prince has distracted your loving husband making it possible for us to possess you for always."

Ripping the hand away from its hold, Angeline thought to move about his menacing strength only to find herself caught in the band of restraining arms, "what are you doing, Stephen, don't you realize what the Count is capable of?" With the issuance of such words, a blood-curdling scream was heard to echo through the halls of Illevante'. "Oh, Sweet Jesus, what have you done?"

Opening the door to the main gathering room at first Angeline was overwhelmed by the smoke filling the room, the smell of burning flesh which assaulted her senses as a fire was seen to be smoldering from the center of the room, "Nickolai!" Angeline screamed as the Illevante' guard filled the room, and she fought to press through the circle they attempted to protect her in, the fires they fought to extinguish. "Nico!" Cried as she felt him reach out to her, sensed him in such terrible pain.

"Countess," Armand was suddenly before her, and the surrounded of guard separated to allow her access, "the Count wouldn't allow me to protect him. Wouldn't let anyone into the room until it was too late." He explained as taking her arm; he led her to the center of the great room. Led through the destruction and smell of death encompassing the room, Armand whispered, "you should prepare yourself, Countess," as he attempted to prepare her for the scene unfolding. Briefly, her eyes went to figures covered by rugs as wisps of smoke were seen to escape the lengths hidden beneath. "Countess, you need to understand what happened here, you need to be strong."

Twisting her arm free of the Captain's leading hold, she felt as if her entire life was suddenly slipping away from her, "Nico?" Escaped as no more than a pained whimper as she recognized him to be the one his guard attempted to comfort on the floor. "Nico?" Weakly Angeline dropped to her knees before his length as it was apparent all the blood which seeped into the marble tile was that of her husband's. Trembling hands attempted to pull the torn and bloody tunic back about his weeping chest as her hands pressed to close the gaping wounds marring his flesh. "Why would he have done this to you?" Looking up into the concern of the Guard, she questioned, "Why?"

Reaching up, Nickolai touched the tears as they streamed over her pale features, "listen to me, little one, and heed the words I will share with you. The time we have is limited." The blood seeped endlessly from the wounds that tattered his clothing, each attempted breath brought forth a
thickened, hot, rush over hands which couldn't quench the flow.

Uselessly Angeline pressed her hands against the ravage of his chest; fought to control the hysteria that rose thickly within her as voices could be heard to be rushing at them even as his blood continued to pool. "Nico, please, what is happening? Why is it happening?" She cried her tears spilling from her cheeks to drip into the crimson pool surrounding her,

Vaguely she became aware as selected Illevante' Guard quickly searched the home for further betrayers, Deleon shouting orders and securing the surroundings as the wail of an infant could be heart to rise from the room beyond. "Nickolai, what am I to do? What can I do?"

"You are the only one to save us." The blood bubbled to Nico's lips, sprayed from his mouth as a weakening cough erupted from lips, "they have cursed me as they have cursed the others of my family. You will end this curse, little one. When the dogs of war are named from the planet of blood, so shall the curse be lifted; so, shall you return to me. You will believe yourself to suffer a hundred thousand nights without me, but I will be with you, I will always love you. You will return to me---to us. Keep yourself safe. Armand will be with you; he will keep you unto us." Shifting his stare from wife to Captain, Nickolai reinforced, "I charge you to keep her safe until you are both returned to me, do not fail me, Armand, remember all I have empowered you with." Weakly he touched the tears as they streamed over her cheeks, tracing the path with a slight smile coming to bloodied lips, "you are always crying." The blue eyes turned from her, and a shuttered breath seemed to heave the ground beneath her. The skies opened, and the ancients of Illevante' exploded in a wail of sorrow.

Contemplating the fierceness of the sudden storm as it battered the Keep with thunder and lightning Armand closed his hand about her arm attempting to draw her from her husband's side, "Countess," from the blood seeping into an encircling puddle about the Count's body. "It is his wish that we leave this place now that you are kept safe."

"My daughter, bring me, my daughter." Struggling from his leading hold, Angeline demanded, "my daughter, bring me, my daughter! Bring me, my daughter." She screamed as the infant's cries silenced.

Staggering into the room, Martine struggled to manage the final steps till she fell from lethal wounds, "I'm so sorry, Countess," cried as the battered infant's body was held to her dying length, "I tried so hard to save her. I tried."

The scream leaving Angeline swelled from the darkest recesses of her soul and reverberate over and through the halls of the great Illevante ` Keep. Those that occupied the room would later swear that it seemed the very walls wailed to the injustice, that tears could be witnessed to seep from the stone surrounding them.

Falling across the breadth of her husband's chest, Angeline drew the cold stillness of her infant into her father's arms; attempted to bring Nickolai's hands up in protection of Nicole, "he will keep her safe, he will hold her!" Came in carefully controlled hysteria to those remaining in surround and security to the final moments of their Count and the woman who loved him.

"Countess, it is time for us to leave. It is as the Count so wished." The head shook against anything more than merely remaining beside her husband and child.

"No!" Screamed up at Armand as he attempted to draw

her away, as the Guard moved to place covering over the child's twisted and broken body, "no, he will keep her safe! He will keep her safe!"

"Please, the murderer of your child has been found and will be punished accordingly to his crime. There is no longer any reason for you to remain here."

A trembling hand came to swipe to the tears on her face smearing the features with the darkness of drying blood, "bring him before me." Angeline commanded. "Bring him to me now! I want to see the face of the man capable of such a thing." Looking up as the Guard dragged the accused before her, Angeline stared into the eyes of her brother to ask, "how could you have done this, Stephen? How could you have murdered my husband and child? Taken an innocent life? Did you think this would endear you to me, did you think I would want to be with you, love you?"

His eyes darkened to the hatred found in hers, the body revolt to the woman who remained grieving over one such as Illevante', "you should have been mine. The bastard spawn from his seed was of little consequence when it was my child that should have grown within you, my seed which plowed your fertile womb, the evil---" and the toe of his boot kicked at Nickolai body, "--- deserved to be wiped clean of this earth. You should be rejoicing in the freedom I have bestowed upon you; no longer are you associated with this abomination."

Rising slowly from the clutch of her family, Angeline came from her husband, the dagger which laid at Nico's lifeless chest dragged along with her, without thought or provocation to her actions the blade buried deeply into her brother's chest. Plunged to the depth of his heart with a strength never realized before. Angeline held it deep within him, both her of her hands closed over the hilt as she held it steady till the heart within him was felt to stutter than slow. As the life to slowly ebb from the surprise of his features, "now you too can rejoice in the freedom I have given you. Only you will be going to hell where you have always belonged." Instantly she felt the fire spreading through her length, from hand to heart, the glow of the ring which adorned her finger held her attention as words rushed quickly through her head. *"When blood is shed of one who isn't, so shall you remain to claim your love."* The air gathered, the heat of her body burned, and the hand which held the dagger within Stephan's chest began to bleed. The blood erupted from the wound, flowed in vine about her wrist dripping to her husband and child.

Armand was instantly attempting to pry her fingers from about the guard of the dagger as he dragged her from the room, pleading to her to come with him before the Prince's remaining guard arrived to ask unnecessary questions.

Racing from the Keep, Angeline was barely aware of the path the Captain had chosen or the route they would use as escape until the crash of the tide was heard to penetrate her numbness. The icy rains washing along her flesh, taking the blood of her husband and child in its fury, "where are we going?" She cried, stumbling along in his haste to lead her to safety.

"There is a place the Count instructed me to bring you to," Armand shouted over the battle of heaven as it raged above their heads, the ocean as it crashed in an unknown fury. "Here!" And he drew her deep into the recesses of a darkened cave, nearly falling against a door which guarded the entrance beyond. The key came to be pressed into her hand as a torch was located and put to light. "He instructed you to go inside; I will wait for you at the beach." Seeing her hesitation to all that had happened on such a night, he pressed, "go, Countess, I will see that you are safe."

Trembling fingers worked the key for merely a moment before the heavy door slid soundlessly open, accepting the torch he pressed into her hands, hesitantly Angeline entered the chamber beyond. For long moments she stood in the engulfing blackness till her eyes could adjust, then slowly, she turned to see the markings and crystals which surrounded her. Stepping to the center of the room, Angeline placed the torch into the holder and confronted a throne of gold and jewels. "Sweet

Jesus." Escaped as she turned to realize the history surrounding her. She read of the curse sending descendants of Illevante` and those that they loved into a separate realm, not quite a death but not life. Witnessed markings to a planet of blood, which gave documentation to this very moment in her life, weakly Angeline settled onto the golden throne as the blood from her hand continued to drip to the sands at her feet.

Covering her face, Angeline allowed the sobs to escape, allowed the heartbreak to overwhelm as she slumped weakly from the chair to the ground where she laid for long moments curled tightly about herself weeping to all that she had lost, "Nico!" Screamed as hours seemed to pass and she realized she could no longer sense him or their child, the understanding of such isolation caused her screams to have no end.

∞∞∞

Exhausted, she laid curled in the sand, the wounded hand wrapped in the bandage of her hem as she stared to the likenesses catching her attention. Rising on weak legs, Angeline came to the walls, touched the figures which could be nothing less than that of her husband's ancients, and wondered, "why have you done this? Why have you taken them from me?" *'None has been taken from you, beckon them.'* They implored, *'before you lose them to the shadows!'*

Gently the air about her stirred, the warmth as it crept up her spine in a gasp to its familiarity, "Nico?" Angeline cried as she spun to the nothingness, "where are you?" Demanded as shadows began to play about her, nothing more than a trick to her eye as she turned toward each only to lose them to the flicker of the torch. "Are you here?" When only the silence confronted her, Angeline slid down along the wall, gathered her tortured hand to her breast, and held it to her. "Why can't I feel you?"

'Little one,' came softly, causing her to gasp to the clarity

of his voice, the gentleness of his reassurance, '*I am with you. We will always be with you.*' Reaching up, she touched the coolness of the wall as if he was trapped forever within the rock, '*you must remain with Armand, little one, he has all that you will need to survive. He has all that you will need until you return to me, to us.*'

A sobbed breath escaped her to hear such words, for she knew somehow they were only in her head, she knew he had become one of his cursed ancients, “Nici is with you, isn’t she, Nickolai, tell me she is with you. Tell me I haven’t lost you both.”

Pressing into the air which surrounded her, Angeline felt the gentleness of touch as it came to her tears, heard the words, '*we are together, my love, we will always be waiting for you. Now go, little one, the sun is rising. You must go while it is safe for you to do so.*'

Twelve

1877

Angeline pulled from the bed with a cry to the pain endured, "why do you torture me?" Sobbed as she fought to be from the thickness of air surrounding her, struggled to keep the memories far from her, "do you think even after all these years that I would forget? Do you think it would be so easy!"

Pacing the length of the room in angered strides the readied weapon was confronted, the invitation so intriguing if only to end the madness once and for all. "I can't do this anymore!" Angeline cried into the air about her, to the heaven's themselves, "I can't live any longer; please don't make me." Spinning about as the door to her chambers opened, Angeline stared silently to the man who came to gather her into his arms. "Please, Armand, let me end this for both of us. Perhaps then you can also find peace. You can go on without me."

Caressing the head as it came to his shoulder as she held to him against the madness of her existence, Armand swore, "if that were the answer, I would gladly do this for you. I would end such misery for both of us." Bringing her back to arms distance he led her to the desk where a newspaper came to be laid out before him, "I have a contact at a library in the city, she lets me know when anything is happening in the ways of our predicament."

A snort of disgust came to the eternal hopefulness Armand greeted each day with, to how effortlessly he embraced the changes which came with each of the decades they survived. "What would she know of 'in the ways of our predicament'?" Angeline's eyes quickly read over the many happenings before her, and her head shook without understanding, "this is a paper from the Americas." She stated not fully understanding what she was reading. Nodding, Armand pointed to the article naming a scientist and astronomer commissioned by the United States Naval Observatory, who had begun to make remarkable breakthroughs in the study of planet Mars. "What does this mean to me?"

"I have had a few years to analyze the curse which has surrounded Illevante`, the words the Count used to spare you living without him. A way for you to return to him. Do you not remember the significance of the planet Mars in Illevante`, even in the chamber when he came to you? Don't you remember telling me of the depiction of Mars on every wall, on the clock in the entry." His hand came up as if to stop her words before speaking them, "the blood of the planet, Mars is the red planet. The blood of planets, the Count, had to be speaking of this one happening, we need to see this man. We need to make sure that whatever he is searching for is found that he has the means to continue with his research."

The auburn head shook against the illogical thinking of the man, "you are telling me we have survived for over three hundred years all for the findings of this---Asaph Hall? How many of these fool errands do we have to run to, how much money do I have to invest in imbeciles only to learn that all is futile." She questioned as reading the remainder of the tiny article, "how can this mere man who studies the stars bring me back to my husband and child? There is no end to this curse; there is no way for me to return to my husband. You have to let me do what I must; you have to let me kill myself."

"It's been three hundred and eighteen, to be more exact, and I have given my word that I would take care of you. I would see you safely returned to Count Illevante', I will not break that promise now when the end could be so near. When the answers may be staring us in the face." The man's shoulders could only shrug, "I don't know, Countess; all I know is what I feel, and I know this man, this Asaph Hall," his finger stabbed to the article which laid between them, "is the means to our end. Somehow you are enduring all this time, all this hardship to end the curse which refuses to allow an Illevante` to pass away. This curse is one that keeps them in some other sense of being until you can return to him and therefore setting them free."

"I can remember at least five countries we have visited all in the telling of some astronomer who has an interest in this damned planet!" Settling weakly to the desk Angeline wearily covered her eyes with the palms of her hands as the head shook uselessly to the grasping of such an idea, "I don't know what to do anymore, Armand, I don't know what to feel."

Touching the heave of slumped shoulders, he managed to tease, "we have yet to visit the Americas. Think of it as a great new adventure. They do, after all, call it the new country. Or we could go back to Italy; I understand there is promising work being done there by Schiaparelli."

Allowing a sigh of resignation to release from her lungs with a snort to his persistence, she managed softly, "find out when the next ship leaves for America, book passage on it for two." Angeline instructed as reaching for her handbag a thick of currency came to be pressed into his hand, "you will tell them we are husband and wife, Armand, I have no wish to sink to the bottom of the sea without you beside me."

"Yes, Countess." And with a stiff bow to her instructions, he left the room.

"Yes, Countess." Angeline mimicked as attempting to draw the air to her, to gain a sense of what Nico wanted of her; of them. That this was the right course to take, "Nico?" Cried, as she could not sense him, "please tell me I am doing the right thing, please tell me this is what you were talking about all those many nights ago when you damned me to such hell?" The whisper, '*soon*' swept senses than just as quickly was lost. "Soon!"

She spat as gathering the few belongings they had accumulated over the many years of their endless travels. Hardly a trunk between them remained as both refused to collect anything of importance, as each year, which eased in passing with the hope that soon their eternity would end and either death or salvation would find them.

Thirteen

Angeline remained before the ship's portal, watching the endlessness of ocean as they pressed ever forward in their journey. "Countess," Armand ventured into her solitude, "you haven't eaten in near two days; at least try the fruit. The Captain says we won't have such luxury for long, and you should enjoy it while it is available." Casting her eyes in his direction, she smiled before shaking her head in denial, "it is not wise of you to starve yourself."

"As soon as my stomach becomes used to such movement, I will be fine, now the mere thought of food is enough to cause my inners to revolt." Returning to the view, she rubbed the scarring of her hand absentmindedly, pressed over the wound which never healed correctly to confess, "even after all the years of travel; I'm still not accustomed to the roll of waves."

Chuckling to her admission, Armand added, "I know, right about now, I would surely kiss the ground if we were ever to find any." Crossing the room to settle beside her, Armand drew her hand into the security of his own. For long moments he contemplated the scenery which held her attention before reminding, "you must have faith this will end soon, you will return to your husband and daughter. That we will return to the place we belong, and not in this strange and new land surrounded by so many new inventions. I fear I miss the simple battles of yesteryear, the hand to hand combat, these new-fangled weapons scare me rightly so."

Laughing to hear his vexation, Angeline wondered to the

thoughts which had been plaguing her as of late, "Armand, do you ever wonder what will be in our future. What we will experience, how long we are meant to exist." With a weary sigh she confessed, "I don't want to exist forever, Armand, to wander this earth as a shell of a human. You must promise me you will end this for me, you will end my existence."

Bracing himself from the inevitable thought of ending her life, of ending both of their life's, he placated her demand of a promise with, "we are not meant to remain as such, Countess; you are not meant to remain without your husband and daughter. We will find a way."

Watching as his lips pressed to the back of her scarred hand, Angeline inquired as he stood to leave the room, "have you ever regretted it, Armand? Regretted the day Nickolai came to you and wrought the promise of protecting me?"

"Regretted spending the last three hundred years with you, Countess?" He questioned, as pausing with his back to her, Armand confessed, "I have never regretted a moment spent with you; the wonders we have seen. I believe I have been in love with you since the first moment you entered your father's study at Belaveuta. So young, so innocent, your devotion to the Count was immediate everyone in that room could sense it. Everyone knew the two of you were born to be together, two souls torn apart from the heavens waiting to reunite." He turned to confront her silence, "and he loved you. I had never seen him as such as he was with you; you made him a gentle, caring, and complete man. You gave him hope, and you could do no wrong in his eyes. You changed him; from the moment you came into his life, you changed him. And that is why I love you as I do; even after all this time, all this waiting, you still give him hope, and you still love him."

Pressing the tears from her lashes, Angeline confessed to him, "I would have never survived without you, Armand, I would have given up long ago without your strength and reassurances. Thank you for everything you have done for me; for my family." With a brief nod to the emotion between them, Armand fled the room needing to be from the woman who held his heart more tenderly than any before.

∞∞∞

Carefully Angeline opened the valise's worn and fragile catch to stared upon the letters and instructions Nickolai had readied so many years ago. Reverent fingertips traveled over the parchment if only to know at one time he had touched the pages. She read over the listings of all monies he had hidden all around the world for her. During the many years of their quest, they traveled from villa to chalet, castle to humble dwellings, following the plans Nickolai had drawn out for her. Never had they stayed in one place for more than ten years, and never did they return to a place any sooner than fifty. Over the years, the two repeatedly reinvented themselves as ancestors of the Illevante` lineage. After three hundred years, she had become her own great-great-great-granddaughter and Armand the one of the many who protected her. Returning the letters to the leather valise, once accounts and balances were confirmed, she secured the locks and happened to stare upon the ring encircling her finger. "Nico," came as she searched the air about her, closed her eyes to sense his nearness as she had for over three hundred years, "why have you deserted me, now, why now if we are so close?" And the tears were felt to threaten her line of vision.

∞∞∞

The white lace which collared her throat was tugged nervously as together they stood before the modest brick building. Confronting the many white trimmed windows that stared down in accusation of what she expected them to perform. "Countess?" Armand questioned to see the hesitation when only a walkway separated them from the completion of their fates.

"We have a two-thirty appointment with Captain Gilliss; it wouldn't be wise to be late."

With a determining sigh, the green was crossed, but not before stopping to give the country's capital building it's due. She contemplated the massive dome and the flag which waved there, "it's a young country to have such pride, don't you think, Armand?" Came in observation to all the grandeur which surrounded them.

"Everything is young to us, Countess." Came in tease to her prolonged lingering as the appointment loomed before them. "Trying to ignore this possibility will not help us; we have to investigate all before they pass us by."

Angeline countered impatiently, as she shrugged off his leading hold, "perhaps we should have investigated the Italian astronomer; at least we would have been closer to home, and I would not have to cross an ocean to return there."

"If this Hall person does not do as expected, we will go there next. We haven't been to Italy in at least a hundred and fifty years." He once again tugged her along. “We can return to Pisa see if that tower has finally fallen over! If that ancient thing is still standing, we have nothing to worry about!”

"You're starting to annoy me; do you know that?" The fiery head could only shake to the periods he spoke of as if they were weeks and not the decades they had lived. "After this, I want to return to Illevante` I have been away from home for far too long."

A troubled look was her reward, "you know that it has become a museum. It will only make you angry and melancholy to the changes that they have made. To the myths and legends fabricated, all in the means of selling tickets."

"I want to go home, and it was my decision which made it a museum. How else could I have reserved it without drawing speculation to myself?" The white painted door opened, leading them into the cool interior of a sparse building. Only a single desk occupied the center of the polished wooden floor as a young man stood to her advancement. "I have an appointment with a Captain Gilliss." Stated to his appreciative assessment of her being.

"Of course, Miss, and what name could I give him?" He asked in the strange accent of his tongue.

"Countess Angeline Illevante'." Was snapped with the little patience she managed to piece together for this appointment.

∞∞∞

Her toe-tapping wait was enough to make Armand groan to the impatience settling upon her once they had landed in this country. For days she had paced the hotel room, and then for hours roamed busy city streets neither given to conversation nor acknowledge he attempted to converse with her. "Countess." He pleaded as he could no longer stand her toe-tapping rhythm. "It hasn't been a moment, please."

Emerald eyes cast upon him with obvious contempt as he dared to question her when she was in such a state, "hasn't been a moment!" Hissed coming to where he stood, "it has been a million moments, over a hundred thousand days that I have held in the scream to insanity. It has been three months, and twenty-three days I have not been able to sense my husband and child, so do not tell me to be patient. Do not expect me to accept this lunacy as if it is just another day in paradise." Witnessing the hysteria which rose to the torment bore, the tears which welled without fall, Armand whispered his apologies.

Spinning about as the precise footsteps were heard to clip over the wooden floorboards, Angeline confronted the uniformed man of badges and ribbons with a marked surprise to his age and stature. "Countess Illevante`, I presume?" And his weathered hand was extended in greeting to the woman whose conclusions he hoped would be in their favor. "I hope you haven't been waiting long; it's a rather hectic time of year. We have been reaching out to all for contributions to the further investment of our little Observatory here." He explained, leading with a wave of a hand to his suite of offices. "That is why we were astonished to hear of your interest in us." Following the Captain up a narrow flight of stairs that seemed to wind about a massive telescope, he boasted, "it's the largest of its kind in the world."

Settled in a chair before his cluttered desk, Angeline craned her neck about the piles of paperwork to confront his acknowledgment, "if you know of the Illevante` history, you know how important the study of astronomy has always been. How Mars as always been a guiding force in my hus---families past. I am here, to ensure, all will remember the Illevante's name for their work toward advancing this extraordinary field." Motioning to Armand, who stood to the left of her chair, he stepped forward to present the valise with the contribution, "there are two hundred and fifty thousand in American currency that I would like to contribute to your efforts here." A breath was taken to see the surprise and gratitude which came to the man's expression, "however," sounded, and his eyes landed on her with suspicion, "I want the astronomer Hall to continue with his work in the explorations of Mars."

"Countess---" The Captain began his hesitation slight, "Asaph has been studying the planet for many months now, and unfortunately, it has not proven to be of interest to him. He has stated that there is nothing left for him to seek with this endeavor." Instantly he witnessed the disappointment as it came to the woman's features, immediately he realized his mistake in admitting such. Surely with such a donation dangling before his nose, Hall could be convinced to continue if not for a little while longer. Perhaps if he spoke to Asaph's wife, she could persuade him to continue, at least, until this woman's interests waned.

Gathering leather gloves and parasol into grasp, Angeline made ready to leave, "obviously, I have come to the wrong place." Stepping forward, Armand offered his hand in escort, "we must have been mistaken to think we could find what we were looking for here. I knew we should have traveled to Italy.

The Italians are always so welcoming."

Rising with her disappointment, the Captain implored, "please, Countess, I will speak to Angeline, his wife, she has always been a guiding force in the direction of his studies. Perhaps she can convince him to continue."

"Angeline?" She questioned with a smile to the association, "if she is anything like all the other Angeline's, I have known, she is a powerful factor in her husband's life."

Chuckling to the knowledge of the woman, he reassured, "I will speak to Angeline, or if you would like, we could share dinner with the couple this evening. I could give you a tour of our fabulous capital, and you would get a chance to speak to Asaph personally."

Hiding her surprise to the unexpected invitation, Angeline managed, upon hearing the warning grumble coming from a usually silent Armand, "I'm sure you will be able to impress the depth of my urgency, and if not, I believe Schiaparelli is working in similar fields, perhaps his benefactors would be more agreeable to my demands." Tugging on the leather gloves, she cast the smallest of smiles to the Captain in dismissal as she concluded. "Armand will complete this business. He has my complete trust and is so directed to sign needed paperwork. Please don't disappoint me in such matters, Captain, I would hate to have to pull my donations because of dissatisfaction."

Nodding in agreement with the results he would make happen, the Captain reassured, "thank you for your generosity, Countess, and I assure you, on behalf of the United States Government, you will not be disappointed nor dissatisfied." The scar contemplated as it met his touch.

"It is a reminder to a time long ago," Angeline explained to see the curiosity of such a marking. "Please excuse me, Armand, I will be waiting for you on the green. Please see that all agreed upon."

Alone in the park, Angeline settled on a bench close to the bubbling fountain as a continuous flow of water erupted from an urn held in the arms of an unrecognized Greek goddess. Her fingers tugged impatiently to the ribbon under her chin then drew the lacey bonnet from her head. For long moments she fought the pins that held her hair into the ornate styling of curls before it was allowed to fall free down her back. Fingernails scratched over the ache of her head to carry such weight and sighed to feel the subtle headache as it eased to her administrations, "Countess Illevante?" Questioned softly, causing Angeline to spin about to face the small, pale woman who stood beside the bench. "I hope that I am not disturbing you." Nervously the woman clutched a pile of papers to her thin chest as she stood staring at the woman who contained a beauty, she couldn't quite fathom. A self-assuredness that had always somehow eluded her except in the private company of her husband.

"Do I know you?" Angeline questioned, and sensing the women held no malice, pointed to the space beside her on the bench. It took a moment for the stranger to decide if she wanted to sit or remain where she was.

"Countess, I am Angeline Hall; please call me Angie." Her dark eyes immediately appreciated the recognition of the name, "I understand that you have come to contribute to the development of the Observatory. But most importantly, to the work that my husband is interested in." Seeing the surprise to the speed which news traveled, Angie explained, "the Captain immediately dispatched a note to me concerning your stipulations. He's very concerned with the loss of your generous funding."

Smiling to the explanation and all that it clarified, Angeline reiterated her needs, "I am here to see that your husband continues with his studies to the planet Mars." She watched as the women settled beside her, continued to cling to the papers as if they were her child. "It is essential he continues on the path he is following."

"Why is it important?" Angie inquired. "What is it that my

husband must find for you that you are willing to fund him so generously?"

Exhaling wearily Angeline turned to the woman and smiled, "let me say that his study will allow me to return to a life I have always known. Will allow me to return to a husband and daughter I have been without for far too many years."

Nodding to the confession, Angie unclenched her hands from about the materials held fast and presented them to the Countess, "when the Captain came to Asaph a few days ago, informing him of your appointment, I became curious." A guilty smile parted otherwise stern lips to find cautious emerald eyes trained upon her, "the name Illevante` was a little challenging to investigate. There have been no documented birth records in years. I learned of the myths and legends which represent the name, of the speculations to magic and supernatural phenomenon which have surrounded the Illevante` Keep. I even went as far as to research the museum Illevante`; Countess, you have been missing for three hundred and eighteen years." She presented the facts in wonder to the woman who sat beside her. "If you are not Nicole Illevante`, the only known descendant of the Count Nickolai Illevante,' then you are three hundred and thirty-eight years old. Countess Angeline."

Laughing out loud to the speculation in the woman's voice, Angeline began, "I have come all this way only to meet another Angeline as stubborn and as curious as myself." Seeing the intrigue coming to Angie's features, Angeline shared, "in the month before my wedding, I researched Illevante' as well. Even then to there was little to no history to my husband's name, even less to his mother's side of the family." Drawing the pile of papers into her hands, Angeline quickly leafed through the notes, dates which stood out to Nico's birth, her own and Nicole's. Simple sketches of the Illevante` Keep, lands, and the village which surrounded it in her time, "I would like to see the source of your references if you wouldn't mind."

∞∞∞

In the silence of the Capital Library, Angeline looked to the many books which came to surround them. The many volumes the Hall woman continued to present her, "is there a likeness of Nickolai?" Nodding Angie flipped through pages till a photograph of the portrait which hung in their gathering room was found, "I have never thought to look in such; it has been so many years that I have seen his face. Sometimes I even doubt my memory." Fingertips traced the line of his lips, the rise of the cheekbone in loving memory. "Are there any others?"

"There is one of---his wife Angeline; there is a legend that the portrait suddenly appeared one day, hanging next to his." Quickly the pages were turned, and a photograph of herself presented. "It is you, isn't it?"

Unwillingly Angeline nodded to the tentative question, "it's the gown I was wearing the day my family became lost to me." Settling weakly to the desk chair, Angeline cast trusting eyes to the woman before her, as she intreated, "I need your help, Mistress Hall, I need you to convince your husband to continue with his work. I need the dogs of war to be seen by the human eye, and I need him to do this as quickly as possible. I don't know how much longer I will be able to survive as I am if your husband doesn't continue with his work."

Looking upon the wonder and curiosity of the woman who continued to stare at her, Angeline began softly, "Nickolai and I have always been destined to be together. From the night of my birth, past the moment of his death, we have sensed each other, carried each other's thoughts, memories, feelings. When we were together, together as husband and wife, we nearly read each other's minds. We knew what each was thinking, feeling, our emotions were never private." Reaching into her handbag a linen was found and pressed to the tears as they continued, "the myth and legends which surround Illevante` have always been true. The '*ancients*,' as Nickolai referred to them, drew us together, forced an unbreakable bond between us. These '*ancients*' knew I would be the one to end a curse surrounding Illevante' for hundreds of years." Returning to the image of her husband in the book, her fingertips continued to caress what she so desperately yearned for. "I know Nickolai tried to spare me this future; he felt so guilty as if he had somehow deceived me in our marriage. His sense of guilt was a near tangible thing between us, but whenever I attempted to confront him, he had an excuse for such feelings. How could he possibly begin to explain, to a nineteen-year-old girl she was to live for three hundred years? Everyone she had ever known or loved would die about her, and she would never get to hold her child or husband to her heart again. How could he without me running from him as if he had lost his sanity right then and there?" A reluctant laugh escaped to the images provoked. "On the night Nickolai was murdered, which by the way, was by Prince Andrew and his elite guard, I was speaking to my stepbrother in the adjoining room, Martine, my woman, summoned me as Nicole, my daughter, needed me. While I was arguing with my stepbrother, Andrew's guard overtook my husband and murdered. No matter how he fought, how he defended himself, there were too many of them. Stephen, in the meantime, murdered my daughter and woman. Nicole was barely two months old, and he snapped her neck." Deep breaths came to fight the tears as they rose. "Nickolai beseeched me with the words, '*when the dogs of war are named from the planet of blood, so shall the curse be lifted; so, shall you return to me.*'

"Phobos and Deimos." Angie managed as the final pages of her research came to be laid before Angeline. "Asaph has already witnessed the two satellites which orbit Mars; we are simply waiting to chart and calculate their path for his study. His findings are being written for publication as we speak. But how could you have known of the names in which he decided on only the night before last? It has been more troubling to him than the actual research." Came with a new lightness as it was now about her husband they spoke.

"Life has a way of orbiting in a path much like a moon, I suspect." Standing as a settling satisfaction came to claim her soul; Angeline knew she had completed her journey. It was time to return home. "Mistress Hall, I want you to use the money I will donate to the Observatory in any way you deem necessary. And I want to thank you for your time and consideration."

"I hope in the next few days that you will find your destiny secured, Countess, that what you came searching for is what was needed to return your family."

"As long as you keep your husband moving in the right direction to these discoveries, all will be as it is meant to be." Enfolding the woman within her arms, Angeline held to her as whispering, "if there is a way for me to let you know of my success, I will. Don't ever forget your interests, and don't ever forget what you have done for me."

"Countess." Armand appeared at her side. "I see you have found the library.

With a smile and nod to his inference of such a find, Angeline turned from the woman to confront her companion, "yes, and it was a wonderful find." She whispered as taking his arm; they walked from the building out into the sunlight. "Did you know that there are books with photographs of Nickolai's portraits in them?" Angeline wondered to all sheltered from, with his reluctant nod, she reassured, "I don't believe I was ready to see him again until today. I don't think I was strong enough to remember why we are here."

"And why is today different, Countess?" Armand wondered as he waved down a hack, and directions to the pier were given.

"Because now I am strong enough to go home, to know whatever may happen, I have done everything possible to free Nickolai and Nicole." Resting against the strength of his formidable shoulder, Angeline confessed, "and I have always loved you as well, Armand."

Fourteen

Walking silently through the house, which had been her home Angeline clung to the hand holding securely in hers. Only briefly, she was able to cast her great emerald eyes to the man beside her as different points of interest came to be explained by the young woman who guided the tour they had paid to experience. It wasn't until they ventured from the entrance hall to the gathering room that she felt the slight stirring in the air, the warmth as it swept up about her length and across her cheek. Her hand clenched tightly about Armand's, and he looked at her in surprise to her reaction, "he's here." Angeline shared, feeling as if the very life returned to her heart. "I knew it was right to come home; I knew I would be able to sense him here."

For extended moments, Angeline listened to explanations of the night that had taken the Illevante' line from the world. "And what of the Countess?" A voice from the back of the gathering questioned. "You hardly give a moment in your history to her." The question was nearly dismissed by the guide who wished to keep to the itinerary as explained to her, "they say she sacrificed herself for the keeping of her husband and child."

"There is little information available to the Countess Illevante', sir. They say she was barely twenty years old on the night her husband was killed and ran away with her lover. The Captain to the Illevante` Guard never to be seen again, there are testimonials that the Captain offered no help in guarding the Count. He alone was responsible for the murder." She answered as the man pressed his way through the crowd surrounding them, "however, if you are interested---" the woman looked upon the towering handsomeness of the man as he came from the group to stand before her, felt herself become lost to the depth of blue eyes as the sternness of a perfect mouth curled ever so slightly into a cruel, exacting, smile, "---in the history of Illevante` we have a gift shop at the end of the tour which has many interesting books to the history of the Keep."

Angeline turned slowly to the voice as it rose steadily in its progression through the sightseers, detangled herself from the hand which clasped hers as a breath was felt to lodge in the base of her throat till she could see the man pressing his way toward the inner circle of the sightseers. "I have no interest in such a Keep's history, young woman, only of the Countess. And I assure you the young Countess had no lover except for her husband, to which she has always been faithful." Stepping before Angeline, a soft smile met the tears that began to fall over her cheeks. "Little one, are you crying again?" Teased as he gathered her into his arms, held her to his length as it seemed all time and separation slipped slowly away.

"Nickolai, is it you?" Sobbed as her arms clasped about his neck, her hands buried in the length of raven hair, holding him closer, tighter to her. "How have you come here to this place to this time?"

"I have come to bring you home, little one." He managed drawing the attention of Armand so he could lead them from the gathering to the privacy of what was once Antony's chambers. "We have one final piece of business to see to, my love. Armand." And a hand clasped to the man's shoulder. "I want to thank you for seeing to her safety all these years, I know it has been a trying time, but I always knew you were the only man I could trust with such an impossible situation."

Nickolai brought Angeline's scarred hand into his own and she watched as the flesh began to bleed as if from its own volition, watched as the tunic upon her husband's chest was found to seep with blood. The chest returned to its ravaged state by the many knives which found his heart that fateful night so many lifetimes ago. Pressing her hand into the injured flesh to his chest, Nickolai signed with building gratification as her blood was felt to mingle with his own. "Come back to me, Angeline. Remember the night we were taken and return to me." Was managed softly as before her eyes, the figure of the man she loved without reason, without end, vanished.

"Nico." Gasped as she staggered to the encounter. Clung to the breadth of shoulders as Armand was before her, holding her against the weakness as it threatened.

"Excuse us!" The tour guide appeared with a gasp as the door to the tiny office was opened, and the two found in its secured confides. "I'm sorry, this is not part of the tour. You can't be in here."

"Forgive us; we became lost." Armand apologized as he gathered Angeline's trembling length closer to his own, held her to a stance only by the arm which surrounded her waist. "Please, Countess," he pleaded as they fell into the back of the tour group, and he nearly dragged her along, "please, if only till we can leave this place."

Room by room, Angeline was forced to confront the memories, room by room made to hold back the emotions as they built until Nicole's nursery was faced, and Armand had to hold her back physically. The bright, airy room redecorated into a lacy, fluffy room of pink and white. "What have they done?" Angeline questioned pressing through the entrance as the very fiber of her fought such heartbreak, "this isn't right---" and the statement caused the group to confront her, "this room is for a little girl. Nickolai always believed we were to have a son; the room was made ready for a little boy. If you knew anything of the Illevante` history, you would know there was never a male child born to this Keep. Nicole was a miracle unto herself, a way for life to go on."

Pressing the curiosity of the gathering away, Armand attempted explained her outburst, "she has been studying this

Keep her entire life, there are few details she doesn't know of the Illevante'." And he escorted her from the room, "Countess, there is much these people don't know about Illevante' but you are in no position to enlighten them, least you inform them to your disposition."

Pointing in the direction of her daughter's room she insisted, "but it's not right, Armand, none of this is right." She cried wearily against the brace of his shoulder, "the furnishings are all wrong, the history is incomplete, and they think you and I are lovers. That I ran away from Nickolai and Nicole when they needed me most, that you, his most trusted Captain, had a hand in his murder. How could all this be so wrong." Pulling away from Armand's' arms, she ran the length of the hall to burst into the master's chambers. For long moments she stood in the center of a room that had somehow remained as it did when she came to him as a bride. Slowly she circled the room, felt the impressions of him as it caressed her, adorned her with remembrance. "Nico, how do I return to you?" Questioned as her eyes opened, and Angeline confronted the portrait which was first seen in the library book.

"Countess!" Gasped, as Armand stumbled into the room moments before the remaining group followed, "come, she will have you thrown out if you persist."

"Armand," whispered as the portrait was pointed to, the image of her seated upon a golden throne, the markings of Mars surrounding her, "it's the cave. We have to return to the cave." She managed to step back into the shadows as the rest of the group tramped into the room. "The cave." Repeated urgently to the clue Nickolai had left her.

Following the tour guide, as the final stop was among the gardens, Angeline quickly slipped away as she became lost among the many paths of the now overgrown gardens which surrounded her. Quickly she ran to the beach and nearly stumbled upon the ancient door as it remained untouched in the three hundred years of her last breaching its hidden chamber. Fumbling for only a moment for the key she wore secured about her neck by ribbon, the door swung silently open, and hesitantly Angeline stepped into the cool darkened confines. "Armand?" She questioned as he remained just beyond the room.

"Three hundred years ago, I stood in this very spot protecting you; this is where I belong, Countess, when you are ready, this is where I will be waiting." With a nod, Angeline turned into the chamber and closed the door behind her.

Fifteen

The torch's light flickered a single time then extinguished, and Angeline found herself eclipsed by the blackness of the secret chamber. Drawing herself along the walls, uselessly, she searched for Nickolai, "why aren't you here! What have I missed?" She cried desperately as the absolute silence of the cavern became realized. There were no phantoms, no emotions for her to sense. All were gone. "You promised we would be together; you promised this would end!"

Turning to growing sounds of storm beyond the closed door, Angeline followed the wall till the door was found and opened to the rage beyond. Standing in the door's frame, she questioned to the hours which she could have remained in the room, it was barely midday when she had entered could it be the dead of night already? "Armand!" Cried as she ventured to where he was found to be keeping guard to the entrance, "how long have you been waiting? Has it been hours?"

"No, Countess, only moments." Looking out over the surf, Armand shared in awe to the conclusion of their journey, "when you entered the cave, it was the day, and then---in a blink, it was the night." He commented, drawing the injured hand into his own, carefully the bandage she had fashioned out of hem was released, and he stared to the seeping flesh before him, with a steadying breath, he confessed, "all has returned to the night when it began."

Lifting the held hand as a flash of lightning suddenly split the sky, Angeline, too realized the flesh, also understood the implication of such a revelation. "It's all been true, hasn't it," a trembling hand pressed down into the blood-stained gown as it once again hung limply about her, the dark seeping of blood as it clung to hem, "all of it, it was true?"

Shrugging shoulders and shaking his head to all that transpired he confessed, "I don't know, Countess, it all seems like a dream that I've only now woken from." And Angeline realized the fear which radiated from the man, "what if it's the same night and nothing has changed. What if we return to Illevante` only to find your husband and child dead upon the floor as we left them."

"It couldn't be all for naught." Angeline forced him from the relentlessness of the crashing shore, the misty spray which showered over them time and time again, "Nico was there, he said it was time to come home. I held him in my arms; it couldn't have been a dream." Looking to the path before her, the sudden flood of emotions swamping her caused her to nearly stagger in relief. "It was no dream." Climbing her way back up the path through the gardens, she entered the silence of the home. "Nico!" She cried as Armand was left behind to search the halls, "Nico, where are you?" Came as no more than a breath to the silence of the Keep surrounding her, the hem of gown bunched into fists as she raised it to run the many halls keeping her from her destination. "Nico!" She cried running through the great room, the death and destruction confronting her horrifying to its implication of finality. "Nickolai!" Screamed and the sound allowed the name to expel from her lungs, from the very bottom of her soul. "No!" Staggering before the fallen length, she dropped to her knees as the blood seeping into marble veins congealed into a pooling dark mass, the smoke acrid and burning of those littering the floor. "No!" Ripped from her lungs as her body came in cover to the man and child, "this cannot be! I have kept them in my heart, I have fulfilled the prophecy, you promised to return to me!" Screamed to the very walls surrounding her, to the shadows that seemed to swirl and chatter all to the demands made, "you must keep your promise as I have kept mine!"

Racing into the gathering room Armand came to where the family remained, the smoldering ash of prince and crumbled body of a stepbrother, to that of his Count and the child Nicole. Still, the death persisted; the time did nothing to reverse the wrong. "You must have freed them, Countess." He offered as he came to a single knee beside her. "We have done everything we could, you have freed the Illevante' ancients, no longer will they roam these halls." Armand attempted to draw her once again from the destruction from the futility of their journey. "It is not wise for us to remain, allow me to bring you to safety."

Wringing herself free from his attempts to draw her once again from her family, Angeline struggled to bring her husband and child into her arms, "I will not leave them, not again." Burying her face in the ravage of Nickolai's chest as the very Keep about them seemed to shudder to the intensity of her heartbreak, to the very soul as it left her. "I will never leave them again."

Staggering back from her grieving length, Armand looked to the walls which surrounded them and he whispered with reverence and fear, "Countess," caused Angeline to lift her head and confront the man's awe, "sweet Jesus, do you see, or is it just a trick of my eyes?"

Turning her head in the direction he stared, Angeline watched as the walls about them came to life, the whispering intensified as a warm wind stirred the air about them. Then from the very depth of stone, they emerged at first nothing more than shadows, wisps of smoke, and mystery to take on more solid form till no longer did they appear to be a trick of the night. Before her, about her, they stood, looking down welcoming and as suddenly as they came to form, Nickolai's ancients, disappeared. "Nico." Whimpered as tears were brusquely pressed from cheek and nose, as her breath came in the torture of the loss settling upon her heart.

"Countess, let me get someone for you. I'll send my men to Belaveuta, tell your father to the happenings here tonight, you can't be alone any longer." Looking down as her hand came to fill his, Armand surmised, “you have ended the curse, Countess, the Illevante’ are free.”

Nodding to the sense of the man beside her gently she pressed the hair back from Nico's forehead, drew the small length of her daughter closer to the protection of father's body, "Armand," managed in awe and wonderment as her hands moved to caress the perfection of Nicole's face, "how can she still be warm?" Ripping open the silken nightgown about her tiny length, a gasp of breath left Angeline to see the tiny chest heave to returning breath, a pitiful cry left the lungs, and chubby hands rose in reach of her mother.

"Oh, my God!" Rushed over lips as the bundle was brought into her arms, "sweet Jesus, thank you!" Cried as kisses pressed to the innocence returned to her, "Armand, she's alive!" Passing the child into his disbelieving arms, Angeline caressed the cold stillness of her husband, clawed to the ragged tunic covering his chest, the breast only moments ago ravished and torn now could be seen to heal and repair, and the heat felt to stutter then pound in mounting beats.

Trembling fingertips came to the warmth as it slowly invaded features, touched to the lips as the color restored, and Angeline allowed a haggard breath to gasp as blue eyes opened to look upon her, "little one." Managed as his arm rose, his hand to caress the dampened cheek with a caressing touch, "you're here." Nico whispered as his fingers buried in the length of hair, "you managed what none other has before, my love; I knew you would never disappoint me."

Pressing back Angeline touched the perfection of his face under trembling fingertips, explored the mouth and cheek before pressing down over the length of neck and the breadth of shoulder, "it is you, and you’re not a ghost or a shadow. No longer just a voice in my head." Whispered as if in awe of the moments between them, "Nicole," came with a gasp, "she is here. You're both here."

"It is you who have freed us, my daughter." Turning to the

woman who came to her side Angeline instantly recognized the resemblance between Nico and the woman, "my granddaughter has missed you greatly, daughter."

"Granddaughter?" Angeline questioned watching as Armand nearly stumbled back from the woman's appearance before him, readily allowed her gentle hands to bring the child into her arms, "but how can this be?" Angeline asked her eyes of wonderment and joy going from the woman to her husband.

Turning into the caress as it came to her cheek, Angeline brought Nico's hand into the two of her own, held it there as he managed, "Angeline, allow me to introduce my mother, the Countess Illevante`, she has been waiting quite impatiently to meet you."

Drawing Angeline up from the floor and into her arms, the Countess snapped, "Nico, such formality to my daughter in law, I am known simply as Josephine, but I would like you to call me Mother." Between the press of their bodies, Nickolai managed to squeeze his daughter out so Angeline could better return the embrace his mother proceeded to smother her in. "We can never tell you how grateful we are. And as soon as Nickolai's father has finished inspecting the house, Nico was kind enough to redecorate for him; he will insist you call him father." Coming from the embrace of her daughter, Josephine looked to the adoration seen emanating from her son's eyes to the young woman and she suggested as the child was drawn once again into her arms. "I have quite a bit of catching up to do with my granddaughter, why don't the two of you get freshened up before the King's Guard arrives and we're all answering questions to the nonsense this night has brought."

Slowly the tunic came from his shoulders as she pressed her hands over the chest as it confronted her, "there were so many wounds," whispered as her lips pressed to the pound of his heart, "the blood was everywhere. Your blood was all around me. How is this possible for you to be here, for Andrew and Stephen to be dead and not you?"

"It is because of you that I am here, little one." Nickolai explained, "because of you Illevante' history has been rewritten, all that was is now changed. The ancients have been freed, and my parents allowed to live their lives. To see me happily married and watch our children grow."

"It was so many nights, Nico, so many endless years. The wonders Armand and I have experienced, it doesn't seem that it should be real." Looking down to her palm, she found only a small pink scar remained where it was a gaping wound moments ago, "None knew what had happened here, how you had lived, how you had died. I don't want to be known as the woman who ran away from you and Nicole when you needed me most. All they knew of me was that I left with another man, a man thought to be my lover."

"You shall write our history, little one; you will fill journals to the life we will share. To the adventures we have shared, so all will know the true legend of Illevante`, so all will know how you and you alone have ended the curse which plagued our family for hundreds of years." Ripping the bodice, quickly followed by the gown from her length, both were thrown into the fireplace were a fire instantly raged about the material, "for you are the one who has found us. You are the one who returned to us." He whispered as the lacings of undergarments were quickly released, and her glorious naked flesh filled his searching hands, "it feels as if It's been a thousand years since I've last made love to you, last held you in my arms." His lips trailed hotly over the arch of the throat, the expanse of the collarbone, lower till the already taut pink flesh was drawn into the suckle of his mouth, pleasing him to feel her instant response to the touch.

Closing her arms about his shoulders as she led him back to their bed as she teased, "only three hundred and nineteen, my love." And she arched to the depth he penetrated in a single thrust to the love he projected to her endlessly as she moved flesh against flesh to the release so long denied them. With a cry to the intensity of the reunion now complete, Angeline held to him as he emptied himself deep within her womb. "Don't." She whispered as he moved to gather her into his arms, "stay in me, just like you are. Don't leave me just yet; it's been so long that I've dreamt of this moment I don't want it to end, at least not yet."

Closing his arms about her nestled length, he couldn't help but smile to the request made, "I seem to remember the first time we made love, and I stayed within you, laying still didn't last very long." His lips teased over the soft parting of her mouth, the plain of her forehead as his hands buried in the depth of her hair, tugged her even closer to his covering length, "I want to bring my sons into this world, Angeline, I want them to know what it is like to love a woman as endlessly as I love you."

"All six of them?" She questioned.

"All six to sixty of them." He reassured.

Angeline Hall opened the book she found on the library table and flipped thoughtfully through the many pages of history confronting her. It wasn't until the name Illevante` caught her attention that she stopped with a frown to the curiosity of what the name should mean to her. A trembling hand turned the next few pages as she scanned the early ancestors of the title until a portrait caused her to pause. On a golden throne, a beautiful woman sat, her hand holding that of the man who stood protectively at her shoulder, and about the woman seven children gathered. Six fiery-haired boys were surrounding a single raven-haired daughter. And the image brought a sudden tear to Angeline's eyes as she realized the woman in the portrait had managed all that she promised.

Afterword

I hope you enjoyed the first book of Illevante' Curse, Angeline:

Now Available:

Angeline

Coming Soon:

Joelly

Leanora

Andrea

Elzbieta

Made in the USA
Columbia, SC
01 July 2022

62579495R00164